THE GIRL WHO IGNORED
Ghosts

THE GIRL WHO IGNORED

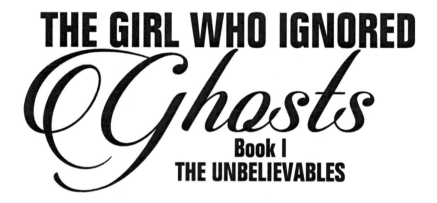

Ghosts

Book I
THE UNBELIEVABLES

K.C. TANSLEY

BECKETT PUBLISHING GROUP, LLC

THE GIRL WHO IGNORED GHOSTS

The Unbelievables Book One

Trade Paperback Edition / August 2015

Beckett Publishing Group, LLC

www.beckettpublishinggroupllc.com

Written by K.C. Tansley

Created by Anthony Dvarskas and K.C. Tansley

Edited by Jessica Jernigan

Cover Art by Creative Paramita

Internal Design by Nick DeSimone

Author Photograph by Brett D. Helgren

ISBN Paperback: 978-1-943024-00-1

ISBN Ebook: 978-1-943024-01-8

Printed in the United States of America

To Anthony Charles Dvarskas,
for dreaming up this world with me when we were children
and letting me run wild in it as an adult.

"Some mysteries were built so intricately, it took centuries to unravel them. Others remained forgotten, left to gather dust in the memories of the dead. Castle Creighton waited over a century for its chance."

—Professor Astor, *The Price of Power: The Curse of America's Uncrowned Aristocracy*

Chapter 1

The two weeks leading up to finals were the perfect time to do research at Gilman Library—if you needed to be surrounded by people. Bustle and noise didn't distract me anymore. I was much more likely to be disturbed by quiet. Or, at least, what the quiet conjured up. Old buildings like Gilman were the worst.

I made my way to the library's elevator. My progress was slowed by the twenty pounds of research material that I carried. I slid my thumbs under the straps of my backpack, trying to relieve my aching shoulders, while I waited.

Professor Astor's classes were unusual—even by McTernan standards—and his paper topics were insane. But he was a prestigious university professor willing to teach prep-school kids, so the school let him teach pretty much whatever he wanted. This semester was "The Lore and Lure of Historical Places," which might sound innocent enough, but Astor had me investigating a notorious double murder that had happened in 1886.

The professor expected McTernan students to do as much as his students at Georgetown, but he helped anyone willing to do the work. For my latest assignment, he'd loaned me some incredible resources from his personal collection. I couldn't wait to explore the books in my backpack, but investigating a grisly mystery and a family curse meant that I had to take some special precautions. Working alone in my dorm room was out of the question. I needed the frantic energy of my classmates preparing for finals.

Once the elevator arrived, it was a short ride to the fourth floor. The place was packed, just the way I liked it. I found a free chair at a table with three sophomores. They didn't look happy about my intrusion, but I was a junior, so they had to deal.

I had a lot of work to do. If I was going to discover anything new about what happened at Castle Creighton, I had to start by reviewing what was already known. While I read, I needed to look for blank spots and anything that had been overlooked. Professor Astor's willingness to believe that I might be capable of unraveling a 129-year-old mystery was one of the reasons he was my favorite teacher.

I slipped on my headphones, cranking up some Taylor Swift. I needed happy music to explore something this dark and scary. Then I pulled out my binder and reread my notes on Castle Creighton.

The castle sat in the middle of an island just a few miles from the village of Wright in Connecticut. It felt a world away from the hustle of Washington, D.C. I'd only seen a few photos of the place, but my first thought was desolate and creepy. Maybe it was the isolation of the island or the Medieval Gothic architecture of the castle, but the place seemed designed to provoke bad dreams. I couldn't help envisioning what I could face there—an endless line of restless ghosts, waiting for someone like me.

I shuddered. Ghosts were something I'd actively avoided for the past eight years.

Ghosts didn't just appear to anyone. They could only break through to our reality if we believed in them. The unbelievers were the lucky ones. They would never see what they refuse to believe in. They would never feel what a ghost could do. They would never know what a ghost did to me.

There were ghosts in my earliest memories. They rocked me in the cradle, and they sang me to sleep. They were a constant presence throughout most of my childhood. Some even became my friends. As I grew up, they told me more about their world, the world of the unbelievables. I discovered a little bit about how curses and spells worked. Like how they could only be cast by the living. Ghosts needed the living for a lot of things, especially for making amends and resolving unsettled conflicts. This was usually what the ghosts wanted from me. A reckoning.

Most of them were harmless, but not all of them.

Forget everything you've learned from movies and TV. Ghosts weren't troubled souls waiting to "cross over." If only it were that simple.

Death shattered souls. This is the first thing you need to know. The largest chunk of the soul moved on. I'm pretty sure it reincarnated, but the ghosts were kind of cagey about that part. The ghosts themselves were the biggest pieces of what was left behind.

Then there were the shards from the ghost chunk that were called "spirits." They were attached to a specific location and a particular event. They were mostly just a nuisance. They didn't have any real thought processes or intentions. They just repeated a moment. Maybe it was the last thing they thought about before they died. Maybe it was the moment of death. Either way, I did my best to avoid spirits.

Some ghosts just needed something simple—something an elementary school kid could actually handle. But most of the time, their reckonings could get really complicated. And scary. I still did my best to help them. And, they were patient with me. Being that they were dead already, time didn't mean much to them.

But soon after I turned nine, everything changed.

The ghost with the dark hair and silver eyes refused to tell me her name. That meant that I had no power over her. I couldn't just send her away—and I would have, because this ghost frightened me. When she had first appeared to me, I was in bed with a fever, so my first impressions of her had a delirious quality that I couldn't separate from the sickness.

Even when my head cleared, this ghost scared me. She wouldn't tell me what she needed from me. Instead, it was like she was trying to figure out how to *take* what she needed. I had no idea what she was going to do, but I sensed it would be bad. Then I started losing time.

In the beginning, it was just a few seconds here and there, like getting lost in your thoughts and forgetting what you were doing. I was still recuperating, so it was easy to think I was just absent-minded. But it didn't stop there.

Soon it was ten minutes gone from my day.

One second, I'd be reading a book, and the next thing I knew, the book was on my bedside table and I was sipping a cup of soup. I had no memory of setting aside the book or of my mother coming into my room with a tray. I felt like this ghost was taking over my life. Like she was taking over me. And I didn't know how to stop her. It was terrifying.

One night, I woke up to find a new ghost sitting beside me on the bed. She had a halo of red curls and warm green eyes and she smelled like lilacs. I had never met a ghost who seemed so alive.

"I'm Toria," she said. "And I'm here to help you."

I believed her instantly. "What's happening to me?"

"There are ghosts who try to steal life from the living—twisted creatures who can't accept death. They seek out people who are both receptive and weak. You've always been receptive to ghosts, but the fever made you weak. She was able to slip inside you."

"No, that can't happen." If a ghost were inside me, I'd feel it.

"Have you been losing time?" she asked gently. "Are there moments that you can't remember?"

I bit my lip. "Just a few minutes."

"So, you've been fighting her." Toria smiled at me. "But the longer she stays in your body, the stronger she will become. If we don't expel her, she'll start stealing hours, and then days, and then…." Lines of worry crept across her forehead.

"You can't let her do that!" I clutched my covers. I didn't want a ghost taking over my life.

"I won't." She smiled like we shared a secret. "Will you trust me?"

I nodded.

"You have to let me slip into your body. I'm sorry, but it's the only way I can drive her out."

"You'll take over my body?" I hesitated.

Toria nodded. "Only for a few moments. As soon as she's out, I'm out. I promise."

"Isn't there another way?" I asked.

"No."

I had no reason to believe her, but I did. I took a deep breath. "Okay."

"It's going to hurt." She reached for my hand.

I braced for the cold uncomfortable feeling I always got when a ghost touched me, but it didn't come. When Toria touched me, it was warm. Her fingers were almost solid.

She murmured words I couldn't understand. I stared at the ring she wore. It had a dark blue stone with a white star in the center. As she spoke, the star grew brighter and the whole ring began to glow. A bright light wrapped around us. The light stung, burning through my bones. Toria turned to white smoke and slipped through my skin.

I convulsed. So much heat inside my body. I kicked the covers away, but the air didn't give me any relief. It felt unbearably hot against my skin. And then something ice-cold ripped through me. I collapsed back on the bed. Toria emerged from me like steam rising from a cup of tea. Then she resumed her familiar shape.

"Is she gone?" I panted.

"I drove her out."

Toria stroked my forehead. Her fingers chilled my skin. The way a ghost's fingers should.

"But she'll come back."

My voice quavered. "How do I keep her away?"

Toria looked sad for a moment, but sounded adamant. "You have to stop believing in us. You have to deny that ghosts exist. You have to refuse to let them into your reality."

Push them all away? They'd been by my side all my life. "But they need me for reckonings."

Toria smiled. "My sweet girl, it's very kind of you to think of us. But if she takes your body and gains full control, we'll lose you forever. You'll never be able to help us again. We need you safe and beyond her grasp."

"But what about you? Can I help you, at least?"

Her smile turned wistful. "I can wait."

For the next three nights, Toria stayed by my side, keeping the silver-eyed ghost away and teaching me how to become an unbeliever.

Her first lesson: Life repelled the lifeless. By surrounding myself with other people, with animals, with plants—seeds, even—I weakened the ghosts around me and made it harder for them to approach me. Toria explained that stones were helpful, too. They weren't alive, but some of them contained protective energy from the earth.

Her second and third lessons were just as important. She told me to never, ever speak of the unbelievables. Talking about ghosts and spirits gave them power. It made them more real. I should make sure that the people I surrounded myself with were unbelievers. The unbelievables couldn't enter the reality of people who didn't believe in them, so the presence of unbelievers would shield me.

On the third night, Toria tucked my hair behind my ear. "This will be our final lesson."

"You have to go?" I'd never wanted a ghost to stay this much. I'd grown to love her.

"It's time."

I blinked back tears. "Will I see you again?"

Her voice was reassuring. "I hope so."

She squeezed my hand and said, "I'm going to teach you words of power. They will be your ultimate weapon against ghosts."

I nodded and focused, preparing to memorize a complicated incantation. Probably in Latin.

Instead, Toria said, "Ghosts don't exist. They can't touch me. They can't hurt me. They aren't real."

"But that's a lie."

She cradled my face in her hand. "Oh, my sweet girl, you have to believe that it's true. You have to say the words with such conviction that no one and nothing can doubt you. You have to say them until you don't even doubt them yourself."

She released my face and took my hand once more. I looked at our intertwined fingers, trying to memorize every detail of the star-sapphire ring she wore. It seemed to wink back at me.

I didn't want to do it. I didn't want all the ghosts to disappear. I didn't want Toria to disappear.

"I don't want to," I whispered, rubbing a tear from my cheek.

"This is the only way for you to be safe. Please, do it. If you can't do it for yourself, do it for me," she pleaded.

It took hours of repeating those words before anything happened. One moment Toria was there, and then she wasn't. Those words became my reality. Between one sentence and the next, the ghosts were gone.

Toria was gone.

Sometimes, I wished I could talk to her one more time. I wished that I could help her. But, if I let Toria in, I let them all in. Including the ghost who possessed me. So I said my words of power until they sounded true. But deep down, I knew I was lying. And the ghosts knew it too.

Digging into a pile of antique books written about an unsolved Victorian murder was a potentially hazardous situation for someone like me. That was why I needed to surround myself with other students who were brimming with end-of-the-year energy. Finals-week panic was a potent protective force. Still, I rubbed the black tourmaline worry stone in my pocket before I got down to work.

I eyed the piles of books in front of me. I decided to start with the thinnest and work my way to the heftiest. Best way to build up an impressive bibliography. As soon as I opened the green leather cover, I sneezed. Great. Just what my allergies needed—dust from the last century.

Reaching for the wad of tissues in my backpack, I read the table of contents. It was vague. I flipped to the back of the book, but there was no index. Now I knew why this book hadn't been opened in ages. I skimmed the chapters for something of value, but didn't find anything I could use for my paper.

I moved on to the next book. It talked about the Radcliffes, who were the owners of Castle Creighton and the family at the center of the murder mystery. In terms of American dynasties, the Radcliffes predated the Rockefellers and the Roosevelts. At one point, their fortune rivaled the U.S. Treasury. They had it all until the night that everything changed.

Sebastian Radcliffe had been destined for greatness. At least, that was what all the newspaper stories said after he disappeared. His bride, Cassie Mallory, didn't get a quarter of the press he did. The reporters were too busy lamenting his death to pay much attention to the second victim of the tragedy.

This book followed the standard storyline, beginning with a fawning history of the Radcliffe family and ending on Sebastian and Cassie's wedding night with an empty room covered in blood. The author basically repeated the only official statement offered by the family.

> *This terrible crime showed every sign of being orchestrated by enemies of the Radcliffe family and its interests. The removal of the bodies suggests an inhuman level of animosity. Both the Radcliffes*

and the Mallorys hope that they will one day be able to put their loved ones to rest.

Nothing new here, but at least I could add another title to my bibliography.

The moldy old books were aggravating my allergies, so I decided to shift my focus to my folder full of articles. The first printout on the stack was a translation of an article from a defunct German magazine called *Das Veritas*. Attached to the translation was a copy of the original article browned with age and dated 1910.

The headline read, "Double Murder Hides Single Death."

Now, this was something new. I read the translation.

What's most interesting in this case is that the authorities refuse to even consider a simple fact: Sebastian Radcliffe is the perfect suspect. He could have murdered his bride in a fit of rage. Given Castle Creighton's location on the remote Isle of Acacia, he could easily have thrown Cassie's lifeless body into the ocean and disappeared from sight. All while revelers celebrated his marriage into the early hours of the morning. The guise of a double murder protects Sebastian Radcliffe from being convicted of a singular killing.

Finally, I was getting somewhere. Professor Astor loved this kind of stuff. I took some notes before grabbing another book.

Ah, yes. The Radcliffe Curse.

If a high-society wedding at an isolated castle ends in a double murder, it would have to be on account of a curse. That was what the locals believed, anyway: that something unseen and unheard crept up on the family and took its revenge on them. Why? The explanations varied.

This was outside the scope of my paper. And dangerous ground for me. I snapped the book shut and looked around. There weren't as many students in the library as there had been earlier, but the trio of sophomores still sat at my table. Good.

Ghosts don't exist. They can't touch me. They can't hurt me. They aren't real. I said it three times in my mind, trying to reinforce it in my reality. But, in that instant, I felt it. Something inside me said that there was no rational explanation for the murders at Castle Creighton. My mouth went dry and my pulse sped up. I knew in my bones that Castle Creighton was a place where the unbelievables thrived.

I shoved the thought away, took a deep breath, and flipped to a clean sheet of notebook paper. I decided to create a timeline of the murders—a neat, orderly, fact-based timeline. A good two hours existed between when the bride, Cassie, left the reception to go to her room in the south turret and when a wedding guest, Drew Nolan, discovered her room drenched in blood.

So many things could have happened. Anyone at the wedding could have slipped away from the festivities unnoticed. The list of guests and servants totaled 153 people—and those were just the people who were known to be in the castle. There would have been plenty of opportunity for a stranger to sneak in. I skimmed through several books trying to find clues about what might have happened during those crucial hours after Cassie left the reception. My pen scraped and my handwriting scrawled across the page.

I was on my third page of notes when the lights hummed and buzzed over my head. Then they dimmed, flared back to daylight brightness, and flickered. I dropped my pen and yanked off my headphones.

This shouldn't be happening. It hadn't happened since I was nine. I looked around and realized I was alone. I'd gotten so caught up in my research, I'd lost track of everything else. My watch read 8 p.m. Where had that last hour gone? I should have been nicer to the sophomores. Maybe they'd have said goodbye before they left me all alone.

The lights flicker-flared three more times. A chilly burn prickled against the base of my spine. My neck muscles tightened. The shadow of the bookcase in front of me thickened. The inside of the shadow shimmered. The way it did when a ghost was breaking through.

To keep the ghost from appearing, I repeated, "Must be a stupid soccer player pranking me," until it became my reality.

The air returned to normal, but the books around me rattled on their shelves. Three fell to the floor. I didn't want to look, but I had to. The books had nothing in common, but each spine had cracked open to chapter nine.

Nine. My age during the last ghost attack. *Ghosts don't exist. They can't touch me. They can't hurt me. They aren't real.* I said it like a prayer. It was the last weapon I had to keep this ghost away from me.

Please don't let this be the night it fails me.

I shoved most of my stuff into my backpack and threw it over my shoulder. Swept the rest of my books into my arms and ran for the exit.

Row by row, the lights behind me went out. Sweat broke out across my upper lip. My heart pleaded, *Not again, not again.* A chair darted into my path. I dodged to the left and sprinted down the aisle, trying to stay ahead of the growing darkness.

I needed light. I needed people. I needed life around me.

I ran to the elevator and hit the button, giving it three long seconds before I hightailed it to the stairs.

Ghosts don't exist. They can't touch me. They can't hurt me. They aren't real.

Cold air blew against my neck. The ghost was so close to me. I didn't turn around.

"It's just a breeze in a drafty old stairwell," I whispered over and over again.

A few more stairs to go. I stumbled out of the stairwell and onto the main floor, crashing into Morgan.

She grabbed me to steady herself. "Kat, what's wrong?"

"I…nothing." Bright lobby. Morgan. Safety. I tried to laugh it off, but it came out more like a gasping hiccup.

"I was just coming to find you. The library's closing." And Morgan's work at the circulation desk was done. "Lights flickering upstairs?" Morgan closed the floor several nights a week. She knew everything that went bump at the library.

I nodded, studying the floor tiles.

"You were alone and got spooked?"

I nodded again.

"You know what finals do to the jocks. They can't help playing tricks on the smart kids. Makes them feel better. Or maybe it's our resident ghost." She was half-kidding. She didn't really believe, which made it easy to joke about the possibility.

I looked up, straight into her aquamarine eyes and lied, "Yeah, stupid jocks." My heart still thrummed in my ears.

"You should study in our room. It's quieter." She tucked her jet-black hair behind her ear, exposing the Medusa ear cuff we'd picked up yesterday on M Street.

It had been years since a ghost came that close to appearing. Why was this happening now?

She peered at my face and swept my blonde bangs to the side. "You okay?"

I clenched the books to my chest to keep my hands from shaking. My voice cracked. "Can we go, please?"

"You're really freaked."

"I'll be fine." *As soon as my heart stops trying to break out of my rib cage.* I needed fresh air. Plants. Life. Lots of people. All the things ghosts shied away from. I needed layers upon layers of ghost armor.

Morgan slung her messenger bag over her shoulder. "All set."

When we stepped outside the library's doors, I breathed in the rose-scented air and listened to an owl hooting. I pressed my palm against the nearest oak tree, resisting the urge to drop my books and wrap my arms around it.

My heart started to settle down, but this wasn't enough. I still needed people. Lots of people. "What party are we hitting?"

When McTernan Academy's famous neighbor, Georgetown University, reached Thursday night, the weekend kicked off. Morgan loved seeing how many college parties she could talk her way into.

She laughed. "First, we drop our stuff off and get prettied up. Then we see where the night takes us."

Normally, I'd beg for a night in with a good '80s comedy and Pop-Tarts. Instead, I forced a smile. "Sounds awesome."

Morgan did a double take. "You really don't want to be alone, do you?"

I shrugged. "I could use a night off."

Morgan didn't know about the ghosts and me. No one here did. And I wanted to keep it that way. I denied the ghosts' existence every day to have a normal life. I had no idea that this was the day that normal started to wither away.

Chapter 2

While Morgan picked out our outfits, I accessorized the ghosts away. Every ring, earring, necklace, and bracelet I owned was made of real metal and stones—things from the earth. The past few years, they'd been relegated to cool accents for my clothes. I had coasted by, doing the bare minimum to keep the ghosts gone. Tonight, my jewelry returned to its original purpose as ghost repellent.

I hung necklaces of garnet, moonstone, and labradorite around my neck. A bracelet of turquoise and another of amethyst slid onto my wrist. I added a silver charm bracelet. Fumbling through my rings, my fingers grazed the blue velvet box I kept hidden in the back of the drawer. I pulled it out.

The box had arrived on my seventeenth birthday. Inside was a ring with a star sapphire encircled by diamonds and set in a white gold band. It was the only thing my father ever gave me. For most girls, it would be a cherished gift. For me, it was a reminder of what I didn't have.

Seventeen years without a word from him. Then the ring showed up with a handwritten note that said, "Know that I love you and that this is yours. Dad."

Tears blurred my vision. I blinked them away. I never wore the ring. It felt like that would be accepting his absence and I couldn't. I hadn't opened the box in months. But tonight, when I looked at the ring, I noticed how similar it was to the one Toria wore. When I touched the star sapphire, I felt the echo of her protection. Like the ring belonged on my finger and it didn't matter that it came from my dad. The stone had found its way to me and that was where it wanted to be. I couldn't help myself. I slipped it on. A perfect fit.

Mine.

Morgan squeezed my arm. "You okay?"

"Yeah, fine." I pretended away the pain. It was weakness and ghosts exploited weakness.

"It's all in your eyes, Kitty Kat." She waited for me to say something.

I couldn't say it out loud. Wouldn't admit how much it hurt. Couldn't let it be part of my reality.

Her tone softened. "It was a beautiful birthday present." Her arm slipped around my shoulder and gave a squeeze.

I said, "I'm okay," willing it to be true. And it would be because I had Morgan. We instantly connected at freshmen orientation and were besties by the end of the first week of school. "What would I do without you?" I leaned into her.

"Probably still be sitting at orientation, too petrified to speak to anyone." She laughed and grabbed my hand, tugging me over to my desk. "Time to put your contacts in."

"I hate wearing them," I muttered. I was so much more comfortable in my tortoise shell glasses.

"You need to stop hiding those gorgeous green eyes."

I smiled. "They aren't nearly as gorgeous as your turquoise eyes."

She wagged her finger at me. "No compliment competitions."

There wasn't much of a competition. No matter how much she tried to make me stand out, next to Morgan, I faded into the background. But after my awkward ghost years, it was a relief to feel utterly unexceptional.

After I got my contacts in, I stared at the outfit she'd laid out on my bed. "No way."

She picked up the red halter-top and pressed it against me. "It's perfect."

It was the size of a handkerchief. "If I want to look like the Pillsbury Doughboy."

"It'll show off your curves." She stretched the top across the front of me.

I looked down at my bloated belly. Way too many carbs today. "That's what I'm afraid of."

She shoved it at me. "Try it on."

I chewed my bottom lip. "Not with those jeans." I pointed to the skinny jeans lying on the bed.

She wiggled the jeans in front of me. "They give you the best butt."

They were a size twelve and only fit thirty days out of the year. To please Morgan, I hopped around the room, squeezing into them. Sucked in my belly and yanked up the zipper. I'd have a permanent button mark on my stomach. Twisting in front of the mirror, I frowned. "My thighs look massive."

"With your blonde hair and peaches-and-cream skin, guys would line up around the block to date you in El Paso." Morgan's eyes softened the way they did whenever she thought of the first half of her life. She'd lived there right up until a spinster great-aunt died and left her mom the house in Wright, Connecticut. Morgan still hadn't forgiven her great aunt for dying.

I stared at my hips. They were so wide. Morgan swore I had a belly dancer's body. "Unfortunately, we're in D.C." Where thin meant everything.

Morgan rolled her eyes. "These will make your legs look longer." She dangled her three-inch heels from her fingers.

I waved them away. "Guaranteed twisted ankle." Georgetown was filled with uneven brick and undulating cement sidewalks. Plus, those shoes turned me from über-tall five-foot-nine to Amazon-queen six-feet.

She tried to hand them to me.

I folded my arms across my chest. They were designed for her delicate five-foot-fiveness. "How can such a tiny person have such big feet?" I asked.

"The better to torture my roommate with," she mwahahahaed and dropped them beside her spiked collar, black miniskirt, fishnet tights, and a "Cure" T-shirt she'd remade into a punk masterpiece with safety pins and a leather cord.

She shoved a pair of one-and-a-half-inch platform shoes at me. "Better?"

I wrinkled my nose.

"There's always my thigh-high pirate boots."

I sat on my bed and shoved my feet into her platforms. "It's your fault if we get caught sneaking out."

"Not like we haven't pulled this off before." She smiled with her Mad-Hatter confidence. "Our dorm head won't be waking up until morning."

I almost felt bad for the teacher who lived in our dorm, forced to be a substitute mom to fifty girls. "What did you do?"

"Made her some brownies." Morgan threw her clothes on the floor and shimmied into her outfit. The T-shirt exposed her flat stomach and sparkly belly button jewel. Her amber-colored skin blazed like an Aztec goddess's against all that black.

"Laced with?" I asked as she sashayed in front of the mirror.

"Tylenol PM." She grabbed her brush and divided my hair into six sections.

In the mirror, I watched Morgan twist my hair into mini-buns and pin them in place. Usually, I loved when she did my hair. But tonight, as I sat still, my mind wandered back to what had happened in the library. Why would the ghosts be trying so hard to get through now? After eight years of normal. What had changed?

I wanted to think I'd gotten cocky and let my guard down. That would be easy to fix. I could just focus, be more diligent. But what if all my protections were losing their effectiveness? Or maybe something about Castle Creighton had triggered the ghosts' return?

I didn't realize how lost I was in my own thoughts until Morgan said, "Kat? Earth to Kat."

"What?" I blinked.

"What do you think of your hair?"

It was done already? I looked in the mirror. "Love it."

"I wonder what Evan the Terrible would think of you now?" she asked.

Evan was the college sophomore TAing my class with Professor Astor. McTernan girls swooned over him and his British accent. He was half British and half Chinese. Probably one of the best looking guys at our school too. The fact that he had grown up on two continents and spoke fluent Cantonese completed his trifecta of coolness.

I faked a bad British accent and said, "Bollocks. Kat should be working on her paper, not partying."

Morgan laughed and leaned into the mirror. She painted her lips Vamp, a dark-purply red. "You remember what we have to do?"

I nodded and ticked off the steps on my fingers. "Crawl on our bellies to avoid the motion detectors. Slam the exit door hard to short circuit the alarm. Avoid the night watchman and the Dean's house."

"Piece of cake."

"If you're training for the CIA."

"Wait until senior year." She winked at me.

Chapter 3

Morgan always said that the harder you play, the better you rest. Which might explain why, four nights later, she was snuggled under the covers gentling snoring while I was wide awake and hunched over my desk.

My paper on Castle Creighton was almost done. I wasn't entirely happy with it, but there wasn't much I could do about it at this point. Morgan's family lived in Wright and her dad's friend at the police department was supposed to send me copies of the official report on the Radcliffe murders. I'd waited for his email as long as I could, but it never arrived. In the end, I did my best to cobble together something new from secondary sources.

I sighed and stared at my growing plant collection. Morgan had quirked an eyebrow and asked, "Going greener?" when my plant collection grew from three to more than a dozen. Not that she minded. She loved plants and immediately moved them to spots where they'd get just the right amount of sun.

The four cacti were thriving on the windowsill. The orchid and bonsai tree kept watch on the nightstand beside my bed. The fern, ficus, and palm crowded my desk. Maybe it was time to smuggle a beta fish into the dorm? Anything to maintain a ghost-free zone.

The episode in the library had shaken me. It was very possible that the ghost trying to get through to me that night was harmless. If it had been like most of the ghosts I'd known growing up, it would have gone away as soon as I helped it with its reckoning. But my skin crawled when I thought about the silver-eyed ghost and what she wanted. She had watched me, stalked me, preyed on me in my moment of weakness.

Toria told me I wouldn't just disappear if a ghost gained a permanent place in my body. Maybe I would stay inside my body, stealing a few moments of control whenever I could. Or maybe my soul would be pushed out altogether and simply wander. If that happened, I'd be trapped in this reality forever. I'd be a soul without a body. Not alive, not dead. Not human nor ghost. A tremor ran through me when I thought of what would have happened to me without Toria.

I looked down at my star sapphire ring. It looked so much like hers. It made me feel closer to her. It felt like mine and more than mine. Ours. I wanted to see Toria again. To tell her how much she helped me. How grateful I was to still have my body. How much I appreciated the eight years of normal she had given me.

This might have been the moment that I realized those years of normal were all I would ever have.

My gaze slid back to the laptop screen. My fingers tapped on the keyboard.

My plan for turning a bunch of notes from secondary sources into an *A+* paper on the Radcliffe murders? Dazzle Evan the Terrible with footnotes. I rubbed the tiger's eye stone on my desk for courage. My stomach gurgled. Great. Heartburn at seventeen. I grabbed some Tums and prepared to pull another all-nighter. I had to have this paper in by 8 a.m., which left me five hours to work some footnote magic.

"You gave me a *B* because of a few grammar mistakes?" I asked.

Evan's long fingers toyed with his pen, reminding me that my future was Play-Doh in his hands. His refined British accent couldn't conceal his mockery. "That sums it up, and jolly succinctly for a change, Kat." He was only three years older than me, but he acted a decade smarter.

"What about the fifty-six footnotes? Do you know how much time I spent checking them?" I asked.

"Time management is your issue, not mine."

Was he kidding or condescending? I studied his face. His hazel eyes reminded me of labradorite, except they were mostly amber brown with flecks of green. They glowed against his golden skin. His expression was absolutely unreadable.

"Professor Astor doesn't care about footnotes. He's much more interested in primary sources."

The blood pounded against my temples and pulsated into my hands. I wanted to jump out of the chair and ram my paper down his throat. "You have no idea how hard I tried to get them."

"But you didn't get them, did you?" He pushed his dark brown hair out of his eyes and sighed. "A *B* is ace, especially for a junior." My face must have betrayed my confusion over his use of British slang, because he added, "Downright amazing, actually."

I gritted my teeth. "Do you understand the consequences of a *B* on my final paper?" It was fifty percent of my grade in that class.

McTernan was my stepping-stone to Georgetown. To the future Mom and I dreamed of. She worked at a private museum for a wealthy benefactor. He paid generously and she embraced every special project he sent her way, spearheading more archaeological digs than most PhDs. It still wasn't enough to cover my tuition. We needed my scholarship, and this *B* put it in jeopardy.

"I'm fairly certain the world will continue as it always has and someone will learn to work harder," he said.

I wanted to scream, but I clenched my jaw shut. Morgan's advice ran through my head. *When facing difficulty, a girl has four options: crying, flirting, blackmailing, or honesty.*

Tears wouldn't work on him. And flirting was out, too. Evan clearly regarded me as an alien life form.

I tried honesty.

"I need at least a *B+*. Is there any extra credit I can do to make that happen?" I asked.

"It's too late in the term for that." He spread his hands before him.

Cornered animals do whatever it takes to survive. So do scholarship kids. Blackmail it was. "Maybe we should take this up with Professor Astor."

The smugness evaporated from his face. "We don't need to bother the professor."

"I think we do." I hated playing the Astor card, and I wouldn't have if Evan hadn't been such a jerk.

"Don't expect the professor to be more lenient because he likes you."

I leapt to my feet, snatching my paper off his desk. "I bet you anything, Professor Astor thinks it deserves a better grade."

"Then you'll lose." He sifted through the papers in front of him.

Was he reading them now? While I was standing right here? I tapped my foot on the floor and cleared my throat.

Finally, he glanced up. "I thought this meeting was finished. Is there something else you want to ask me?"

Yes. Why did he have to be "such an arrogant jerk?"

Evan's eyes narrowed.

My hand clamped over my mouth twelve seconds too late. Did I really say those last four words aloud?

Right about the time he started clenching his jaw, I grabbed my paper and darted out of the room.

Chapter 4

I followed Mom's advice about waiting three days after an argument before making a move. On day three, I checked my email and found an invite from Professor Astor to stop by his office on Georgetown's campus at 4 p.m. He wanted to talk about my summer research for him. The email went out to me, Morgan, Evan, and someone named Seth Fitzgerald.

I was supposed to do off-site research on Castle Creighton this summer while I stayed with my grandparents here in D.C. I figured I'd be spending most of my time parked in the Java House, pouring over old books, but I hadn't really thought about it lately. Ghost-repelling required a lot of concentration. Between that and preparing for finals, I was taking life hour-by-hour.

Things were so different back in March, when the professor first asked for my help. I'd leapt at the chance. It was exactly the sort of thing admissions officers loved. This could be my golden ticket to Georgetown. At the time, I hadn't worried much about the topic of the professor's book: the curses surrounding America's richest families. I'd almost convinced myself that the "curses" were just a series of bad decisions that no one wanted to take credit for. There hadn't been any ghost issues in years. I'd been pretty sure that I could do a little research on the Radcliffes without making myself vulnerable.

But I'd been wrong.

After what happened in the library, I couldn't spend my summer reading about Castle Creighton. I had to stay far away from the unbelievables. I needed to surround myself with people and other living things and think about baby pandas and rainbows, not unexplained deaths and family curses.

Constant vigilance wasn't easy, but there had been zero ghost events since the library. I wanted to keep it that way. All the ghosts needed were a few minutes of me alone and unfocused. A single moment where I allowed myself to believe in the unbelievables again. This project was just too dangerous. I had to find a way out of it.

The day flew by in a blur of study sessions for finals. At 3:45 p.m., I still didn't have what I needed—a good excuse to get out of the Castle Creighton project. I knocked twice on Professor Astor's door. No answer. I sat on the floor to wait, anxiously trying to come up with a reason I couldn't work for the professor this summer. I twisted my star sapphire ring around my finger. Touching the stone made me feel better when I was nervous or worried.

Semi-coherent muttering and frenetic tapping on a phone interrupted my thoughts. Professor Astor had arrived. His head of unruly salt-and-pepper hair screamed *brilliant physicist,* but his neatly trimmed beard and impressive sweater-vest collection said *humanities scholar*. His eyes were the lightest blue, like the larimar stone I'd added to my rock collection last week.

He threw open his door and the mountains of papers in his office shivered, threatening an avalanche. "Come in, come in," he said with the soothing voice of a therapist.

Four new piles of research were stacked around the room. The shortest was a foot tall. The largest, and most unstable, was the height of an average second grader. "Four new projects?"

"Three, actually." He pointed to the tallest pile. "The shortest is a continuation of that one." He weaved his way to his desk. "All ongoing projects."

Ongoing could span decades. Floor-to-ceiling bookcases lined the walls beside his desk. Only here could Cunningham's Wiccan magic book,

Earth Power, sit beside *The Search for Modern China*, Spense's book on China's history.

I edged toward the chair in front of his desk, trying not to disturb the layers of documents scattered over his work area.

He ignored the blinking voicemail light on his phone. "You're earlier than usual. What's on your mind, Kat?"

"I had a quick question about my final paper."

"Have you talked to Evan about it?" he asked.

"He was...unable to resolve the confusion."

"Let me take a look."

I handed it to him. Professor Astor shoved his wire frame reading glasses onto his nose. They were crooked, but he didn't notice. Normally, I'd have laughed. Today, I held my breath, hoping I wasn't wrong.

His brow furrowed as he flipped through my pages. It smoothed out when he came to the last page. "He didn't factor in the curve properly. The *B* should have been changed to a *B+*."

My breath rushed out.

"Your paper was one of the best in the class. I actually learned something. Too bad about the lack of primary sources." Professor Astor reached for his red pen and fixed my grade. "We wouldn't want a silly math error to mar your GPA or jeopardize your scholarship." He handed the paper back to me. "I'll have him update the grade book."

"Thanks. Sorry to bother you."

"Evan's TAing both my classes at McTernan Academy. You know how it goes, chomping off more than you can digest."

Or just being an arrogant jerk. I forced a smile and nodded.

"By the way, I loved that term you used for the paranormal—the unbelievables. How did you come up with that?"

I didn't. It's what they call themselves. "I'm not sure. I must have stumbled on it somewhere."

"I plan to use it in my book." Professor Astor settled back in his chair. "How's your mom doing? No surprises in Africa?" He chuckled.

Mom only called him when a dig uncovered something unusual or inexplicable. Those were his specialties. Professor Astor and my mom had been colleagues years ago, but he'd quickly evolved into a close family friend.

"It's one of the more typical ones, I guess." That was what she'd said when we'd video chatted last week. "How are things progressing on your next book?"

"I've got some great news." He looked at his watch. "Let's wait for the others to join us."

There was only one other chair. And no way to bring more in without toppling the stacks of papers. "Will they fit?"

"I was hoping Morgan and Seth wouldn't mind standing," he said.

"Morgan's cool sitting on the floor, but I don't know Seth."

"He'll lounge against something," the professor assured me.

Before I could ask what that meant, Evan arrived.

He took the seat beside me and asked, "This is the meeting you mentioned last week about Castle Creighton?"

Professor Astor nodded.

Evan's brow knit together. "And you invited Seth?"

"He's an expert in architecture," Professor Astor said. "We can use his input."

If Evan was asking questions, so was I. "And Morgan's your contact in Wright?"

"She knows everyone in town, and she's the current Radcliffe Scholar," the professor said.

One of the few perks of being from Wright for Morgan. Every year the Radcliffes held an essay contest and awarded a full scholarship to McTernan Academy to one deserving eighth grader.

Evan sounded confused. "I thought we were doing independent studies. Are we all working together?"

I guess the professor hadn't kept any of us in the loop on that new detail.

The professor looked past him to the doorway and smiled. "Seth, Morgan, please shut the door and join us. We've run short on chairs."

I turned around and caught Morgan's eye. She gave me her what's-going-on eyebrows. I shrugged. She sat down on the floor beside me.

Seth shut the door and leaned against the wall. His eyes were gray, like hematite. He had the most symmetrical face I'd seen outside of a magazine ad. With the kind of messy dark brown hair you couldn't help wanting to touch. When he caught me looking at him, he gave me a half-smile that made my stomach do a cartwheel.

"Trying to get me to study more, Evan?" Seth asked. He had one of those deep and gravelly voices that made a girl go tingly.

Evan smiled. "It's the professor's plan, not mine. I swear."

In his roundabout way, the professor began explaining, "Kat's last paper on Castle Creighton was extremely insightful. Not only did she provide an excellent summary of what we know, but she also identified the areas we need to explore further if we're going to form a reasonable, evidence-based hypothesis about what really happened the night of the wedding."

Morgan patted my leg. When I looked down at her, she gave me a thumbs up.

As an aside to Evan, the professor said, "Oh, and I need you to fix a mistake in the grade book."

Evan asked, "Mistake?" in the tone most people reserved for unicorns and other imaginary phenomena.

"The curve wasn't factored in properly when you graded Kat's paper," Professor Astor said.

Evan groped for an excuse.

The professor held up his hand to stop him. "We changed the curve a few times. I should have reminded you to double check the formulas in your spreadsheet."

"I'll recheck everything." Evan's voice was smoother than maple syrup on pancakes, but his fingers curled into fists.

Mr. TA did not like being wrong. Or maybe it was me being right that bothered him.

I heard Seth sigh and shift against the wall behind me as if the conversation already bored him.

"I've assembled research teams for each location and each family in my book. The funding came through for the entire project. It's much more than I expected, so I've decided to send each team on-site. The four of you will be working together at Castle Creighton on the Radcliffe family." Professor Astor paused to let us process the change in plans.

I didn't trust myself thinking about curses in a crowded coffee house. There was no way I could go to an isolated castle and investigate a mysterious double-homicide.

"Your mission will be two-fold. First, you should do everything you can to find out what really happened at Castle Creighton. My hope is that, in this part of the book, we can offer a satisfying solution to the mystery—or at least a well-supported hypothesis," Professor Astor explained.

"But I also want you to study the curse. Slip on your folklorist or anthropologist hats. You're not trying to prove or disprove the curse. You're simply collecting stories and finding out what the local people have to say. Whatever skepticism you might have about the reality of curses, set it aside and just listen." Professor Astor's gaze shifted to me. "Kat, you've always been open to the unbelievables."

What? I'd spent half my life cramming them in a closet and locking the door.

"Unbelievables?" Evan asked.

The professor turned to him. "Yes. It's Kat's word and I like it. That's how we'll refer to anything paranormal or supernatural in the book. Unbelievables."

Evan gave me some serious side-eye. He hated when the professor picked me over him.

The professor returned his attention to me. "Your openness comes through in your papers. You understand that reason and sound scholarship don't preclude a belief in the inexplicable."

I guess I wasn't as good at unbelieving as I thought I was. Despite how stuffy and overheated the professor's office had been, I felt chilled.

"I want you to bring that sensibility to your investigation of the facts of the case. And I asked Evan to take on the curse precisely because he doesn't believe in it. I want his scientific rigor. Now, I'm hoping that all of you, working together, can use a combination of these approaches to create a comprehensive account of Cassie's and Sebastian's deaths and the Radcliffe Curse," the professor said.

The professor leaned back in his chair to look at all of us. "This work is an important component of Evan's thesis. For Seth, it's a chance to earn some much-needed extra credit." Professor Astor paused to give Seth a pointed look. Seth just smiled, charmingly. "And, Kat and Morgan, I don't have to tell you that doing this level of research in prep school will undoubtedly help you to get into the college of your choice."

No, he didn't have to tell me. But I still couldn't do it.

Professor Astor kept talking, but I wasn't paying much attention. I was busy thinking of excuses for why I couldn't do this. Helping out at grandma's antique store this summer. Family road trip to the national parks. Joining Mom on a dig. I considered each one and tossed it aside. None of them felt good enough to get me out of this situation.

I did manage to catch Evan's objection to being shackled with high-school students. "I chose Georgetown so that I could work with you. Why would I want to work with kids?"

I almost laughed. It would be too much if Evan's attitude turned out to be my ticket back to my nice, safe, ghost-free world.

"Evan, you are best suited to lead this project." Professor Astor let his words sink in. "But you can't do this alone. Morgan is from Wright. She knows the village and she knows its people. Her help should prove invaluable when it comes to interviewing locals. And, even though Kat is young, she has more experience doing fieldwork than you do."

For once, Evan had no reply.

The professor continued, "Kat's mother is Dr. Valerie Preston."

"The same Dr. Valerie Preston who wrote the brilliant paper on Kiffian burial practices at Ahafa?" Evan asked excitedly.

That paper had been published in the *African Archaeological Review* two years ago. In academic circles, Mom was a rock star. To the rest of the world, she was just that weird woman who dug up old pottery.

The professor nodded. "Kat's been going on digs since she could walk. It's rare that I would ask someone so young to do this kind of research, but she is uniquely qualified to work with you."

My cheeks were hot from the praise. And my stomach hurt. The thought of letting Professor Astor down made me sick. But I didn't have a choice.

While I tried to come up with a plausible way out of this situation—one that wouldn't disappoint the professor too much or ruin my future—Astor kept talking.

He said something about architectural plans and hidden passages as he gave a sheaf of blueprints to Seth. Professor Astor told Morgan that Joshua Radcliffe had specifically requested her presence on the team when he offered to open the castle to researchers. My attention drifted away again until I heard the professor say, "...and Toria Langley."

Toria.

The professor slid a photograph across his desk. I reached for it with shaking fingers.

There she was. Toria. My Toria. She was standing next to a bride who had to be Cassie. And on Cassie's other side was the ghost who had tried to possess me.

I struggled to keep my voice from quivering. "Toria Langley and...? What's the other bridesmaid's name?"

"Leanna Burnsby."

Leanna. Now I knew her name.

They had been there. They were in the Radcliffe wedding. They were there for the double murder.

Over the years, I had rarely let myself remember Toria. It hurt to think of her. But, when I did, I suspected she'd been placating me when she said that I would be able to help her one day. Now, I realized she had been telling the truth.

I didn't want to go to Castle Creighton. I didn't want to leave the safe little world I had created for myself. But I owed it to Toria. And after what happened in the library, my safe little world wasn't that safe anymore.

Chapter 5

Our journey from McTernan Academy to Castle Creighton required more forms of transportation than I would have imagined possible. Mostly because Evan was super cheap and Morgan knew how to make the trip as inexpensive as possible.

We bused across D.C. to Union Station. Switched to Amtrak for the train ride to Penn Station. Walked across Manhattan to Grand Central, where we caught a Metro North commuter train heading toward Connecticut. On the train, Evan snagged a four-seater so we could have a project meeting.

"Let's begin with the Radcliffe Curse. It seems to have a distinct pattern," Evan said.

He sounded like he was discussing an algorithm, but the word *curse* sent a chill up my spine. I was going to talk about curses as though they were real. I was opening that door to the unbelievables. I was decked out like a carnival fortuneteller in crystal necklaces and silver rings, but I knew it was only a matter of time before the ghosts got to me. Right now, my hope was that Evan was such an unbeliever that he could hold the unbelievables at bay for a little while longer. Evan was my last hope. *Evan.*

I was so screwed.

"Did everyone read the research notes that I sent you?" Evan asked.

Morgan and I nodded and fumbled in our bags for our printouts.

Seth said, "Must have missed that email."

"I figured you might." Evan handed him a copy.

Seth slipped it into his backpack. I had a feeling he was never going to look at it again.

"The curse only affects the first-born sons. If they marry before they turn twenty-three, they die on their honeymoon. If they remain single, they die on their twenty-third birthday. In both situations, the circumstances of death tend toward the bizarre."

Evan had put together the timeline of these untimely deaths. He seemed unimpressed by curses, but he had a lot of respect for orderly mathematical patterns.

Cassie and Sebastian had been murdered in 1886—just after Sebastian, the twenty-three-year-old first-born son, had gotten married. The following year, Phillip Radcliffe married Leanna Burnsby. They had two daughters and two sons born between 1888 and 1898. Evan had traced their lives through public records and newspaper tidbits.

In 1915, at the age of twenty-two, their elder son, William, married. During his honeymoon at the family cabin near Cooper Falls Mountain, both he and his wife died in a terrible rockslide.

The Wright Chronicle offered few details about these deaths, but Evan had unearthed a geology student's dissertation that referenced the event. The paper said, "It took several days to discover the bodies, which were mangled under tons of rubble. No other documented rockslides occurred in that area." The student couldn't find a scientific explanation for the tragedy.

Evan had tracked down the paper's author. During a video chat, she described the accident as "an unnatural natural disaster."

Phillip's second son, Nicholas, inherited everything. All the evidence Evan had found suggested that Nicholas had led a good life. His obituary stated, "He leaves behind his beloved wife, precious children and countless friends." Nicholas died at home, of a heart attack, at the age of fifty-seven.

Nicholas' first son, Howard, and his wife, however, met a bizarre end. *The Wright Chronicle* headline read, "Plane Crash Kills Local Businessman." The article mentioned engine failure after a bolt of lightning struck the private plane carrying Howard and his new bride to their honeymoon.

In 1956, Nicholas' second son, Brian, married. Like his father, he led a relatively peaceful existence. Evan had requested a copy of Brian's death certificate from the town clerk's office. The document said that Brian had died at sixty-eight of natural causes. He left behind three children, Gregory, Christopher, and Helen. Christopher married in 1987, and his son, Joshua

Radcliffe, was born in 1992. Joshua was the current heir.

Gregory was a bit of a black sheep. Evan passed around a five-page color spread in *Paris Match* detailing Gregory's affair with the French president's eighteen-year-old daughter. Gregory remained a bachelor until he died on his twenty-third birthday in 1982. *The Wright Chronicle* attributed his death to drowning, but Evan had found a much more detailed account of Gregory's death in a French newspaper.

Evan translated the headline, "Jelly Fish Attack Immorality." Then he read a bit of the article aloud. "It wasn't the season for jellyfish. But while American playboy Gregory Radcliffe snorkeled in the crystal waters of the Côte d'Azur, a swarm of mauve stingers attacked. While the venom of these creatures is generally nothing more than an irritant, the sheer volume of stings Radcliffe endured proved to be fatal. Marine biologists cannot explain why there were so many jellyfish in this part of the Mediterranean in October, nor do they understand why the creatures attacked en masse. No one else was injured, and the swarm of jellyfish disappeared as mysteriously as it had arrived."

With his older brother dead, Christopher became the heir to the Radcliffe fortune. In 1994, Christopher's second son was stillborn and his wife nearly died in childbirth. Christopher and his wife had no more children.

"That leaves us with Joshua. The first-born and only son of Christopher. He's twenty-two now."

Evan's tone was matter-of-fact, but he was talking about an actual person, a twenty-two-year-old man facing a death sentence.

"I can't imagine living with something like this looming over my head," Seth said.

A heaviness filled the air. As if the weight of Joshua's fate hung over us.

"Doesn't it make you wonder what they did to bring something like this down on their family?" Seth asked.

Morgan's eyes slitted. "No one deserves to suffer like this. To have their death date carved in stone before their birth."

I tried to bring the conversation back to our work. "What about the female Radcliffes?"

"Neither *The Wright Chronicle* nor Google searches on their names found anything out of the ordinary. I reviewed copies of death certificates from the town clerk's office to be sure. Most of the women lived past their fifties, some to their seventies. All died from old age or the excesses of extravagant living," Evan said.

"So the curse's pattern is that it kills married first-born sons on their honeymoons and single first-born sons on their twenty-third birthdays, whichever comes sooner, and always under strange circumstances," I said.

"As far as I can tell, yes." Evan said.

Morgan asked Evan, "So are you really a complete unbeliever?"

"Pretty much," Evan said.

"Like no curses or ghosts or time travel or aliens?" Morgan asked.

"I believe in science. So, no to curses and ghosts, but maybe aliens and time travel." Evan smiled at her.

"But, the Radcliffe Curse—how do you explain the pattern?" she asked.

"I'm still collecting data," Evan said.

When Morgan laughed at his prim tone, Evan blushed a little. Evan blushing. Now that was unbelievable.

"Look," he sounded testy. "I believe that curses are real to the extent that they can become real in people's minds. So, maybe the Radcliffe heirs are unconsciously seeking to repeat the pattern. Maybe, as their twenty-third birthdays approach, they take stupid chances. Maybe the reporters writing stories about their deaths make the circumstances seem more mysterious than they really are. Tabloid articles and local legends aren't hard evidence."

"So we've got an unbeliever versus a believer. I'm sensing a smackdown." Seth grinned at me.

"I never said I believed," I said.

"But you never said you didn't." Seth winked at me. "I myself am on the cusp of believing. I wonder what else we have in common?"

Now it was my turn to blush.

"Stop flirting with underage girls," Evan muttered.

Morgan snorted. "That's like asking him to stop breathing."

"Speaking of dangerous ages. How close is Joshua to twenty-three?" Seth asked.

Morgan gazed at the landscape flashing by the train window. "His twenty-third birthday is July 30th," she said softly.

Five weeks away. Our school project was his impending death. It was eerie how easily we had talked about the curse. Like the lives lost were just historical curiosities, not people that had died.

"I hope our research helps," I said. But I was afraid of what helping Joshua—and helping Toria—might mean for me.

"Let's move on to Bertram's journal. Has everyone read it?" Evan asked.

Bertram Mallory was Cassie's uncle and guardian. His diary was exactly the kind of primary source that would have gotten me an easy *A* if I'd had a copy before my paper was due. Unfortunately, Professor Astor didn't share this with us until after finals.

"Skimmed it," Morgan said.

Seth shook his head and ripped into a bag of Doritos.

I yanked out my copy. Of course I'd read it. Three times, surrounded by potted plants and my favorite stones, hoping to discover more about Toria. I hadn't had much luck, but there was one passage that stuck with me.

> *She is too young. How can Toria be ready for what she must face? She has only had a few years. If only Julia had not died. The responsibility is too great for Toria. Damn this alliance. How many more must we lose to it?*

I showed it to Evan and asked, "What did you make of this?"

He shrugged. "I didn't make much of it."

"But what about this alliance thing?"

"Marital alliances were very common in that era. Families bonded together for business, for territory, and for strength." He was silent for a moment, thinking. "Though a woman being a key player, rather than just a pawn, is weird. Maybe we should ask Joshua Radcliffe about it."

I nodded and flipped to my first Post-it marked page. "Bertram's notes on the wedding party read more like he was a private detective than the man giving the bride away. He wrote a short description of every single wedding guest. It's almost as if he was already looking for suspects."

"Definitely odd," Evan said. "He noted such peculiar things. Before the wedding, he barely mentioned the bride's best friend, Leanna Burnsby, but, after the tragedy, he spent several pages describing her relationship with the groom's younger brother, Phillip."

I flinched when he said Leanna's name. As if saying her name could somehow summon her ghost. I was still hoping that Evan's ferocious unbelieving would protect me. He was my human shield.

I tried to keep my voice calm as I read a passage aloud.

> *The night of the wedding reception, Leanna ensnared Phillip with the ruse of finding her gloves. Ever the gentleman, he spent an hour assisting in the search. He would have searched all night if not for the murders. A tragedy that shattered my family and his somehow bound them together. A most unnatural attraction bred in a time of misery and loss.*

"Bertram wrote a great deal about the best man, Alistair Kingsley, too." Evan thumbed through his photocopies and pointed to the entries he'd underlined in pencil. "He wrote, 'Alistair was born to protect Sebastian. Decades of training and he broke his oath.'"

"What do you think he meant?" I asked.

"Maybe Alistair was some sort of bodyguard?" Evan said.

It had crossed my mind when I read Bertram's journal, so I had to ask, "Could Alistair be a relative of yours?"

"I had the same thought." Evan smiled. "The Kingsleys are a large family. There's a distant connection between the American and the British Kingsleys. A third cousin four times removed, actually."

Evan followed every lead to its conclusion. He was a good researcher. A jerk of a TA, but a good researcher.

"Bertram hated Toria Langley's date, Drew Nolan," Morgan said. I wasn't surprised that she had focused on the soap-opera aspects of the story while she was skimming. Morgan loved drama—watching it unfold and being a part of it. She'd had a leading role in a few of the breakups at McTernan this year.

"Yes, but did you notice these?" Evan pointed to the symbols in the margin of the page Morgan had dog-eared.

When we nodded, he asked, "Do you know what they mean?"

"Nope," I said.

Morgan shrugged.

"They're Ogham, a medieval alphabet used for writing in Old Irish. As near as I can make out, they suggest an oath of fidelity between Drew and Bertram's family," he said.

"Wait, you read Old Irish?" I asked. I loved languages. I'd studied French and Chinese, and I hoped to take Russian in college.

"Language gives you insight into how people think," he said. "I speak and write several."

Morgan cocked her head the way she did when something intrigued her. "That's pretty cool."

"Is it?" he asked.

"I speak three languages. English, Spanish, and the language of love." Seth waggled his eyebrows at Morgan and me.

Evan gave him a dirty look. And it suddenly clicked. Seth wasn't flirting with me. He was trying to get a rise out of Evan and I was just the way he did it.

"I know, I know. Part of your job as team leader is to keep the lovely Kat out of my clutches," Seth said.

Heat rushed to my cheeks, but I also kind of enjoyed watching Evan get annoyed.

Morgan laughed. "Or maybe the professor expects Evan to keep you out of her clutches."

I didn't trust the glint in Seth's eyes. Morgan could eat him for breakfast. Me, I was more likely to be on the table beside the bacon.

The bus we caught in New Haven dumped us off on the outskirts of Wright, where ten-foot-tall shrubs formed a natural barricade between the road and the sidewalk. I couldn't find a way in. As a local, Morgan knew the spot where the bushes overlapped and allowed people to slip through.

I pulled out my parasol for sun protection.

Seth snorted. "A spoonful of sugar, Mary Poppins?"

I rolled my eyes. I was done letting him intimidate me. "So original.

Wow."

"She is rather pale. She might catch fire in the sun," Evan said.

"Vampires don't catch fire anymore. They sparkle," Morgan said.

She led us down a narrow dirt path. Gigantic pines and thick bushes surrounded us, completely obscuring the view of the ocean. The path curved a few times, quickly hiding the route back.

"In town, we use bicycles. Cars are parked near the outskirts. It's a tiny town, so you can bike everywhere," Morgan said.

"I prefer driving," Seth said.

She pointed to the plant life. "The town council is all about protecting the fragile ecosystem. Wright's a natural habitat to several endangered species. As a bonus, it helps keep tourists away."

"Wouldn't tourists be good for the town?" Evan asked.

"Not for Wright," Morgan said. "The Radcliffes are very generous to those who help protect their privacy."

With my horrible sense of balance, I kept my feet on the ground as much as possible. I had a scar to remind me of every time I broke that simple rule. "How about walking?"

"Biking would be faster," Evan said.

"I can rent you a bike," Morgan said.

I glared at Morgan. She had seen me fall off two-inch heels.

She added, "But walking might be the best way to get to know people in town, easier to talk to them about the curse."

We rounded the next bend in the path. The trees and bushes fell away, revealing the tiny town below. Colorful Victorian houses and small cottages dotted the shore. A perfect rectangle of grass formed the town green and miniature shops burst up along Main Street. My gaze wandered over the town, toward the water.

I'd seen pictures, but they didn't prepare me for my reaction. Like I found something I'd always lacked. Something I couldn't name but always needed. The castle shimmered under the rays of the late afternoon sun. I got why historical accounts dubbed it "the jewel of the ocean." I couldn't remember seeing anything more awe-inspiring. Castle Creighton throbbed with a life of its own.

Chapter 6

I lurched to a halt when I saw Morgan's house. How could the girl who introduced me to studded leather wrist cuffs have grown up in a gingerbread fantasy? Her house was a lilac-colored Victorian. Buttercup yellow shutters and white icing accented the windows and roof.

We had barely started down the walkway to the house when two children raced out the front door. I recognized Jaime and Marisella from Morgan's photos. They orbited their sister all the way to the front porch. Then they dashed inside to announce her arrival.

Morgan's mom bustled out in a floral apron and flung her arms around Morgan. "*Mija*, you look too thin. Don't they feed you at school?" Before Morgan could reply, her mom's face scrunched up. "*Ay Dios mío*, what did you do to your hair?"

Morgan peeked at her mom through her long lashes. "Added a little color."

She had streaked it azure blue right after finals.

"But your beautiful hair…"

"Is fine, *mami*. It washes out," Morgan turned to me. "Mom, you remember Kat?"

"Hi, Mrs. Sanchez. Thank you so much for letting me stay at your house," I said.

"We're happy to have you." Her mom hugged me like a long-lost daughter. "Do you like tamales? Chorizo? We can have hamburgers and hotdogs too. How about eggs? Or do you like cereal? We have lots of cereal."

"We lived off dining hall food all year. Kat will eat anything homemade," Morgan said.

I nodded. "I love tamales. And chorizo and eggs."

Mrs. Sanchez beamed at me. Morgan introduced Evan and Seth. Her mom hugged them and herded us all inside.

As she rushed off to the kitchen, Morgan's mom sang out, "Miguel, Morgan's home."

I used to wish for one power as a kid. Invisibility. Just so I could wander into a home like this and see what a family did. To taste what I was missing out on. To pretend I was a part of their world. And for a week or two this summer, I would be.

Morgan's dad sat in his brown recliner, digesting Morgan's scaled back goth-punk attire—black razor-cut T-shirt, short plaid pleated skirt, and black boots that laced up to the knee. Finally, he said, "At least you didn't pierce your nose."

Morgan danced over and gave him a peck on the cheek. "I have to save something for Christmas."

"You tell Marisella that your hair was an accident. Otherwise she'll be begging us to get hers done," he said.

"Sure, Dad," Morgan looked around for her siblings. "Where'd they disappear to?"

"Probably sneaking cookies in the kitchen."

Morgan introduced Evan and Seth. They sat down on the couch near her dad.

Seth started the conversation off with "The turret roof on your Queen Anne is in great shape. How do you maintain it?"

Her father's face lit up. Seth and Evan fell into a nodding contest while Morgan's dad described his recent repairs. Morgan and I slipped off to the kitchen to help her mom.

It was nearly nine when Morgan and I walked the guys over to the bed-and-breakfast where they'd be staying. The manager was a friend of Morgan's mom and let Morgan show Seth and Evan to their room. Morgan opened the door to the room and winked at me.

Two twin beds were pushed against opposite walls. Images of giraffes and monkeys danced across their comforters. The room had a desk painted powder blue. The lamp on the desk provided excellent lighting, but a circus clown sat at its base. Toys overflowed from a box in the corner.

After a semester of Evan killing dozens of red pens on my papers, Morgan had found a way to get back at him.

She gave Evan a sympathetic half-smile. "I figured you wouldn't want to spring for separate rooms. This was the only room with two beds."

Evan nodded and let his bags fall to the floor. He was adamant about not wasting his budget on accommodations.

I had to get out of there before I cracked up. "Morgan, we should get back to your house and cheer up Marisella."

Morgan's sister had been quietly sulking about giving up her bed so I could share the room with Morgan. Luckily, Jaime didn't seem to mind having his sister as a roommate.

Morgan smiled. "I'm thinking we do her hair and nails?"

"Sounds perfect," I said.

We shut the door as Evan asked Seth, "Can't you use your credit card to book your own room?"

"Professor Astor promised room and board." Laughter brimmed over in Seth's voice. "Maybe a game of Chutes and Ladders would help?"

Evan groaned. We heard a pillow make contact, most likely with Seth's head.

Seth's muffled voice said, "Physical violence solves nothing."

The next day, Morgan's walking tour of town ended with lunch at the local pub, The Blind Unicorn. Every time I glanced at the bar from our booth, I caught a redhead staring at us—well, at Morgan. There was such intensity in his citrine brown eyes. I planned to ask her about him later, when Seth and Evan weren't around. For now, I'd eat my greasy cheeseburger and crispy fries and wonder.

As soon as he'd paid our bill, Evan was all work again. While we were passing the bar, he reminded me, "You need to go pick up a copy of the investigation notes from the murders." To Morgan he said, "We might as well start lining up interviews with locals this week."

"I'm on it," Morgan said.

The red-haired guy pushed his way toward us. Freckles dusted the tip of his nose. He might have been cute if he hadn't looked so disgusted.

He ignored Evan and said to Morgan, "Word around town is you're asking questions about the Radcliffe Curse. What are you up to?"

"Adam, I'm not up to anything." Frustration crept into her words. "This is part of a research project. That's it."

Adam snorted. "You're the Radcliffe Scholar. Is private school tuition the going rate for your soul? Do they own you like they own the rest of this town?"

"Nobody owns me." Morgan threw her hands up. "Stop dreaming up conspiracies that don't exist."

Adam stepped toward her.

Evan put himself between them. "That's close enough."

"Stay out of it." Adam's eyes sought hers. "I can't believe I ever trusted you. One day, you'll see what the Radcliffes are."

"And one day, you'll realize how wrong you are about me," she said.

I pulled Morgan toward the door. Evan blocked Adam from pursuing us and Seth backed him up.

I dragged Morgan out into daylight. She broke free of my grasp and stormed back to the dirt path. She swerved off the walkway and plunged into the trees. By the time I caught up with her, tears streaked down her cheeks.

I rubbed her back and softly chanted the words we all need to hear, even if they're a lie. "Everything's going to be okay." I reached into my purse and fished out a wad of tissues.

She grabbed a few to wipe her face.

"Who was that?"

"Adam. He was my best friend," Morgan said.

"What happened?"

"Everything got twisted up after his mom died." Morgan's face collapsed and fresh tears filled her eyes. "She was awesome. She never said anything mean. Ever. And she loved him so much."

"What happened when she died?" I asked.

"Adam became an orphan. His dad had died in a car accident when he was three. He barely remembered him. Adam clung to his grandfather—he was the only family Adam had left."

"So Adam moved in with him?"

She nodded. "Adam believed every word his grandfather said about the Radcliffes. He really thinks they're murderers who must be punished." She gulped back a sob.

I squeezed her hand.

"He had this stupid idea that hurting Joshua would make his grandfather proud." She wiped her nose. "He waited until the July 4th picnic when all the Radcliffes were in town. He wouldn't tell me what he planned to do." She gnawed on her lower lip. "I've never seen the Radcliffes harm anyone. I couldn't let him injure Joshua over something that happened a century ago, so I watched Adam all day."

"You did what you thought was right."

She sniffled. "If I hadn't, Joshua would have gotten really sick."

"What did Adam do?"

"Joshua has a severe peanut allergy. Adam snuck ground peanuts into his sandwich. If Joshua had taken a bite, he'd have ended up in the hospital." Her voice became a whisper. "I knocked the sandwich to the ground and threw it away before Joshua could touch it. Then I gave him mine. Adam said I ruined everything and ended our friendship."

I hugged her. "Morgan, you didn't do anything wrong."

Her voice broke. "I turned on my best friend."

"He could have killed Joshua." I'd seen a classmate go into anaphylactic shock from a food allergy. It was terrifying.

"I couldn't believe that the boy I knew could do that. Would do that. Adam was my first friend when I moved to this town. He made it okay to be here. When I see him, I can't help remembering who he used to be."

"He isn't the same boy you loved."

"Kitty Kat, I miss him so much." Her lips trembled.

"Is there anything I can do?" I knew the answer. Nothing helped that kind of pain. Being abandoned by someone you loved. Time didn't make it better. You just got used to living around it.

The following morning's research almost got derailed. *The Wright Chronicle* was only available on microfiche before 1890 and we needed access to older issues to make sure the Radcliffe Curse started with the double murder. The librarian, however, refused to let us use her precious microfiche machine without giving us a tutorial. But she was the only one working the circulation desk and couldn't leave her post.

It took an hour for Morgan to convince the librarian that she could train us. Seth used that time to wheedle out of working with us, claiming he needed time alone to study the blueprints of the castle. More likely he was heading out to the beach to sunbathe.

We ended up in a tiny windowless closet with three chairs. If anyone wanted to move, that person had to announce it so the others could shuffle out of the way.

Evan decided to go back fifty years before the double murder and check for any bizarre deaths amongst the Radcliffe's first-born sons to make sure the curse started with Sebastian's death.

While our eyes scanned thousands of pages of newspaper, I discovered Evan read slower than me. Every time I turned the page, he switched it back. Our hands accidentally touched, and he gave me a shock. I jerked away and almost hit Morgan. Finally, I gave up on the controls and began intoning "Next" when I felt the page should be turned.

Evan scowled. "Are you skimming the page or just trying to annoy me?"

"I read fast. Not my fault if that annoys you."

I jotted down key dates or interesting snippets in my notebook. My notes were a combination of Chinese characters, mathematical symbols, and my own abbreviations. Virtually unreadable to anyone but me.

"What are you doing?" Evan snapped.

"Shouldn't someone jot down our progress, the dates, and what was in the paper? A timeline of non-events to prove the curse's pattern didn't exist prior to the murders," I said.

"Well, continue then," he muttered.

"Will do, Chief." I saluted him.

His eyes narrowed.

We worked for another hour before we took a break.

That's when Evan asked Morgan, "So, Adam. What's his issue with the Radcliffes?"

Morgan didn't answer so I jumped in with "It's nothing."

"It didn't sound like nothing," Evan said.

"Adam is a Nolan, and the Nolans think the Radcliffes are evil." There was a slight tremor in Morgan's voice.

Evan didn't push her, but I knew he had a new thread to pull on in the Radcliffe tapestry. And he would be tugging at Adam for the truth.

Our research continued a few more hours. It got really repetitive. So many non-events.

My eyes ached from staring at that dim screen. "How many charitable foundations can one family run? I'm surprised the pope didn't fly over to speak with them about managing non-profit organizations."

"You were expecting Hollywood intrigue?" Evan asked.

"Not until after the murders," I murmured.

Chapter 7

I tiptoed down a deserted stone corridor, desperate to escape. Afraid of discovery. There had to be a way out. An opening loomed on the left. Inside, there was a spiral stairwell. Icicles pierced my fingertips. The cold burned up to my knuckles, shooting pain into my wrists. Ghosts. Ghosts were everywhere. And they were strong. So much stronger here. They were coming for me. Something in me screamed, *go back*. I turned around, but darkness had devoured the hallway. If I stepped into that darkness, they would break through. They would break me.

I had no choice but to go up. A snowball of fear lodged in my throat. It refused to melt. I couldn't swallow it away. The stairs were freezer-chilled. They stung the soles of my feet and the cold seeped into my bones.

Through the blur of tears, I couldn't see where I was going. I stumbled and caught myself. I kept going until the stairs plateaued in front of a rounded door with black metal hinges stabbing across the wood panels.

The knob twisted in my hand, but the lock wouldn't budge. No key in sight. I threw my weight against the door. Nothing. I touched the keyhole. Suddenly, the lock slid out of place, and the door swung open.

A candelabrum blazed to life in the corner. A four-poster bed and armoire dominated the room. A delicate vanity sat beside the armoire. Gleaming against the stone wall, a large, antique mirror begged for a closer look. I shuffled onto the wood floor. My feet started to thaw.

I was halfway across the room when I felt something coming up the stairwell. Not Leanna's ghost. No. Something different. Something even more menacing. Something I'd never encountered. Dread encircled my waist. Fear paralyzed me. I couldn't hide. Couldn't even turn around to face what was coming. But I knew it was the worst unbelievable I'd ever encountered and it was coming for me.

I awoke drenched in sweat and tangled in my sheets. *Just a dream*, my mind chanted. Didn't help. Morgan's clock said 5:43 a.m. I sat up in her sister's bed and looked at Morgan. She was curled around her Winnie-the-Pooh bear, sound asleep.

Here in Morgan's house, there were so many people and so much life. Up until now, I'd felt safe, even as we researched the curse and the murders. I'd never had so many family meals. Breakfast was a noisy festival of fruit and eggs. Every morning, Jaime and Marisella came up with new questions to fire at me.

Dinner was my favorite meal. The whole family talked about their day. Sometimes at the same time. A mom, dad, and three kids all together. I loved the way Morgan's mom finished her dad's sentences. I wondered if my parents ever had that. And what had destroyed it.

There were so many layers of protection here. Not just my stones, but Morgan's family, her mom's garden, Evan's unbelief. I had never felt safer. But that dream was a bad sign. I didn't want to think about what it meant. I needed to clear my head. A shower. I needed a shower. I snuck out of our room and headed down the hall.

While I waited for the water to warm up, I stared at my reflection in the mirror. Anxiety was etched into my eyes. Worry lines slithered across my forehead. The ghosts were getting stronger. The unbelievables had found a way into my dreams. All my deterrents were just temporary hurdles for them.

The bathroom mirror fogged over. I lost sight of myself. I dropped my clothes on the floor and stepped into the shower. The water danced over my shoulders and dribbled down my back. I rotated until the water hit me in the face. I rubbed my palms over my cheeks, trying to wash the confusion away.

The dream still clung to me. Like at any moment it could tug me back there. Why did that corridor and room feel familiar? Not dream-familiar, but lived-through-it familiar. Where was it?

On our third afternoon in the microfiche dungeon, we picked up a few days before the wedding tragedy in 1886. Only a few more years of microfiche to go.

Evan flipped the microfiche forward and back a few times. "No newspapers on the four days following the wedding tragedy—that's quite peculiar."

"Look at this." I pointed to the obituaries section and read aloud, "'The Mallory family and Radcliffe family will hold a joint memorial for their beloved children, Cassie Mallory Radcliffe and Sebastian Radcliffe.' When parents lose a child, they search for someone to blame. Why didn't Bertram Mallory blame the Radcliffes for Cassie's death?"

"Bertram's journal alluded to them being victims of some greater tragedy," Evan said.

"Could he be any cagier about what it was?" I asked. "What's the point of being secretive in a journal?"

He stared at me. "You look tired." His hazel eyes didn't miss much.

"Bad night's sleep."

"Try warm milk," he offered.

Milk. That would keep the ghosts away. I choked on a laugh. He had no idea what this project was doing to me. How my reality was unraveling.

We went back to reading the microfiche screen. We had gone forward a year when I stopped him.

I flipped through my notes. "Wait, stop. That's Phillip Radcliffe and Leanna Burnsby's wedding announcement."

"And?" he asked.

"Look at the wedding date. That's Cassie's birthday."

"A tribute?" Evan asked.

"You think?" I asked. A person's birthday is the one day of the year that belongs to them. If ghost Leanna would steal a human body, why wouldn't human Leanna take her best friend's birthday and make it her anniversary?

After we finished up with the microfiche, Evan hunted down the librarian. "*The Wright Chronicle* is missing for the four days following the Radcliffe tragedy."

"No papers were printed on those days," she said.

"Why?" Evan asked.

"Out of respect for the family."

There wasn't anything else to say so we walked away from the reference desk. While Morgan cleaned up the microfiche room, Evan tapped away on his phone.

I started to walk away, when he asked, "Any luck with the investigation notes?"

I sighed. "Police procedures were pretty weak back then. And the tides made it impossible for the police to get out to Castle Creighton until the next afternoon."

"So nothing?" he asked.

"They measured the radius of the bloodstain on the floor. It was four feet."

He whistled. "That's a circumference of twelve-and-a-half feet. That's a lot of blood."

What had happened to Cassie and Sebastian? I cringed to think about it.

"Anything else?" he asked.

"Back then, they didn't take photos of the scene or dust for fingerprints. Any evidence that might have been there was lost."

"Thanks for looking into that," he said.

"It's my job."

"You do pretty good work," he murmured.

I never expected to hear him say that. "Thanks?"

"I'm interviewing Adam Nolan's grandfather tomorrow. You might want to come along to take notes," he said.

"What about Morgan?" She was supposed to do interviews with him.

"There's too much teen drama there," he said. "And I have to follow every single lead."

As Morgan's friend, I didn't like him going near Adam. But, as Professor Astor's researcher, I understood Evan's decision. I almost admired it. I nodded. "Yeah, I'd like to be there."

47

At 6:55 a.m., Evan and I strode up the Nolan's driveway. Their house may have once been pristine white, but now it was dingy gray. The gutters hung precariously from a roof that looked like it couldn't withstand another storm. On the porch sat a weathered, old man sipping from a mug in his rocking chair. A shotgun rested in his lap.

We both froze in place.

Evan recovered first and shouted, "Hello. I'm Evan Kingsley. Is this the Nolan residence?"

The old man inclined his head. The shotgun remained in his lap. Evan hesitated. So did I.

Adam came out onto the porch. "Are you coming up or do you conduct all your interviews from twenty feet away?"

Relief tiptoed through Evan's words. "Wasn't sure we had the right place. May we join you on the porch, sir?" He directed his question at Adam's grandfather.

Adam laughed. "You Brits sure are polite. If Grandpa meant to shoot you, he'd have done it as soon as you came into range." Adam pointed to the shotgun. "That's for the possums under the porch."

Evan continued up the front walk and mounted the steps. I followed him. He introduced me to Grandpa Nolan. The old man stared at me like he was sizing up my soul. Then he nodded, granting me permission to be there. I took the seat closest to Evan. I didn't want to be near the old man.

Grandpa Nolan asked, "Son, Adam says you want to talk about the Mallory murder. Why should I tell you anything?"

He was the only person to call it the Mallory murder.

"I'm interested in the truth, not what some powerful family says is the truth," Evan said.

"Well, I'll tell you what I know. What was told to me by my grandfather. What I've seen over the years. What the Radcliffes don't talk about. What nobody around here talks about," Grandpa Nolan said.

The old man fell silent. He leaned his head back against the chair and stared up at the morning sky. When he spoke, strength flooded his voice. "Drew Nolan was my grandfather. He loved Cassie Mallory. He went to the wedding to change her mind. If he couldn't, he was willing to let her go—provided she was happy. He warned her that Sebastian could destroy her, but she wouldn't listen. Maybe she loved Sebastian. Maybe she was more afraid of not marrying him than of marrying him."

"Did Sebastian have a temper?" Evan asked.

"My grandfather said he did, but nothing ever made it into the papers. You want to hear the story or not?"

Evan, chastened, nodded.

"The guests were still downstairs celebrating when my grandfather decided to turn in. That's when he heard a scream from Cassie's room in the south turret. He ran as fast as he could. When he got to the top of the stairwell, he found her bedroom door ajar. Inside, he saw something no amount of whiskey could wash away. The bed was covered in blood. It dripped off the sheets and pooled on the floor. To his dying day, he whispered how he'd never seen so much blood."

Grandpa Nolan paused for effect, clearly relishing his role of storyteller. "He called out to Cassie, but the room was empty. He swore that the mirror sparkled and shimmered at him like it was alive. Anyhow, he ran back to the great hall and alerted everyone to the murders. By the time they rushed upstairs, the mirror was back to normal. Those Radcliffes, they tried to blame him. They owned this town then as much as they do now. They hushed up any talk about Sebastian being behind Cassie's murder."

A shadow appeared next to Grandpa Nolan's rocking chair—a shadow that shouldn't have been there. The darkness inside the shadow shimmered, and a chill swept over me. Grandpa Nolan was definitely a believer. His belief was strong enough to counteract Evan's disbelief and my feeble attempts at protection. And whatever it was coalescing there on the porch, it wanted very badly to break through. It needed to break through.

White wisps of smoke emerged from the shadow. They gathered into a vague form: a man in a frock coat. My heart skipped a beat. This man leaned close to Grandpa Nolan's ear. I couldn't make out what he was saying, but I didn't have to. Grandpa Nolan repeated everything to us.

His voice shook with the ghost's conviction. "Sebastian must have found out that Cassie loved Drew. In a fit of rage, he killed her and threw her body into the ocean. Her body was never found, but the currents around that island would've carried it off. Sebastian disappeared out of humiliation. Scandals are unacceptable to the Radcliffes. My grandfather used to say that was the night the Radcliffe Curse began."

The ghost looked satisfied. As if he needed us to hear his words. He had to be Drew Nolan. I didn't want the ghost to know I saw him so I tried not to look directly at him. But he nodded at me anyway.

Ghosts don't exist. They can't touch me. They can't hurt me. They aren't real. I repeated my mantra in my head until he faded away. He wasn't gone. I just didn't see him anymore. The only sign that he remained was a shimmer in the air.

Grandpa Nolan leaned toward the shimmer, listening to Drew's words. He told us the whole history of the curse working over generations of Radcliffes. His account matched everything we'd already put together. Evan tried not to look smug.

I guess we didn't act shocked enough because Grandpa Nolan said, "But you knew all this already."

Evan nodded.

"Joshua's the last of them. The Radcliffes are dying out. That's their curse—for what they did to Cassie and to my grandfather." Grandpa Nolan's voice trailed off.

I tried to focus on what he'd told us. A man betrayed by his wife wouldn't be content with her death. Sebastian would want her lover gone too. The question flew from my lips. "Why would Sebastian let Drew live?"

"Losing Cassie was the worst thing that ever happened to Drew. Second only to living a long life without her," Grandpa Nolan said.

"Why stay here?" Evan asked.

Grandpa Nolan's voice hardened. "Nolans keep their promises. My grandfather swore to find justice for Cassie. On his deathbed, I promised to carry on for him. Adam will stay here until the Radcliffes finally pay for their crimes." He tilted his head toward where the ghost had been and added, "Best stay clear of the castle." Was that Grandpa Nolan's warning, or the ghost's?

With that, the old man slumped in his chair. I knew how he felt. Even the most benign ghost has to draw energy from the living to enter our world. I used to take a lot of naps.

As Evan stood up to go, Grandpa Nolan stirred one more time. His hand snaked around Evan's wrist, and he pulled him in close. Grandpa Nolan's voice lowered to a rattling hiss. "The curse is real. Don't matter how much you don't believe it." He released Evan's arm and gave me a piercing look. "She knows. She knows the truth. Ask her."

Evan said, "I will, sir."

Then we left. We walked in silence down the driveway.

When we got to the road, Evan asked, "What did he mean about you knowing the truth?"

I shrugged. "He must think I'm a believer too. Like Professor Astor does."

"So, are you? You haven't actually said."

I chose my words carefully. "I think anything's possible."

"So you do believe in curses and ghosts?"

"No one has proven that they aren't real," I hedged.

"Nice try, Kat." He trapped me with his gaze. Today, his eyes looked more green than brown, like labradorite catching the light and going from dull to gorgeous in a moment.

Nervous laughter spilled from my mouth. "Are you asking if I've, like, actually seen a ghost?"

"Yes," he answered quietly.

I had never seen Evan like this before. He was seriously interested in what I had to say. Maybe Grandpa Nolan had shaken him. Maybe he'd felt something when a ghost had materialized just a few feet away from him. Maybe now was the time for me to tell him the truth.

"If I say that I have, will you believe me?" I asked.

"I'll listen."

Then he folded his arms across his chest, and the spell was broken. I could feel him pulling away. Away from me. Away from believing.

He'd listen to my words, but he wouldn't hear them. He'd listen so he could disprove whatever I said. I was surprised by how disappointed I was. "I'll keep that in mind."

Maybe when we got to Castle Creighton, I'd be able to explain. Or maybe the castle would find a way to explain for me.

With a loud clack, I sank the eight ball in the right corner pocket. Another win, the third of the night for Morgan and me. Morgan danced over and gave me a baby five, her fingertips just kissing mine. We were the undisputed champions of The Blind Unicorn.

Neither Seth nor Evan had listened when the pub owner tried to tell them that Morgan knew how to play. And I had neglected to mention that pool was my grandfather's favorite game, or that he and I played every day until dinner was ready when I was in middle school.

Back at our booth, Morgan and I devoured our prize: chicken fingers and seasoned fries, paid for out of Evan's meal allowance.

He still found ways to make us pay. We wouldn't be allowed to enjoy our deep-fried meal without talking business.

"Yesterday's rain gave Seth more time to pour over the castle's blueprints. He came across some interesting stuff," Evan said.

Seth leaned back in his chair. "The castle is riddled with secret passageways. All the upper turret rooms have a hidden corridor to another room. These turret rooms are the most isolated rooms in the castle so the passageways are like escape hatches." He sounded excited. "I wonder what sort of mechanisms trigger them."

"So Cassie's room in the south turret is linked to...?" I asked.

Seth smiled. "Sebastian's bedroom."

Sebastian. Cassie's groom.

A hush fell over the table.

"Do any of the passageways intersect?" Morgan asked.

Seth shook his head. "That's the weird thing. One entry point and one exit to each passageway. So you can't cross between them."

But someone still could have moved completely undetected between the bride's room and the groom's room.

Evan pulled me out of my thoughts, by saying, "I spoke to Professor Astor about our progress. I finished up our interviews this afternoon. We've done what we can here in town, and Joshua's ready for us. We'll pack our bags and head out to the castle tomorrow."

Tomorrow. I would be at the castle tomorrow. This might be my last moment of normal. Everything I'd run from for eight years, I was running toward. But maybe I'd find Toria. That was the only thought that made any of this okay.

My voice squeaked. "When do we leave?"

"At 8 a.m.," Evan said.

Morgan ran her finger over the table's edge. "Afternoon would be better."

"I want an early start," Evan said.

Morgan dipped the tip of her chicken finger into a pool of honey mustard sauce. "Are we swimming there?"

"Of course not." Evan frowned.

"I can't walk on water. And the sandbar that links to the castle won't appear until 2 p.m. tomorrow." Morgan's voice vibrated with repressed giggles.

Seth erupted in laughter.

"That's problematic," I said.

Evan stared at Morgan. "You could have told me."

"I just did." Her lips curved into a delicious smile.

"We'll meet at noon for lunch and head out to the island after that," Evan said.

"Why can't we take a helicopter?" Seth asked.

Morgan pointed to Evan. "Have you met Mr. Budget?"

"Walking is great exercise," Evan said.

"Did you just call us fat?" Morgan asked.

"No, I, no. We're all fit enough for a hike." Evan's neck was mottled with pink spots.

I smiled at Morgan. She winked at me.

Seth raised his glass. "To the castle and the curse."

We clinked glasses.

My ear tingled and went cold a few seconds before something whispered, "And the unbelievables."

Chapter 8

"A few more minutes." Morgan shielded her eyes with her hand and squinted at the horizon.

My toes burrowed deeper in the sand. The waves receded, revealing the sandbar, only to charge the shore and cover it over again. I gazed down at my castle-storming clothes: a white and navy gingham print blouse, navy shorts, and brown sandals.

"Stop worrying. You look great." Morgan looked me up and down. "A little matchy matchy, but great." She kept her eyes trained on where the sandbar would emerge. "It's too late for second thoughts."

"I know." And clothes should be the last thing on my mind. But I used them to avoid thinking about what was coming. I eyed Morgan's black Grecian sandals, short black skirt, and fitted T-shirt. Her favorite blue butterfly wing pendant hung around her neck. Three snake rings writhed across her right hand. She'd twisted and braided her long hair to keep it off her face. Morgan conservative.

I was as ready as I'd ever be, slathered in sunscreen with my UV-coated parasol shading my face. My backpack was stuffed with everything I needed to work at the castle. The wheels on my suitcase were useless on the sandbar. I planned to carry it all the way out to the isle and the castle. A place filled with unbelievables. Ghosts. They were going to make their way into my world. I prayed Toria's ghost was waiting and not Leanna's.

Seth started to venture into the water, but Evan's words stopped him. "The rip tides are less than twenty-five meters from the shore."

"We call this stretch of water Lorelei's Way," Morgan said.

"I'm sensing a story," Evan said.

"Legend has it Lorelei lived out there on the Isle of Acacia with her family," Morgan said. "She had her pick of guys. But fell in love with Ian."

"Let me guess—the only one her father didn't approve of," Evan said.

"Her father forbid her from seeing Ian, but he snuck out to the isle to meet her." Morgan's tone tugged us back in time. "He was halfway there when the tides turned on him. The waves completely swallowed the sandbar. Ian tried to swim, but he was no match for the current. Screaming Lorelei's name, he disappeared under the water. Lorelei waited for him by the cliffs. She heard him cry out, but never saw him again. Cursing the tides, she threw herself into the water. No one has ever passed safely there since. During storms, some say you can hear the lovers crying out for each other."

My skin tingled like an army of microscopic ants had marched over it. "How awful."

Despite the summer sun, coldness swept across the back of my neck.

A voice whispered, "It was."

I twisted my ring and stepped closer to Evan.

The ghost chuckled. "You can't keep this up."

Icy fingers danced over my arm and I shivered. I didn't sense the darkness of Leanna. This was a new ghost. And she knew how close I was to losing everything.

"You'll see me soon," she whispered.

I didn't doubt it.

Evan stared out at the horizon. "That tale was probably created to warn children of the dangers of drowning."

His words caused the ghost to gasp. The pain of an unbeliever. She disappeared. The sun warmed me again.

I adjusted my parasol to protect my face. "Way to ruin a legend."

"I suppose you still believe in Santa Claus?" Evan asked.

Before I could reply, Seth winked at me. "Want to be my Lorelei?"

"You run into the water and drown. I'll be right behind you," I said sweetly.

Evan laughed.

With perfect timing, the sandbar emerged.

For two hours, we plodded across wet sand. Sweat poured down the gully of my spine and soaked my shorts and shirt, cementing them to my skin. As we got closer to the isle, I noticed a mountain of rocks blocked our path. "Why didn't we see this from Wright?"

"Probably not the best time to mention we have to climb to the top of the cliffs." Morgan patted my arm.

The muscles in my arm already ached and burned from lugging my suitcase this far. "Why did you let me bring this luggage?"

"I told you to pack just the essentials." She had one duffle bag that she'd slung across her back.

I wiped the sweat from my brow. "But after the climb, we're at the castle?" I asked.

"Once we hike a ways inland," she said.

I groaned.

For the next few hours, we climbed rocks, traipsed through sea grass, and hiked into the woods. Pieces of hair escaped from my bun and plastered themselves against my neck and face. I was a mess by the time we reached the twenty-foot-high stone wall surrounding the castle. We took a water break and Morgan fixed my hair. Then she led us to the opening.

Evan raised his hand to knock, but the wooden door creaked open.

There was no one there.

Still, Evan knocked on the door four times.

We waited for a response, but Seth didn't wait long. He stepped just inside and shouted, "Hello? Anyone here?"

Evan tried to grab him before he could go any farther, but he sailed right in.

"He's on his way to the castle's front door," Morgan said.

Evan dashed through the opening.

This was it. *Courage, Kat, courage.* I grabbed Morgan's hand and followed Evan.

The front of the castle rivaled any European estate with its formal French garden. Roses and hedgerows were groomed to intricate spiral designs. Green lollipop-shaped trees lined the cobblestone walkway to

Castle Creighton's entrance.

Evan shouted a proper greeting, but no one was around to hear him. Suddenly, the door in the wall slammed shut. I jumped and grabbed Morgan's arm. Turning to face our captor, I coughed to cover my laugh. A fifty-something groundskeeper menaced us with a rake. From the looks of him, he didn't part with his clothes until he'd worn a hole through and patched it twice.

Evan introduced us and explained why we were there.

The groundskeeper rested the rake on the ground and looked us up and down. "Wasn't expecting a group of kids."

"Cheap labor," Seth said.

The groundskeeper nodded. "You best behave yourselves here."

The castle door opened and an auburn-haired woman descended toward us. Her hair hung loosely around her shoulders, not a strand out of place. The red in her hair contrasted perfectly with her ivory skin. A model would envy her high cheekbones. I'd swear she was Pygmalion's Galatea, a sculpture brought to life.

The groundskeeper said, "Miss Olivia, they're the research team."

"Thank you, Perkins." Olivia nodded. "We were wondering when you'd arrive. Did you walk here?"

Evan nodded and she laughed.

"Joshua would have sent the helicopter for you," Olivia said.

Seth made his told-you-so face.

When Evan introduced us, Olivia's azure blue eyes trailed over each of us. They were the shade of winter sky that lures you outside with the promise of warmth only to plunge you into frigidness.

"Please come inside, Joshua is waiting to meet you," she said.

I swallowed and looked up at the castle. Every window had shadows. Shadows that shimmered with an unbelievable waiting to break through.

Twenty minutes had passed since Olivia deposited us in a sitting room that Austria's Empress Maria Theresa could have decorated. Morgan and I shared the periwinkle brocade sofa in the center of the room. Evan sat to our right in an Edwardian chair. Seth had picked a beech bergère chair by the window.

My grandmother would have delighted in every knickknack in this room. She'd be able to tell you its story—where it came from and what influenced the artist who created it. She was a walking Wikipedia of old furniture.

But it was a nightmare for me. Being inside an old castle surrounded by so many personal objects. They might just be pretty trinkets. They might be family heirlooms, dense with emotional history. They might be enchanted. I didn't know what to do with myself. I tried not to touch anything.

A marble chessboard sat on the coffee table in front of me. It looked fairly new. Innocuous. I reached for the rook and accidentally knocked over half the pieces. Morgan's sharp intake of breath and Seth's snort were followed by a frustrated sigh from Evan. I tried to fix it, but took down the rest.

"Relax. I got it." Morgan fingers weaved through the pieces, returning each one to its proper square.

The double doors opened and Olivia floated into the room. "Joshua will be joining us soon." She settled gracefully into the chair across from Evan.

"Thank you," he said.

A couple minutes later, the doors opened and a maid entered with sandwiches and tea. I automatically accepted the plate she offered. I took a few bites of my sandwich and swallowed, but my stomach was already full of anxiety.

Fifteen minutes of small talk ticked by before the doors opened again. A man with jet-black hair strode into the room. He had to be six-foot-four-inches of lean muscle.

"Welcome to Castle Creighton. I'm Joshua Radcliffe."

Evan introduced each of us. When he got to me, Joshua trapped me in his gaze. His eyes were the darkest blue I'd ever seen. Almost as dark as his pupils—no, more like the deep violet-blue of iolite. It was impossible to look away. Scary part? I didn't want to. I wanted to be near him. It was the craziest urge and it was really hard to ignore.

Joshua smiled at Evan. "I appreciate your eagerness in hiking here. How about we start off with a tour? Then we can talk about the project in more detail." Joshua's cell phone rang. He frowned. "I need to take this. Olivia, can you show them around?"

"Of course, dear. I'll have Cook push dinner back to nine?" Olivia said.

He nodded and pinned Evan with his gaze. "We'll talk further tonight."

When he left the room, I felt something weird. An emptiness. Like I'd just said goodbye to my best friend. Which made absolutely no sense. I turned my ring a few times. I hoped I wasn't already cracking up from the ghosts.

Chapter 9

After the servants took our luggage, Olivia whisked us to the castle terrace. From there, a courtyard stretched a thousand feet from the building. Closely-trimmed grass and swirled flower beds lined the gravel walkway to a massive water feature that rivaled the Trevi Fountain in Rome. The only difference was that the Radcliffes had gone with Poseidon rather than Oceanus—I could tell by the trident.

Seth strayed from the group, wandering toward a hedge maze. Olivia warned, "Don't go into the labyrinth alone. We've lost a few friends over the years."

Seth eyed the entrance, but Evan shook his head.

Olivia laughed. "Forgive me. I love to scare visitors."

Olivia led us behind the fountain and through the trees to the south door in the wall surrounding the castle. An apple orchard filled with semi-dwarf trees stretched just beyond the castle wall. She said, "They grow the sweetest apples I've ever tasted. The Radcliffes planted the first tree more than two hundred years ago."

Beyond the orchard, a bunch of rocks loomed like ruins. I had to ask, "What are those?"

Olivia puckered her lips. "I'm not sure. As kids, we built forts there."

I filed it under something to ask Joshua. I couldn't wait to see him again. It was more than that. I needed to be near him. I'd never felt a pull like that to anyone. Well, except Morgan. The first time she smiled at me, I felt it. I had to know her. To be her friend. It was the same with Joshua.

Seth trampled the underbrush, and Olivia said, "Stay on the paths at all times. There are rare plants and animals here."

Seth jumped back onto the stone walkway. "I would hate to endanger the isle's ecosystem."

Seth was on the flirt again. Same game, new target. Maybe Olivia would be a good distraction for him.

Olivia pointed to the southern tip of the island. "And avoid that area. There's a stretch of unstable marshes where the ground feels like quicksand."

South is bad. Good to know.

Olivia led us back through the south gate, across the courtyard and into the kitchen. From there, we turned left onto the main hallway and left again down a short hall to the breakfast room in the western turret of the castle. The four intricate stained glass windows were the coolest part of the room. They captured each season in a riot of color. The circular oak table echoed the room's roundness. By my guess, you could seat eight people there comfortably.

Olivia retraced her steps to the main corridor and opened the double doors across the hall.

We peeked inside the ballroom. It had gilded walls, a frescoed ceiling, a wall of mirrored panels, and an ornate crystal chandelier. Then we followed the main hallway past the kitchen to the dining room.

According to Olivia, "Every generation of the Radcliffes added to the room, giving it an eclectic style."

More like hodgepodge. I could easily imagine dinner conversations turning into a game of name-that-era. On one wall hung an old tapestry that traced the Radcliffe family back several centuries. The opposite wall was home to two Rococo paintings. I recognized Jean-Honore Fragonard's work. The other might be a Watteau.

The dining room table and its thirty chairs were straight out of the Middle Ages. The rug beneath it was Persian. My grandmother would have been able to tell the year and place of origin, but I couldn't. The dishes were fine bone china. I didn't pick them up to check, but I'm pretty sure they were Wedgwood.

"The French doors give a nice view of the courtyard and add more natural light," Seth said.

Pride crept into Olivia's voice. "They were Joshua's contribution to the room."

Across from the dining room lay the great hall, where we'd entered the castle a couple hours ago.

As we paused to take it in again, Seth said, "The castle's main entry was designed to inspire awe. Look at the high ceiling, mahogany panels, and stoic Radcliffe family portraits."

Olivia nodded. "The Radcliffes like to make an impression."

Continuing down the main hallway, we entered the library on the right. A rectangular wood table and six chairs sat in the center of the room. Each corner of the room housed a reading nook. My favorite had a burgundy-brown leather button sofa and two tall stand-up lamps.

The best part? Four solid walls of shelves filled with books. I ran my fingers over the leather bindings. Books flat out did it for me. The smell, the feel, the look—I loved being surrounded by them.

"The library houses many first editions and signed copies," Olivia said.

"Can I look around?"

"A bookworm?" She sounded amused.

I couldn't tell if I'd been insulted or complimented.

"You're welcome to borrow a book or two." Olivia gestured at the shelves. Leaving the library, she motioned to a small corridor that intersected with the main hallway. "That area is off limits."

"Why?" Seth asked.

No wasn't in his DNA. Though the novelty of it excited him.

"Joshua's study," Olivia said.

It was also the south turret, which meant that two floors above the study lay Cassie's bedroom. Invisible fingers tickled my scalp. A cold breeze caressed my hair. I stepped closer to Evan—so close that my arm brushed his and he gave me a weird look. I didn't move away, because his nearness drove away the chill.

Across from the library was the game room, dominated by a billiard table. We passed through it on our way to the eastern turret, where some Radcliffe had built a conservatory.

Olivia stood in front of the orchids. "The castle has most of its original stone walls, but Joshua added more windows and special lighting to maintain my plants year round."

Morgan examined the blossoms. "These hibiscuses are gorgeous. I've never seen anything like them before."

"You won't. I crossbreed them myself," Olivia confided.

Hibiscus was Morgan's favorite flower. Her face bordered on hero worship. Seth lusted after Olivia. Pretty soon Evan would fall at her feet too. Don't get me wrong. I didn't dislike her. There was nothing to hate about her. And that kind of bothered me.

We returned to the game room. "On the other side is the sitting room where you met Joshua," Olivia said.

Retracing our steps to the hallway, we entered a room where two overstuffed white leather couches and a few rows of white leather reclining chairs faced a blank wall.

Seth leaned against the wall, surveying the room. "Nice home theater."

Olivia smiled. "We enjoy it."

Returning to the great hall, she led us up the T-shaped staircase. "The castle's main staircase skips over the servants' quarters."

"It's odd for the owners to trudge up an extra flight of stairs," Seth said. "Usually the top floor is reserved for servants' quarters."

Olivia shrugged. "I wouldn't have designed it this way."

Reaching the first landing, we turned left and mounted another flight of stairs.

At the top of the stairs, Evan stopped. "Where's Cassie's old room?"

"Down that side hallway in the south turret," Olivia said.

"Which is off limits?" Evan asked.

"For now. Joshua wants to go over ground rules before he unleashes you on his home." Olivia turned right onto the main hallway. "This room will be Seth's and the room diagonally across the hall will go to Evan." She pointed to the next door. "This is mine, if anyone needs anything."

Taking a right down a side hallway, she pointed out Morgan's room and my room, which were across the hall from each other.

Finally, Olivia took us to the rooftop. "It's a stunning view. And the perfect place to wrap up our tour."

I was the last one through the side door and up the stone stairwell to the roof. I stepped out onto the rampart. The stones winked beneath my feet.

My entire world fell away.

Everyone vanished. I heard the echo of a child's laughter. It was my laughter. Red curls bobbed in front of my eyes as I chased a dark-haired boy. Our shoes slapped against the stones as we raced over the rooftop. I shrieked in delight when I almost caught him.

I blinked. The stones beneath my sandals glinted in the sun's last rays, but the shadow of red ringlets floated in front of my face. I was in two realities at once. Both flickered, and I felt like either could be mine.

Morgan wavered in the distance. Was she really here? I tried to give her a smile, but my face refused to cooperate. I took a step toward her. My knees buckled and everything went black.

Chapter 10

Darkness blanketed me. Silence roared in my ears. I struggled to remember what happened, how I had ended up here. But the memories wouldn't come. Arctic air whirled around me. The ghosts were moving in.

I squeezed my eyes shut. *Ghosts don't exist. They can't touch me. They can't hurt me—*

A voice interrupted my thoughts. "Not yet."

I shuddered. And then I started all over again. *Ghosts don't exist. They can't touch me. They can't hurt me. They aren't real.*

I repeated those words until Olivia's voice penetrated the haze. "The poor girl must have heat exhaustion."

"Why'd you push her so hard on the hike?" Morgan asked.

"You're her best friend. Why didn't you tell us she couldn't handle it?" Evan asked.

My thoughts ran together. Things started coming back to me. Children playing. Red hair. The blood beat in my ears as I fought to make sense of everything.

The scent of ammonia wafted beneath my nose and I gasped. *Smelling salts?* From some ancestral medicine cabinet, no doubt.

My eyelids fluttered open, and I saw Morgan smile with relief. "Welcome back, Kitty Kat."

"What's up?" I asked.

"Not you." She winked at me.

"Not funny." My head rested in her lap. Stones pressed into my spine. I was stretched out on the castle rooftop.

Evan crouched beside us. "Are you okay?"

"I think so." With Morgan's help, I sat up. "What happened?"

Morgan fussed over me. "One minute you were looking off in the distance, then you turned toward us and passed out."

The redheaded girl. There hadn't been any warning. No sense of a ghost emerging. If she was a ghost. I wondered for a moment if maybe she was a spirit who had somehow managed to suck me into the moment she was doomed to repeat. But she wasn't like any of the spirits I'd known. They were weak, and she definitely wasn't weak. And I wasn't just in her reality—I was her. I thought about the time Leanna had taken from me, and I felt sick. The unbelievables were so strong here. It was impossible to say what they were doing to me.

Everyone was looking at me, expecting an explanation. I mumbled something about low blood sugar.

"I told you to eat more at lunch," Morgan said.

She wouldn't let me get up until a maid had been summoned to bring me a glass of orange juice. Morgan watched me drink it all down. By then, I was feeling like myself—and just myself—again.

"Sorry to worry you." I stared at the stone floor and played with my ring. Touching the stone calmed me.

Morgan lifted my chin up and examined my face. She murmured, "The color's back in your cheeks." She let go of my chin and told everyone, "She's fine."

"We should probably freshen up before dinner." Olivia headed toward the stairwell.

While we descended back into the castle, Seth said, "Otherwise, we'll start dropping like flies. Joshua can't catch everyone."

I had no idea what Seth was talking about.

Morgan saw the confusion on my face and whispered, "It was straight out of a movie. You swooned and Joshua caught you."

I blushed. I couldn't believe I had been that close to him and couldn't even remember it. "Where'd he go?"

"You were out for ten minutes, Kat," she said.

Ten minutes. That was not good.

When we reached my room, I got rid of Morgan by saying, "I need a shower."

What I really needed was time to figure out what had happened to me. Was happening to me. After I shut my door, I sat down at the dressing table and tried to remember everything that had happened on the rampart. I pulled the pins out of my hair as I went over the scene in my mind.

There hadn't been any warning signs—no coldness, no tingling between my shoulder blades, no feeling of wrongness. No sign of a ghost. One second I was me, and then I was a little girl with red curls.

My chest constricted and my breath came in wheezy gasps. Panic pushed me to move. I threw open the window and tried to suck in some fresh air. A light summer breeze brushed past me. I caught a faint scent. Lilac.

Toria's scent.

That little girl. She was Toria.

For a moment, *I* was Toria.

All those years, I had kept the ghosts away. I hadn't wanted to keep Toria away, but I had no choice. Now she was back, and I wanted to be happy, but I wasn't. I was scared of what the unbelievables were doing to me in this place. What they could do to me. What they would do to me.

My gaze darted around Joshua's book-lined study. He sat at his giant mahogany desk barely noticing the information filling up his four flat-screen monitors. It looked like every line on his phone was blinking, but he ignored it.

All his attention was focused on Morgan, Seth, Evan, and me. He steepled his fingers and stared at us.

My hands trembled. I held them together to hide it. I had chosen to be here. I had come to help Toria and Joshua. I couldn't turn back now.

My shoulders sagged. It wasn't relief. It wasn't relaxation. It was resignation.

Morgan touched my arm. A reassuring reminder that she was here.

"I wanted to go over a few ground rules for your stay. You will obey Olivia and my staff. You will stay close to the castle unless you have permission from Olivia or me to explore the island. Absolutely no wandering off." Joshua paused. "If you want to see the tunnels beneath the castle, you must go with a guide."

Evan and Seth exchanged a covert glance. Professor Astor hadn't said anything about tunnels. They must not have been on the castle blueprints that Seth had studied either.

"I have never opened the castle to researchers before, but you are my guests, and I want you to feel welcome here. I need for you to understand, though, that my privacy is very important to me. This study and my private suite are off limits without an explicit invitation."

Evan nodded.

"I'll show you Cassie's room tomorrow," Joshua said.

"Excellent," Evan replied.

I had a sudden, ridiculous urge to confide in Joshua about what had happened on the roof.

Joshua stared at me like he knew something was clawing its way out of my mouth. "And?"

Don't tell him about the roof. Instead, I blurted out. "Um, thanks for catching me."

"You're most welcome." His warm voice rippled over me, and his eyes didn't leave mine. He was waiting for something else from me, but I had no idea what.

"I was wondering if I could see the rock fort," I said.

"That path isn't well marked. One wrong turn and you'll end up in the ocean," Joshua said.

"Oh."

"But I'll take you," Joshua said.

"Thanks!" I sounded way too excited. My cheeks burned. "Do you think it's a ruin?"

Joshua leaned back in his chair. "There is a hot spring nearby, and an old fire pit, so maybe. But my father thought that it was the remnant of a child's fort—or, rather, generations of forts built one on top of the other. It could be both, of course. The first Radcliffe children to play there might have been building on top of an older structure."

"The best of both worlds," I murmured.

Joshua's lips relaxed into a smile. "I couldn't have put it better myself."

A rush of pleasure spread through me. I wanted him to like me. I wanted it more than I had any reason to.

Evan pulled out his copy of Bertram's journal and put it on the desk. "We found a passage that talked about an alliance involving Toria. Do you know what it means?"

Joshua skimmed the section. "The Mallory, Langley, and Kingsley families had many business ventures with us. Personal and professional intersected all the time."

"It was quite rare for women to be involved in business back then," Evan said.

"It may seem strange, but the Langleys were very forward-thinking."

"Why would Bertram be worried about losing Toria?" I asked.

"He probably meant a metaphorical loss. If she failed, he worried how it would affect her," Joshua said.

His explanation sounded reasonable. I wanted to believe him. But Bertram was the king of understatement. If he sounded worried, it was because it was really serious. There had to be more to this alliance. But Joshua wasn't going to tell us.

"What about the origin of Lorelei's Way?" Evan asked.

"That's a favorite of the townspeople. There may be some basis in truth, but, who knows?" Joshua glanced at me. "You can work on that mystery after you resolve the Radcliffe Curse."

I dropped my pen. It thudded on the hardwood floor.

Joshua leaned forward. "I'm well aware of the gossip surrounding my family's history. I gave Professor Astor permission to send you here because I was hoping that he—and you—could put the rumors to rest. Living with this castle's infamous past can be…difficult." His eyes swirled with emotions. Before I recognized them, he blinked and swept them away.

"We'll do everything we can," I promised. I meant it too.

"So you don't believe in the curse?" Evan asked.

Joshua's laugh sounded hollow. "If I believe in it, I have four weeks left to live."

Halfway up the stairs, I realized that I'd left my pen in Joshua's study. I would've let it go, but it was a vintage Pelikan that my grandmother had given me.

I was about to knock on the door to Joshua's study when I heard Olivia say, "I won't leave. We're in this together. No matter what."

I should have just walked away, but I didn't.

He sounded resigned. "Seeing you distracts me too much."

Olivia begged, "Let me stay. We have a reason to believe. You saw it, didn't you?"

"It's too early to be hopeful."

"Hope is all we have," she said.

"It's a good sign, but we can't expect too much."

"But…" Olivia's voice cut off.

The door opened. Joshua was just inside the threshold.

I stepped back. "Sorry, I left my pen in here."

Joshua turned sideways to allow me through the doorway. Passing by, I wanted to hug him and make this better for him. It made no sense. I made no sense. I darted by him, retrieved my pen from the floor, and tried for a quick exit.

He blocked my path. "That's a beautiful ring."

"It was a birthday gift."

"May I see it?" he asked.

"Sure." My hands shook so much, I nearly dropped it. Joshua caught the ring and my hand in his. His touch sent a jolt through my fingers. I gasped. It was like touching someone I'd loved and known forever. He felt that familiar and that important. It was nuts.

He flipped the ring over, revealing the four intertwining branches on the band. "Lovely. Easily several hundred years old."

He gave me another one of his piercing stares as he placed the ring in my palm. "So, how are you liking Castle Creighton so far?"

Dead people had been whispering in my ear since I got there and I thought I was possessed by a ghost I used to know—or I possessed her—and then I fainted.

"It's… great. Just really… great." I tried to sound like I meant it.

Joshua and Olivia exchanged a look I couldn't interpret.

Then they wished me a good night.

I forced a smile and left the room. A good night was not something the castle would ever allow me to have.

Disturbing dreams plagued my sleep. I was a child. A warrior queen. I betrayed a friend. I was Lorelei standing on the cliffs, cursing the ocean. As my body hit the water, I sat up in bed with the sheets twisted around me.

I fought my way free of the bedding and wandered to the window. The moon cast shadows that danced around the castle grounds. A chill crept up my spine. In the garden, I saw a girl with a mass of red curls sneaking out with a dark-haired boy. Their fingers were laced together.

He wore trousers and a silk waistcoat. She wore a green dress with a bustle skirt. Their clothes dated from the 1880s. They almost looked like living people until the moonlight flashed through them.

Toria stopped, pulling the boy to a halt beside her. She looked up at me and smiled.

I wanted to call out, but I was afraid of waking the others.

She looked up again. I swear she said, "Soon."

Then she and the boy disappeared beyond the castle wall.

The moonlight cut a white six-pointed star across my star sapphire stone. I wanted to run into Morgan's room and beg her to tell me that everything would be all right. But even if she did, it wasn't possible—not in this place. At Castle Creighton, the unbelievables were in charge. They were able to bend reality to their will. I had never been more vulnerable in my life.

I couldn't sleep after seeing Toria. I spent an hour in the library, looking for books that might bore me back to sleep. I pulled out a book called *British Lore*. I skimmed the table of contents, hoping for a boring academic approach. Instead, I found chapters on ghosts and hauntings and curses and spells. Exactly what I didn't need tonight.

I quickly slid the book back onto the shelf. It popped back out and fell to the floor. I picked it up and tried again. It wouldn't slide into place, like something already filled the spot. I pulled the book out, reached up, and checked to make sure nothing was blocking the spot. It was empty.

When I tried to slide the book in a third time, it suddenly quadrupled in weight. I had to use both hands to lift it. Clearly, something wanted me to have this book. And if I kept fighting, who knew what would happen next? I didn't need any more unbelievables coming at me. Fine. I put the book at the bottom of my pile and kept searching. I ended up with a stack of books that included three volumes on the military history of Great Britain, one book on the evolution of ants, and a tome on ocean currents.

I brought them back to my room and settled into bed. But not even tide tables were tedious enough to overcome my anxiety and apprehension. By the time the sun broke through the shadows in my room, I'd gotten about two hours of sleep.

Breakfast came way too quickly. I played with my eggs. I knew I should eat. I needed food to keep me strong, but I couldn't put it in my mouth.

The wind beat against the castle walls. The windows clanged in their frames.

Joshua's forehead creased. "A hurricane is making its way up the coast. Stay inside today. We don't know when the worst of it will hit here."

Evan stirred raisins and brown sugar into his oatmeal. "What are we looking at?"

"Winds up to sixty miles an hour with heavy downpours and flooding," Olivia said. "Maybe hail. It'll be much worse here than when it hits the mainland."

Morgan stopped buttering her toast. "Is there anything we can do?"

"The staff's already done everything to prepare. If the power goes out, we have a back-up generator and plenty of flashlights and candles. The pantry is fully stocked. We should be fine," Olivia said.

Seth savored his poached eggs, oblivious to all our worries.

I envied him. "No concerns about the storm?"

Seth's voice dripped with condescension. "I lived through a tsunami in Thailand. This doesn't faze me."

"Fair enough," I murmured.

Evan sipped his coffee. "It won't affect our work. We don't need electricity to investigate and take notes."

"I admire your focus." Joshua's smile transformed his face. It was full of life. I wished it could stay like that forever.

But, in four weeks, he would be dead. Unless we could help him.

Chapter 11

T he coming hurricane derailed our plans for the day. Joshua had pressing business he needed to conclude before the wireless got spotty. He had to postpone our visit to Cassie's room. I expected Evan to be disappointed, but I think he was as geeked out as I was to spend the day in the library. My excitement at seeing so many first editions almost eclipsed the fact that we'd found nothing we didn't already know about Castle Creighton or the Radcliffes.

We'd left Seth and Morgan in the breakfast room. They'd volunteered to spend a few hours helping Olivia in the conservatory. By now, they were undoubtedly wrist deep in plants. I had expected mulch to fly while Morgan and Seth fought for Olivia's attention. What I hadn't expected was shouting. Or the bang and thud of furniture being overturned.

Evan left to investigate. I followed him to the great hall—partly out of curiosity, and partly because I didn't want to be alone. Two hulking men dressed in gray were subduing a red-haired guy. *Adam.* Seconds later, Morgan, Olivia, and Seth came rushing through the sitting room.

Perkins bellowed, "We'll throw you in the sea for trespassing, you dirty little thief!" There was no mistaking the gleam in his eye when he said to Olivia, "Sorry to disturb you, ma'am, but we found this intruder on the grounds. I'll dispose of him immediately."

I rushed to Morgan and slid my arm through hers. She barely noticed me. Her eyes never left Adam.

Olivia gave Perkins a 300-mega-watt smile. "Your loyalty means so much to Joshua. Thank you."

Perkins stood taller.

Did everyone have a crush on Olivia?

Evan stared at Adam. "What are you doing here?"

"Figured you could use some help with your project," Adam replied.

Olivia's voice rose an octave. "He's part of your research group?"

"Absolutely not," Evan said.

"Why are you here?" Olivia asked Adam.

Adam's gaze flickered to Morgan. "I came to make sure they were okay. I tried to leave, but the storm is messing with the tides. It wasn't safe to cross the sandbar back to the mainland."

Morgan tried to pull away from me, but I tightened my hold on her. We didn't need her and Adam making an even bigger scene.

"You'll have to stay until the hurricane has passed," Olivia said.

Perkins harrumphed so loudly I thought he might cough something up. "How many apples did you help yourself to?"

"You caught me. I'm an apple lover. Can't get enough of them." Adam struggled and the men twisted his arms behind his back until he stopped.

"Isn't this an interesting picture?" Joshua's voice came from the shadows beneath the stairwell.

The minute I heard him, I relaxed. He would handle things. That was just what he did.

Joshua stalked into the light. "Why are you on my isle?"

"Stealing apples. Just ask your gardener."

Couldn't Adam sense danger? These guys were serious about protecting Joshua. With all the animosity building in the room, I half expected the portraits to fly off the walls.

"He said he came to check on them." Olivia motioned toward Morgan, Seth and me.

Joshua's gaze went from Adam to Morgan and back again. A slow smile of understanding spread across his face. "As you can see, Morgan's fine."

Adam's lips parted, but then he clamped them shut.

"I can't send you home, but I can't welcome you into mine." Joshua folded his arms.

Fear seeped into Adam's features. It was followed by a flare of hatred.

"There's a dungeon, right?" Adam asked. "Better yet, toss me in the ocean. Or is that only for Radcliffe wives?"

Olivia spun across the floor in a blur of motion. She slapped Adam's face. The sound echoed in the great hall. Morgan moved toward him.

I used both hands to hold her in place. "Stay out of this," I whispered.

"But..." Morgan said.

"Not your fight," I said.

"Never insult Joshua in his home." Olivia's voice, usually so warm and inviting, was icy cold.

Joshua put his arm around her. "It's all right. Let me deal with this."

"I won't let anyone speak to you like that," Olivia said.

I hadn't much liked charming Olivia, but I kind of admired avenging Olivia. And I certainly understood her desire to protect Joshua.

"I've heard your family stands by their word." Joshua stared at Adam, and Adam met that unrelenting gaze. I felt time blur again, as if I were watching a conversation that had happened a hundred years ago—a thousand years ago.

"Nolans don't break promises," Adam said.

"I know what lies between our families, and I won't ask you to betray your beliefs. But if you agree to a temporary truce, you can stay here as my guest."

"And if I don't?" Adam asked.

What was he thinking? Did he think he'd find allies here? Morgan's arm tensed beneath my hand. *Well, all right. Maybe one ally.*

"If you don't agree to my terms, my security team will confine you until it's safe to escort you from the Isle of Acacia." Joshua's voice was calm.

"To keep them safe from this place, I'd make a deal with the devil himself." Adam tossed his head in our direction, but his eyes were locked on Morgan.

"And that will be the last insult." Joshua's voice reverberated up the walls. "You'll treat everyone with respect at Castle Creighton, from the staff to me."

Adam nodded.

Joshua asked, "Do I have your word?"

Adam spit out, "Yes."

Making accommodations for a sworn enemy wasn't easy even after he'd committed to a temporary truce. Ultimately, Joshua decided that Adam should move in with Evan. The castle was full of empty rooms. Maybe Joshua had overstated his faith in a Nolan's word during his parlay with Adam.

To say that dinner was tense was an understatement. The simmering animosity was barely drowned out by the wind and rain lashing against the castle walls.

After coffee, Joshua summoned Evan and me to his study. I was grateful for the break from the tension.

Joshua pulled a black velvet box from his drawer and placed it on top of his desk.

Evan reached for it, but Joshua stopped him. "This is for Kat."

I lifted the lid. On a bed of black velvet lay a brass key. My breath stopped for a moment, and everything else faded away.

Antique keys were a special type of personal object. They held the secrets of their owner. They weren't scary like an object that's been spelled or cursed. Antique keys and I, we had a thing. An instant connection. I reached out and slid my fingers over the cool metal shaft to the rectangular tooth. I could feel the key's secrets stirring. There were so many things it wanted to tell me. But not here and not now.

"What's that for?" Evan asked.

Joshua ignored Evan and spoke directly to me. "Where would you like to go?"

I found the answer in his eyes and breathed out, "Cassie's room."

Joshua gave me one of his dazzling smiles, and my heart sang. I wanted so much to help him, and he was letting me. But I was also afraid—terrified of what might be waiting for me in that turret room.

A darkness descended around us, and it was just Joshua and me. Evan was gone.

"It's time, Kat."

And then the darkness lifted.

Joshua shuffled some papers on his desk, preparing to dismiss us.

"You'll keep the room locked when you're not inside."

"Of course." Evan sounded eager to reinsert himself in the conversation.

Now that the situation had returned to normal, I gave the key in my hand a close look. "Do you have a magnifying glass?"

Joshua rifled through his desk drawer. He pulled out a magnifying glass and handed it to me.

"Amazing. The handle has a triple spiral inscribed with J.D. Morehead's signature," I said.

"And?" Evan asked.

I turned the key slowly, scrutinizing it. "He was one of the best locksmiths of the eighteenth century. No one could pick his locks. Safeguarding secret passageways was one of his specialties."

But the timelines didn't work. I tried to make sense of what I was seeing and what I knew.

"Problem?" Joshua asked.

"Morehead disappeared ten years before this castle was built," I said.

Joshua's voice was a low murmur. "Professor Astor didn't exaggerate." Evan made a noise somewhere between a snort and a hiccup. Joshua ignored him, and, once again, I felt like I was alone with the Radcliffe heir.

"Few would recognize J.D. Morehead's work or catch the symbols he hid in the bow of the key." Joshua leaned toward me. "This castle was his last great project." Something on one of Joshua's monitors caught his attention. "I have to finish up some business before the storm gets worse and knocks out my wireless. Let's pick this up again tomorrow after breakfast."

As we were leaving Joshua's office, Evan said, "I'll take the key." He put out his hand.

I had no intention of giving it to him.

"The key stays with Kat," Joshua said.

"Of course." Evan sounded calm, but his eyes rained fury on me.

Storm winds slammed against the castle walls and rain pelted my window. Lightning flashed through the curtains. Sleep became impossible.

The metal key warmed my hand.

Take me home, it begged.

I tossed the covers aside and paced around the room. Evan would be furious if I went to Cassie's room without him, but he had to babysit Adam tonight. That wasn't my fault. And, anyway, Evan wasn't a believer. He had no idea what I was dealing with.

I got dressed in the dark, put the key in the pocket of my shorts, and picked up the flashlight I'd been given in case of a power outage. I opened the door to my room as slowly and silently as I could. I checked the hallway. No one in sight. I made my way to the end of my hallway and peered around the corner to the main corridor. All clear.

When I reached the end of the corridor, I made a right onto the hallway leading to Cassie's room. I'd been in this hallway before. Not today or yesterday. No. During my dream in Wright, I'd walked down this very hallway.

My legs wobbled beneath me. My world spun into spider webs.

I leaned against the wall and closed my eyes. *Breathe, Kat, breathe.*

When the dizziness had passed, I opened my eyes.

I was still in the same corridor I had seen in my dream. I pushed the panic back down so I could put one foot in front of the other. I didn't stop until I got to the spiral staircase.

In my dream, this was when the corridor behind me disappeared. I turned around. The hallway was still there. *It was just a dream*, I told myself. A really, really detailed dream about a place I'd never seen before.

I touched my ring. It was the only stone I was wearing. I wasn't hiding from the unbelievables anymore.

I entered the dark stairwell. I was as quiet as I could be, but each step echoed in my ears. I kept stopping to look behind me. I couldn't see anything, but that didn't mean that nothing was there.

At the top of the staircase, I faced the wooden door I recognized from my dream. I was terrified, but I also knew that this was exactly where I was supposed to be. After a few seconds of fumbling in the dark, I found the keyhole. The lock resisted, but only for a moment. There was a delicate click when the room decided it was time to reveal its secrets.

Chapter 12

The door moaned softly as it swung inward. I stayed out on the landing, letting my flashlight beam circle the turret room. A four-poster bed dominated Cassie's room.

A flash of light startled me. It took me a couple seconds to realize it was my flashlight beam reflected back at me in an antique mirror on the far wall. My heart slowed down a bit. Wait, that mirror. It was the mirror I had seen in my dream. The mirror Drew had seen sparkling on the night Cassie died.

How could I dream about a place I'd never been? Was it a glimpse of where I would be in the future or somewhere I had been lifetimes ago?

I broke out in a clammy sweat, the kind that seeps into your skin and clings to your marrow.

I needed some distance from this situation. I needed perspective. I needed to observe. Notebook in hand, I jotted down what I saw and felt. None of the other turret rooms had this feel. The breakfast room was cozy. Joshua's study was almost welcoming. The conservatory similar to anything you'd see in *Traditional Home*, that high-end home decor magazine my grandmother subscribed to.

Cassie's room was so different. Despair lived in this room. Hopelessness oozed out onto the landing to greet me. I needed every ounce of willpower to step inside. It took an effort to separate the dream from my reality. I was strangely relieved when I realized that I wasn't freezing, like I had been in my dream. Probably because I wore sandals.

Okay, Kat. Keep observing. This is just research.

I slid my fingers along the wall searching for a light switch, but I didn't find one. Maybe they'd never wired this part of the castle with electricity. A kerosene lamp sat on the nightstand, but there was no oil in it.

I walked over to the vanity beside the mirror. The perfume bottles on it fit Bertram's description. It was as if time had stopped in this room on the night Cassie died. And to this day, the room remained Cassie's.

My pen scraped over the page as I wrote it all down.

On the other side of the vanity sat a dark cherry armoire. I ran my fingers over the floral carvings in the doors. Through tiny windows, I glimpsed the long forgotten clothes inside. Creepy. I almost regretted leaving Evan behind.

Observe, Kat, observe.

Back beside the door, a fireplace's mouth yawned with darkness. Shadows danced in its depths. I tried not to look too closely.

I went over what I knew about this room. The investigation notes included the measurement for the blood pool by the bed. I moved between the mirror and the bed. A huge oriental rug lay there.

I knelt on the floor, set down my flashlight, and rolled the rug back. I had read about the size of the bloodstain, but I still wasn't prepared for it. The stain stretched under the bed. Acid burned the back of my throat. I couldn't swallow away the bitter taste.

You'd think after years of archaeological digs with Mom, this wouldn't faze me. But this wasn't cracked pottery and dusty bones—the remains of lives waiting to be dissected. Cassie's and Sebastian's lives had seeped into the floor. How could anyone do that to other people? Tears stung my eyes. For Cassie. For Sebastian. For everything they had lost that night. For an ending that could never be undone.

"What a surprise to find you here," Evan said from the doorway.

I squeaked like a rusty hinge and wiped my teary face on my arms.

His footsteps rounded the bed. "What's wrong?"

I lied. "Dust in my eyes." I stood up. "I couldn't sleep. I figured I'd take a peek at the room."

He glared at me. Even in the dark, his disapproval was apparent. "You didn't follow our plan."

"I didn't plan on being wide awake in the middle of the night."

He sighed. "You were supposed to wait for me. We were supposed to do this together. Initial impressions are critical."

"Should I have invited you and Adam along?" I asked.

"You should have waited until morning when Seth could play prison guard." He shook his head. "I took you on the Nolan interview. Can't you meet me halfway?"

"I've done everything you've asked. Hours of scanning and photocopying that was a waste of your talents."

Evan gave me what Morgan called the "dude look." It was the look a straight guy gave when he was confused, annoyed, or just couldn't get something. It instantly shifted all weirdness and blame back at the other person.

I hated that look. And I'd have kept fighting with him if this was just about the project. But it wasn't. It was much bigger and more personal. This was about me and the unbelievables. "We can stand here all night arguing…"

"Or?" he asked.

"I'll say I'm sorry and you'll forgive me."

He raised an eyebrow.

"I'm sorry I came up here without you," I said.

"Okay."

"That's it?"

"For now," he said.

"Fine." I took a deep breath. I hated to admit it, but the room felt a little less gloomy with him here. "There's something I need to show you."

"Anything I can do to assist you is a top priority." He didn't try to keep the sarcasm out of his voice.

"Look at this." I trained my flashlight on the bloodstain.

He knelt to examine it.

I remained standing. I didn't want to get that close to the bloodstain again. I could almost feel the pain and sorrow emanating from it. *Researcher, be a researcher.* I directed his attention to the mirror. "You saw how the blood seeped under the bed, right?"

He nodded.

"But it stops right in front of the mirror. It looks like it was held back somehow, even repelled." It wasn't easy to discern in the low light, but the stain was clearly darker just a few inches in front of the mirror. "What stopped the blood?"

Evan took a closer look. "The mirror is a good six inches off the floor. The blood should have gone under it or, at least, further toward it. There's also a faint secondary blood trail, ending a few inches in front of the mirror. It extends beyond the original stain like someone passed through the blood on the way to the mirror. The trail doesn't go behind the mirror. There's not another trail leading away from it either."

"The shadings of the stain are off," I said.

"The edge and center are lighter than the middle band."

I finished his thought. "As if the blood flowed back on itself."

"A slight warping of the floorboards could cause the blood to flow away from the mirror." He rubbed his chin. "The secondary blood trail might mean there's another secret passage behind the mirror. The killer could have bundled up Cassie's and Sebastian's bodies in a blanket or rug and carried them out of the room. That would stop the blood trail."

"A secret passage? There?" I gestured at the window between the vanity and the mirror and the other window between the mirror and the bed. "It's structurally impossible. Unless our killer was a dwarf." I tried not to laugh, but I was too full of nervous energy.

Evan's expression was stormy. I expected his pupils to shoot lightning at me.

"I can examine the area around the mirror for a hidden mechanism." It was a waste of time, but I'd do it to appease him. "We need a marble to test your warped floorboard theory. But don't you think Bertram would have mentioned if a quilt or a rug went missing the night of the murders?"

"He might have missed that detail at his niece's murder scene. But if the killings were premeditated, maybe the murderer brought something to transport the bodies with him." Evan talked about the murders like he was proving a theorem.

The tingling between my shoulder blades climbed the vertebrae to my neck. Being in this room. Seeing the bloodstain. It was a lot different than reading or hearing about it. "A monster lurked among these people."

"Focus on why we're here. Research." He stood up and brushed the dust from his pants.

"She was only seventeen." I couldn't imagine getting married at my age, let alone murdered.

"Murdering newlyweds in their bedroom on their wedding night—it doesn't get more personal than that. And this kind of blood loss is cruel. It guaranteed that their deaths would be all that people remembered of their lives." In the glow of the flashlight, Evan's eyes didn't look completely human.

"They succeeded."

He surveyed the room. "No electricity in here?"

"I couldn't find any switches."

He headed toward the freestanding candelabrum between the mirror and the bed, pulled a lighter from his pocket, and lit its ancient tapers. Their glow dispelled some of the darkness in the room, but the shadows gathered and waited.

"I'll take the armoire. You search the vanity." He opened the doors of the armoire, pushed aside the Victorian dresses, and climbed inside. It was a good way to check for hidden compartments. My grandmother did it at estate sales and made some terrific finds.

I sat down at Cassie's vanity. Old furniture wasn't usually a problem. Though the stuff inside might be. I slid open the first drawer and peered inside. I took a deep breath and let my fingers two-step through the antique hairpins, silver brushes and combs, and lace handkerchiefs.

Nothing happened. These were just old personal objects. Evidence of a life briefly lived, and nothing more. Nothing felt special, beloved, charged with meaning. Nothing was spelled or cursed. After working myself up to deal with the unbelievables again, I was almost disappointed.

I still had more drawers to tackle, so I took a deep breath and plunged onward.

I worked my way down the column of drawers on the left side of the vanity. In the bottom drawer, I picked up a hand-painted picture of two young women sitting together. It was just a miniature, but I felt the echo of friendship in it. The blonde's lapis blue eyes twinkled in her heart-shaped face. On her right sat a reserved brunette with dark gray eyes, the color of galena. Both were attired in proper Victorian afternoon dresses with flounces and knife-pleated skirts. I recognized them from the wedding pictures Professor Astor showed me.

Cassie Mallory and Leanna Burnsby.

I stared at the small painting. Cassie exuded happiness. Leanna looked pensive, but not unhappy. They were so young. They had no idea what was coming.

It had been easy to hate Leanna all these years. She'd possessed my body and tried to steal my life. I'd never known why. I hadn't cared. I was fighting to save myself. But what if she had to take human form to find justice for her murdered best friend or save her descendants from the Radcliffe Curse? Maybe I had just been a means to help those she loved. I wasn't prepared for the rush of sympathy that washed over me.

I turned to check on Evan's progress and found him peering over my shoulder. He was so close I could smell his cologne. Woodsy with hints of amber and pine. I kind of liked it.

His breath warmed my cheek. "Looks like no one stayed in this room after Cassie."

"It's creepy." It was as if the room awaited Cassie's return.

"Make sure you note everything you find in that vanity," he said.

"Already done, boss."

"I'll go through the nightstand." He moved toward the bed. Farther away than I would have liked. The darkness swirled around me again, filling in his vacant space.

I was cataloging all the bottles on the vanity when a flash of lightning reflected in the mirror and grabbed my attention. I couldn't resist taking a closer look. I trailed my fingertips over the ornate frame and accidentally cut myself on a sharp edge. It wasn't deep, but it stung. A bit of blood seeped up. Just enough to make me nervous. I hated the sight of my own blood. Even a drop of it bothered me. I sucked on my finger and grabbed my notebook.

All four corners of the mirror had the same four-headed knot with a circle. It looked like a Celtic design. I sketched it so I could research it later.

Stepping back, I sighed. I loved how forgiving antique mirrors were. They distorted my flaws away. My skin was porcelain smooth. My own green eyes stared back at me, yet they looked like chrysoprase glowing in the candlelight.

I was nearly beautiful.

But something wasn't right about my reflection. It had to be a trick of the candles and the haziness of the old mirror. I laid my notebook on the vanity and went in for a closer look.

I'd been a blonde all my life, but my mirror image seemed to have red hair. I could see the khaki shorts and T-shirt I'd been wearing since morning, but they looked blurry. Then my reflection's image sharpened, and I was wearing a burgundy-colored riding habit. I looked at my face, and it wasn't mine. It was Toria's.

I gasped.

Without thinking, I reached out my hand. She did the same. The mirror's surface was warm beneath my fingertips. My gaze never left hers. I pressed down on the mirror's surface with a couple fingers. She smiled and pushed back, reaching for me. The surface started to give way. Her warm fingertips grazed mine. She grabbed my hand and pulled me toward her. I lost my balance and screamed as I careened into the mirror.

 Chapter 13

I had to be bleeding to death. It was the only explanation for how I felt. Not pain. No. Shock had deadened my senses. Delirium must have set in.

I tried to move, but I couldn't. Like my mind was awake, but my body stayed asleep. The disconnect felt permanent. I was trapped. A tidal wave of fear roared in my head. It engulfed my mind, threatening to wipe out rational thought. So easy to give in to the panic and be swept under.

Focus. That's right Kat, focus on what you can control—your thoughts. Okay, rewind the events. Hit play and...

I went through the mirror. No. I was pulled through the mirror. By Toria.

I hadn't lost consciousness right away. Or at least I didn't think I had. But I had no memory of smashing into the mirror. No shards of glass pierced my skin. No blood poured from any wounds. I felt like I'd been yanked through several layers of super strong Jell-O.

I opened my mouth to scream, but no sound came out. Things had gone cave-in black for a while. And now I was trapped inside my own mind.

What was Evan doing to help? I didn't hear him. Didn't see him. Didn't see anything.

Falling through a mirror was a possibility I'd cling to. I'd accept all the unbelievables over certain death.

I begged and pleaded for a sensation. A clue about where I was. But nothing happened. All I could do was think. What if this wasn't the unbelievables? What if I'd died and become a ghost? Right now, the ghosts might be the only ones who could hear me. The only way to find out was to believe.

Ghosts exist. They can touch me. They can hurt me. They are real.

I repeated the words over and over and over in my mind, but the ghosts didn't come. Maybe I was too close to death to be useful to them anymore. Or maybe I was somewhere they couldn't reach me.

No. Don't believe that.

Those years of training my mind to not believe in ghosts had saved me. Maybe they'd save me again. If belief shaped reality, I would believe I was alive with everything I had.

I have a body.

I concentrated on my skin, willing it to give me a hint about where I was. The first sensation took a while to decipher. A flat surface beneath me. I must be lying on my back.

My fingers twitched.

I have fingers!

Sensations flooded my mind. It wasn't easy to sort them out. I held someone's hand. I heard a voice. No idea whose, but I was still alive. And that was all I needed to know.

I lived.

I gave it a few minutes before I pushed further. Concentrating, I finally got my eyelids apart. Blobs blurred together and melded into shapes. I stared into hazel eyes. Flecks of green clung to his pupils, while his irises remained dark amber. Evan's eyes. But as my field of vision expanded, I realized that I was seeing Evan's eyes in a stranger's face.

I struggled to rise.

The stranger lifted me to my feet. "Toria, what the devil happened?"

I couldn't respond. My mouth moved, but it wasn't my voice speaking. The voice I heard was deeper, richer. It was Toria's voice.

"I had the most peculiar sensation, Alistair. Like returning to reality after a long night of dreaming. Discombobulating, to say the least." I could feel my mouth moving, but the sounds coming out weren't mine.

My hands smoothed out my dress. I hadn't told them to do that. I ordered them to stop. But they ignored me and kept fixing my skirt.

More words spilled from my lips—Toria's words, my lips. "It knocked me off my feet. Give me a moment."

Bats beat against the walls of my belly. My legs were so weak I had to lean on…Alistair, was it? As soon as they felt strong enough, I stepped away from him. Or rather, my body did, swiveling toward the mirror. My fingers weaved through my hair, tucking loose strands back into place with jeweled hairpins. I had no control over these movements.

I caught sight of myself in the mirror. Familiar green eyes greeted me from a face that wasn't mine. A face crowned with red curls. A face I'd longed to see for eight years. Toria's strong chin anchored her pert nose and mischievous lips. Her body was petite and delicate. You'd never know the power she possessed.

Her riding dress weighed me down. It had to be at least fifteen pounds of fabric. This wasn't just an image in the mirror. This was me. But it wasn't me. I still had my own thoughts, and I could feel the body I inhabited. But this body was Toria's, and there was some kind of barrier between the two of us.

I screamed, *What's happened to me?* But those words never left my mouth—because it was Toria's mouth.

While my body twisted in front of the mirror, making sure my hair was fixed and my dress was smooth, I caught a glimpse of my surroundings. I was still in Cassie's room, except it wasn't a creepy monument to murder, but a brightly lit mess. Handkerchiefs poked out of a vanity drawer. Hatboxes tumbled out from under the bed and dresses peeked out of the over-stuffed armoire.

I stared at my companion, Alistair. He had Evan's eyes, but that was the only feature they had in common. He had a strong almost Germanic nose, pale skin, and chiseled cheekbones. Toria knew this man, but I didn't. He was a complete stranger to me.

Images raced through my mind. Memories that weren't mine. People I shouldn't know. Like I'd been thrown into a movie about someone else's life twenty minutes too late.

Toria—that's what he called me, her, us?

But her full name was Victoria Langley. Toria was just her nickname. My nickname? The nickname of the person whose body I was currently inhabiting? This was crazy.

The memories kept coming. He'd called me Toria since we were little.

He was Alistair Kingsley, my close friend and fourth cousin.

Fourth cousin, did that even count?

We'd come to Castle Creighton for Sebastian's wedding. Sebastian was a close family friend. Wait, he was more. Much more than Toria was willing to admit. A wall dropped in front of me. I was hurled out of Toria's memories as though I'd trespassed too far.

Suddenly, Alistair lost his balance and fell to the floor. I didn't know what to do. Toria knelt beside him, chafing his hand. I felt her worry for him. She grabbed a hatpin from Cassie's vanity and jabbed it into her palm. Blood bubbled up. She cupped her hand over Alistair and whispered words I couldn't understand, but her memories showed me that it was a healing spell.

Alistair started coming around. He rubbed his eyes with his palms. When his hands fell away, I wasn't alone anymore. That look of annoyance mingled with blame could be found in only one person's eyes: Evan Kingsley's.

Sitting up, Evan looked stunned to find me worried about him. Tentatively, he reached out and touched my face. When he opened his mouth, a rich baritone said, "My apologies. All those days of travel must have caught up with me. Are you well?"

I wanted to scream, *No, I am not well. I'm not even me.*

Instead, I found myself nodding, and saying, "Never better." Then I winked. I don't wink. Rather, Toria winked and I watched.

Alistair got to his feet. "We need to get out of here before they return." He looked at the blood in her palm. "Are you sure you're all right?"

"It's just a scratch." She grabbed one of Cassie's handkerchiefs.

He grasped her hand and checked her palm. His hands were strong but gentle. "Thank you."

"It will heal quickly." She balled up the handkerchief and squeezed it inside her fist to stop the bleeding.

My thoughts were so clear, but they were in direct competition with Toria's. So far, she was winning.

Something flickered in Alistair's eyes. An ember of Evan. His head jerked.

Evan asked in a hoarse whisper, "Kat, is that you?"

I shoved through the darkness and made my way to the surface. I struggled to whisper back, "It's me. How'd we get here?"

He looked at the mirror. Shock registered on his face. His eyes were his own, but everything else about his reflection had changed. He reached out to touch his hair, which had gone from straight dark brown to medium brown and wavy. The few inches he lost in height, he gained in a broader chest. Evan could verbally take down anyone, but Alistair looked like he could do it physically with a few moves.

Evan's words tumbled out, "You screamed and fell through the mirror...I tried to catch you, and then..."

"Toria pulled me," I said.

"Pulled you?" He raised both eyebrows. Eyebrows that weren't his own. Creepy.

"Sounds crazy, right?" I asked.

"No crazier than us being in bodies that don't belong to us."

He had a point. "How'd you get here?"

"I saw you go through the mirror. It shimmered and sparkled like it was alive. I followed you."

He came after me. Without knowing what awaited us. It was beyond brave. A rush of gratitude stole over Toria's body and made it mine temporarily. My lips quivered and I smiled. "Thanks."

"We're a team." He reached over and squeezed my arm. It might have been Alistair's hand touching Toria's arm, but I felt Evan's strength.

Evan walked toward the mirror. He ran his fingers over the surface and rapped his knuckles against it. "Solid glass."

I looked at the knot work in the frame. It was the design I'd sketched in my notebook last night. "It's definitely the same mirror." The mirror from my dream. The mirror we'd both fallen through. This room was the same turret room we'd left behind, but it didn't feel the same. No dread. No loss. No darkness. Most importantly, no bloodstain.

Evan stared at himself in the mirror. Then he slowly turned in place, taking in the entire room. Finally, his gaze settled on me.

"We traveled back in time," he said.

I had the same thought. But to hear an unbeliever like Evan say it aloud was still astonishing.

Behind Alistair's knit brow, I could almost see the cogs of Evan's machine-like mind whirling through all the evidence, checking that his hypothesis made sense. "Time…"

The bedroom door flew open.

Chapter 14

A wisp of a girl with sun-kissed blonde hair and bright lapis blue eyes came in, followed by a taller girl with light brown hair and eyes that were a startling galena gray. Both girls carried baskets of fresh cut flowers. In my world, these girls were long dead.

When they saw us, their chatter halted.

I clutched Alistair's arm to remain upright. Here in front of me stood Cassie Mallory and Leanna Burnsby. My heart lurched in my chest at the sight of Leanna. She was nothing like the ghost who'd tried to possess me. There was no darkness or threat in her. She was just a girl. A living, breathing girl.

Cassie wore a powder blue dress with a floral print overskirt and knife-pleated underskirt. The bodice was a sea of frills. If I didn't know what Leanna was capable of, I wouldn't have noticed her in her understated pale pink dress.

"What are you doing in my room?" Cassie clutched her basket of flowers.

I couldn't open my mouth. The words crowded onto my tongue and tumbled backward, cluttering my throat. I was shoved into the background as Toria seized control of the situation.

"Sorry to intrude, but it really is all Alistair's fault," Toria said.

Alistair flashed his dimples. "Sebastian probably warned you. Toria has a habit of getting me into trouble."

"Who insisted there was a secret passage in this room?" Toria turned to Cassie, pouting like a frustrated governess. "I told him he was wrong, but he refused to believe me. I figured he might try to sneak in here, so I came to retrieve him."

Looking sheepish, Alistair fell into the role Toria had assigned him. "I swear we played in a secret passageway as children. Remember Sebastian had us stand facing the door? Then he disappeared and reappeared without coming near us."

"That was at Dumbarton." Toria rolled her eyes for Cassie's benefit. Turning back to Alistair, she said, "I was six and you were seven. It was a few weeks after Sebastian's tenth birthday and you were both visiting me."

I could hear the thoughts floating through Toria's head as she talked. I could almost remember her memories. I knew that she was the instigator in most of the capers she shared with Alistair, and that both were practiced at improvising their way out of any resulting trouble.

I thought at her, *Toria, can you hear me*? Silence came back to me.

Toria swiveled toward the girls. "His cockiness has known no bounds since Sebastian chose him as his best man."

"Do you see what I have to endure? She's been like this since birth," Alistair said.

Cassie sounded bewildered. "If you wanted to visit my room, all you had to do was ask."

Alistair laughed. "Such graciousness. I see why Sebastian is so smitten with you. Toria and I take the most convoluted path, overlooking the direct way."

Apologizing again, Toria slid her hand into the crook of Alistair's arm and tugged him toward the door. "And now it's time for you to make good on your promise to take me riding." As she left, she threw over her shoulder to Cassie, "I will do a better job of reining him in."

They descended the spiral staircase without saying a word. Toria headed down the hallway to her room in the east turret. Alistair hesitated to follow. It was improper for him to be going to her room. Ever the gentleman, she thought with a sigh. After glancing over her shoulder to make sure no one else was in the corridor, she grabbed his hand and pulled him up the stairs and into her room. She slammed the door and leaned against it.

Her turret room was done in shades of midnight blue and chocolate brown. A stark contrast to Cassie's pink and white room. A pink and white room that had once been Toria's. Years ago, back when Sebastian was still hers.

Alistair grinned. "If you wanted me in your bedchamber, you only had to ask."

"If I wanted you in my bedchamber, it would have happened already," Toria said.

"No need to be snippy. It was exciting to be manhandled by you." Alistair's eyes glimmered with amusement.

"Alistair, really. Try to restrain yourself," Toria said.

"You have no idea how hard I try."

She ignored his comment. "Well, that was a near thing. They should have been in the garden longer."

"Nice thinking on your feet, my dear."

She basked in his praise.

Alistair crossed his arms. "You are a brilliant storyteller. I have often thought you could be the next Shakespeare."

Toria dropped a curtsy. "Thank you. I'd like to acknowledge Cassie's gullibility. And of course my partner in crime, Alistair, without whom none of this would have been possible."

Alistair let out a deep, rumbling laugh.

She liked the sound of it.

So did I.

"Cassie could have caused a stir about us sneaking into her room."

"She can afford to be forgiving. She gets her happily ever after." I didn't just hear her bitterness; I felt it reverberating inside my soul. The pain of being unwanted.

"Sebastian isn't good enough for you, Toria. He never has been."

"Don't." One word carried so much pain. Toria turned her back to Alistair and headed toward the window.

He grabbed her arm and made her face him. His eyes fixed on hers.

I saw Evan lurking in their hazel depths.

"Kat, I really need to talk to you."

It was like a scene ended, and Toria exited stage left as I stepped into the spotlight. "I can't believe we just met Cassie and Leanna," I whispered.

"Why are you whispering?" Evan asked.

"I don't have perfect vocal control over this body."

"You just have to concentrate."

I sighed and tried again. This time, my voice came out normal. Well, Toria's voice did when I asked, "What's it like? Sharing a body with Alistair?"

"Unsettling." Evan grimaced. "Like someone flicked a light switch to turn me off and Alistair back on. I heard everything, but couldn't say or do anything."

"Do you think Toria and Alistair know we're in their bodies?"

Evan shrugged. "I can't communicate with Alistair."

"I have the same problem with Toria." What was happening to Toria and Alistair while Evan and I were in control? Were they starting to lose time, like I had when Leanna had tried to possess me? I felt goose bumps rise on Toria's arms.

"I want my own body back. How do we get home?" Now I was shouting.

Evan shushed me, but I didn't know who was calming whom when strong hands clasped my shoulders.

"Maybe it's a dream?" That was definitely Evan. He was looking for ways to not believe in what had happened. He paced the radius of the turret room.

"Stand still when I'm talking to you." I meant to shout that time.

He stopped and stared at me.

"We are not dreaming. I know things that I shouldn't. I have memories from Toria's life."

"You prefer the idea of us falling through a magic mirror and traveling back in time?" He threw himself into the armchair by Toria's bed. "I don't believe in the unbelievables."

"How do you explain what's happening?" I gestured at my body. Toria's body.

"Time travel has scientific possibilities. Magic portals, however..." He rubbed his hand over his face. His expression was so conflicted. An unbeliever dealing with the unbelievables.

I bit my lip. There were things that I knew. Things that would help him make sense of this. Things that might help us find a way home. But they were the things I never spoke about to anyone. The unbelievables I'd hidden for so long. Well, they weren't staying hidden anymore. They were all around us. They *were* us.

"There's something I need to tell you," I said.

He dropped his hands. "What?"

"I need you to listen to me. Really listen, Evan."

"I listen to you." He sounded surprised that I could ever think otherwise.

"With a completely open mind."

He snorted, and made a flailing gesture that encompassed both of us and everything around us. "My mind is as open as it ever will be right now."

He was right. This was the moment to tell him everything. So I did. I told him about how I'd seen ghosts since I was a baby. How they came to me for their reckonings. I told him about Leanna's ghost trying to possess me and Toria's ghost saving me. How I had to pretend ghosts didn't exist to protect myself. About all my ghost deterrents. My dream of the turret room. Everything. I told him all the things I'd never shared with another human being.

And he listened to every word. When I finished, he sat there in stunned silence. "It can't be," he murmured.

"It is."

"There has to be something else happening." He sounded desperate. Fear trickled into his features. The world of the unbeliever crashed around him.

"I never wanted ghosts as friends. And I refused to believe in them for years, even though I knew they existed." I looked into his eyes. "They kept trying to break into my reality. I fought them every step of the way. But eventually they found a way in. And here we are."

He shook his head, trying to deny it all.

I walked over to him and dropped down in front of him. "I'm sorry. I really am. I'm sorry that you got dragged into this. I'm sorry your unbelief didn't keep you safe. But Evan, we can't afford to lie to ourselves anymore. We are in the past. We traveled back in time through a magic mirror. We are inhabiting other people's bodies." I squeezed his hand. "And if we are ever going to get back to our own time and our own bodies, we have to accept these things as fact."

"Who else knows about the ghosts?"

His question surprised me. "No one."

"What about Morgan? Professor Astor? Your family?"

"No one but you."

"Just me," he murmured. He stared at me. "You've kept this secret your entire life?"

"Yeah."

"That's a tremendous responsibility." Understanding filled his voice. "You made this happen."

He was right. I did this. It was my fault that we were here. That he was here. The guilt overwhelmed me. Tears blurred my vision. "I didn't mean to. I don't know how I did it. And I don't know how to get us back."

He touched my face. "It's okay. We'll figure this out together."

I blinked back tears. "Okay."

"We traveled through time. We're inhabiting the bodies of Victoria Langley and Alistair Kingsley." He spoke slowly, wrapping his mind around each word.

"Yes."

With that affirmation, something clicked. The project manager returned. "Do you think we're here to stop the murders or to observe what happens?"

"To stop the murders." I was shocked that he would even ask. "Otherwise, what's the point? I don't think we'd be whisked through a magic portal just so we can get an *A* on our project."

"But that would disrupt the time continuum."

Evan might be Mr. Scientific Evidence, but he was a history major, not a physicist. His knowledge in this area was about the same as mine, which meant our source materials were novels and movies.

"If you go back in time and change the past, you disrupt the present, and that ripples into the future. Maybe you create parallel universes. Try to return to your own reality, and you might not find it. Or maybe you find that you don't exist," he said.

"But that supposes a passive universe." Evan wasn't the only sci-fi geek in this nineteenth-century room.

He tilted his head. "And?"

"What if the universe moves toward order, not entropy? Then parallel universes don't exist because the universe will maintain the integrity of the time continuum."

"Meaning any actions we take to change the past won't impact the future?"

"It's possible," I said.

"If you believe the universe can auto-correct itself."

"Which brings me back to my first question. Do Alistair and Toria even know about us?"

"So far, the evidence suggests that they don't." He sounded so logical.

"Maybe we can't stop the murders. And if nobody knows that we're here, are we changing the past at all?"

Evan drummed his—Alistair's—fingers on the armrest. "Maybe not in any meaningful way. Maybe you're right. Maybe the universe can handle minor disruptions in the space-time continuum."

And maybe this whole conversation was pointless. Maybe the usual rules of physics or quantum mechanics or whatever didn't apply when you traveled through a magic portal. I was about to say something to this effect when I was stopped by an outburst from Evan.

"I just remembered something. Or Alistair just thought about it and I heard him. Regardless, Toria wanted to search Cassie's room. Alistair tried to stop her."

Before I could respond, I was yanked off-stage, behind a velvet curtain, as Toria took over again.

She stood up and put her hands on her hips. "Do not be fooled by Cassie's pretty smile. That girl is hiding something."

Evan gripped the armrests. "We need to stay focused. Kat, fight her."

I clawed my way around the curtain. "I'm here."

Evan let out a long breath. "That was a close call. Alistair almost took control again."

"Probably because we're squatters in their bodies."

"We need to figure out how to coexist with them." Evan talked about it like a new project, not a life-and-death crisis. "Since our bodies don't exist in this time, we have to inhabit the body of someone who does."

I flashed back to what Leanna's ghost had done to me. I'd find myself places I didn't expect to be. Minutes lost. I made excuses. But the blackouts got more frequent.

If Toria hadn't stopped her, I'd have disappeared. Now, I was the ghost tormenting Toria. Stealing moments of her life. Time she could never get back.

Nausea dampened my neck.

I closed my eyes. *I'm so sorry*, I thought at Toria. She probably couldn't hear me and would never know how much I regretted it.

"What's wrong?" Evan asked.

"This is what Leanna's ghost did to me."

"You're afraid we'll hurt Toria and Alistair?"

"We are hurting them. We're stealing moments of their lives. We're just like Leanna. And if we stay too long, we might make them disappear." I couldn't stop shaking.

He got up and put his arm around me. "It's going to be okay. We'll figure this out."

I rested my head on his shoulder. Knowing I wasn't alone in this helped. "Why did you follow me through the mirror?"

"I promised Professor Astor I'd keep an eye on you."

I laughed. "I don't think he meant following me one-hundred-twenty-nine years into the past."

"Now you tell me."

"Any regrets?" I looked up at him.

"It's the research opportunity of a lifetime. A hundred lifetimes."

"But what good will it do if we never get back to our own time and our own bodies?" My voice—Toria's voice—rose again.

"Should I concentrate on that question until I'm paralyzed with fear and shaking?"

I winced. Only one of us needed to do that today. "No."

His lips slipped into a smile.

I twisted my ring a few times, feeling calmer. "Can we move—"

My ring. Toria was wearing my ring. I had thought that it was similar to Toria's, but it wasn't. It was the same ring. My father had given me Toria's ring.

Chapter 15

A knock on the door sucked me into the shadows. Toria took control and brought Alistair back.

She dragged him across the room by his frock-coat sleeve and stopped in front of the bookcase to half-whisper, "Get in the secret passage." To the person at the door, she raised her voice and said, "Just a moment. I am not presentable."

A muffled male voice said, "My apologies. Take your time."

Alistair planted himself beside her.

"I can get rid of him. It will only be a moment." She reached out and pulled four books from the bookcase. As she rearranged them, each book slid into place with a delicate click. The bookcase swung away from the wall to reveal the hidden passageway.

Toria grabbed the candelabrum and box of matches and pressed them to Alistair's chest. His hands curled around them, but he didn't move toward the passageway. She shoved him. Before he could protest, she placed her finger to her lips. His expression was resigned, but his eyes hinted at future mutiny as he backed into the passage. She shooed him in until he triggered the closing mechanism. The bookcase swung back against the wall. When it came to rest, it looked as though it had never moved.

Passing her vanity, she stopped to check her reflection. Her ivory skin glowed. A faint pink tinged her cheeks. And not a hair out of place, either. She pranced across the room, reached for the handle, and opened the door.

Drew Nolan lounged against her doorframe. Propriety demanded he send a footman with a message, but Drew wasn't the kind of man who did the proper thing.

"Rumor has it that you're going riding with Alistair." His words came out like a caress. "How about a stroll with me instead?"

His tousled dark blonde hair and maple syrup-colored eyes made most girls melt. She was fairly certain his full lips never had to steal kisses.

Toria savored the image of Alistair trudging down the passageway, unable to remember how to open the entrance to his room. All the while knowing she was with Drew. A fitting punishment for daring to defend Cassie.

"A walk in the gardens would be delightful. I shall change out of my riding habit and make my excuses to Alistair. Meet you in the great hall in an hour?"

"I look forward to it." He took her hand in his. His fingers had a slightly calloused feel, as though they had done something useful most days of their lives. He brushed a kiss across her knuckles. His lips lingered longer than necessary.

Toria knew that she should blush and drop her gaze. Instead, she reached out and ran her other hand along his cheek. "As do I."

After he left, she closed the door and leaned against it. If only the other gentlemen in her life would fall in line so easily. Alistair was proving difficult lately. And Sebastian? He never appreciated the depths she'd gone to for him.

Alistair's anger radiated from behind the bookcase. Might be better to leave him in there. Then again, an angry Alistair could cause problems. When she opened the passageway, he blew out the candles and stomped into the room. She had not made him this mad in…weeks. His eyes took on that animal-like quality she adored. She loved affecting him like this, seeing tangible proof of how much he cared.

He came close enough to share a breath with her. "Care to explain your sudden need to stroll with your wedding escort?"

He had been listening through the peephole. She patted his chest. "There is more than childhood friendship or puppy love between Cassie and him. The only way to find out is by spending time with him."

"Something about him bothers me," he said.

"Could it be his interest in me? Alistair, really, you're being overprotective." She touched his arm. "He still loves Cassie."

"He's not the only one still in love."

Toria's knuckles curled around the sleeve of his jacket. He was on dangerous ground.

"You may not care a fig about your reputation, but think of your parents," he said.

"You're overstepping." Once she could let pass, but she bristled at twice.

"If Drew makes off with Cassie, it will destroy Sebastian."

"I always protect Sebastian." She went over to her vanity and began touching up her face. She didn't want Alistair to see the flush of anger in her cheeks. It wouldn't do for him to know how much his words upset her.

Alistair sighed. "You've done your best since your aunt died."

"I'd give my life for his."

Alistair rested his hands on her shoulders. "I know how much he means to you."

"I must keep him safe. It's not just about family obligations. I protected him before I ever got this ring and all its responsibilities."

Alistair squeezed her shoulders. "Drew is dangerous."

"I'm only interested in his secrets. I know the real threat to Sebastian's happiness is Cassie."

"You think you know," Alistair said under his breath.

"Doubting my visions?"

Alistair raked his hand through his hair. "You take unnecessary risks."

"And you don't?" She stared at him in her vanity mirror. "Being a woman doesn't make me helpless."

"Quite the opposite," he muttered. "You'll keep me informed of your discoveries?"

"As long as you do the same with your investigation of Drew." Toria dabbed her perfume behind her ears. She breathed in the scent of ylang ylang and sandalwood, specially blended for her in Paris. She added an emerald hairpin to her elaborately arranged tresses.

Alistair watched her in the mirror. "Be careful."

"I know how boring your life would be without me." Toria winked at him.

He looked away. "You have no idea."

She turned around in her chair to face him and batted her eyelashes.

"Can you forgive me for delaying our ride?"

"Have I ever held a grudge?" He quirked an eyebrow.

"I don't have time to answer that question."

"I should take my leave before we're found together." He headed toward her door.

"Not that way." She jumped up and grabbed his arm. She didn't need the servants catching him leaving her room. All the adults in their families might consider them closer than siblings, but the servants didn't. She and Alistair were only fourth cousins.

"I can barely make out my feet, let alone the stones in the wall of that dark passageway. How can I get those blasted mechanisms to work?"

"Try harder." She handed him the candelabrum. "To find the opening, count up eleven rows of stones when you enter the passage. Drag your hand along that row until you find the carved stone. Your bedroom is on the other side of the wall."

He nodded.

"From there, move your hand to the right four stones and down four stones. Press the middle of that stone. Go left eight and up eight, tap that stone. Go four right and four down and pull that stone. The wall slides back, and you are in your room." His eyes started to glaze over so she rushed to add, "To close it, you just do the same in your room. Start with the stone that sticks out beneath the shelf in the wall. Then you do four-by-four, eight-by-eight, and four-by-four again."

"I'd rather leave carefully through your door."

She glared at him.

"Not acceptable?"

"Hopefully, this time it will stick, so I don't have to remind you every time you use the passageway."

"Here's something to ponder, why are you so adept at opening and closing the secret passage between my room and yours?" Alistair sauntered into the passageway and disappeared from sight before she could answer.

He was infuriating sometimes. The answer was simple. She had to be, given his inability to remember how the passageway worked. She pulled the cord and rang for her maid.

Her thoughts turned to Drew. He had accepted her invitation to the wedding to be near Cassie. She'd figured he would confide in her. Maybe even enlist her help. But thus far, nothing—which left her with less than a week to uncover Drew and Cassie's secret. Otherwise, Sebastian would bind himself to that simpleton for life. No. She would stop this farce of a wedding. No matter what happened, she would protect Sebastian.

Chapter 16

I was dining with dead people. Okay, maybe they were alive right now, but they shouldn't be. Or at least, I shouldn't be here with them when they were alive. I should be back in my time when they were ghosts.

Sitting beside them, I recognized everyone's names from studying Bertram's journal, but meeting them as flesh-and-blood people was creeptastic. Especially knowing the sinister future awaiting Cassie and Sebastian.

The dining room wasn't the same. It was missing a few things that I had seen on Olivia's tour, like the French doors Joshua added to the room and the Rococo paintings bought by his father. It made sense since neither of them had been born yet.

That was weird and disorienting, but not being able to talk to Evan was torture. Toria hadn't allowed me to emerge for a single second since Drew had knocked on her door. Then again, I wasn't willing to put up much of a struggle. It was wrong to be stealing her body. I couldn't quite bring myself to fight her for something that I had no right to take.

I did eavesdrop on Toria's thoughts, though. And that woman had a lot of thoughts. This had to be what it was like inside Morgan's mind. The constant scheming. They delighted in hatching plans and pulling strings. I couldn't help but wonder how Toria was going to feel when everything started to go horribly, horribly wrong.

There wasn't a single ounce of the patient, selfless ghost I had known in this Toria. I had no idea how they could possibly be the same woman.

Maybe losing Sebastian would change everything for her.

Strangest experience of my day? Besides the whole time-traveling-body-snatcher thing, I mean. Toria's psychic abilities. I experienced her "talent" shortly before dinner when images of the future assaulted her mind and blocked out the present. I lost all sense of balance and fell to the floor in my room. I didn't want to see some symbolic clue about the future and then be slammed back to Toria's reality. To be burdened with that sliver of knowledge and have to interpret what it meant.

Stuck backstage, I waited. I watched. I worried.

Toria's gaze lingered on Sebastian and his brother. As ever, she was astonished that her Sebastian could have sprung from the same parents as Phillip. Sebastian was the kind of man who commanded attention. Phillip came and went without anyone taking notice. Sebastian stood a good head taller than his younger brother, and his blue-green eyes and black curls were arresting. Phillip's dark blue eyes lacked sparkle, and his limp hair was a dull brown.

Phillip pushed his chair back and stood. In all the years Toria had known him, Phillip had never made a speech. It was a testament to how much he loved Sebastian that he was willing to endure this public display of discomfort.

"I am not particularly adept at making speeches." Phillip gestured toward Sebastian. "That task has usually fallen to my far more eloquent brother." A creased piece of paper shook in his hands. "What can I say about my older brother? When I wanted to learn to fish, he spent many summer afternoons teaching me to swim. When I wanted to borrow a book on European history, he took me on a summer tour of Europe. He has never laughed at my dreams, even the outlandish desire to turn a tool shed into a laboratory."

Phillip paused as laughter circulated around the table. Surprise sprinkled across his features. Poor Phillip constantly underestimated himself.

"Sebastian makes anything and everything possible. He sees what you want, and then he gives you what you need to achieve it. Sebastian will make a wonderful husband. And dare I say, an excellent father someday."

Cassie's cheeks turned piggy pink. The girl couldn't handle a hint of intimacy without a fit of the vapors. I didn't just sense Toria's contempt for the girl's delicate sensibilities; it seeped into me. I didn't like her either.

"We have shared so much over the years," Phillip said. "To see all of you here tonight is proof of how blessed we are." He raised his glass to Cassie. "We are honored to have you join our family."

With all eyes upon her, Cassie's blush deepened to magenta. The perfect demure fiancée. Everyone rushed to her rescue, trying to set her at ease. Toria despised her. It was a fiery hatred born from the ashes of her hopes for herself and Sebastian.

It was a kind of hatred I'd never felt before. I didn't want to be immersed in it, but what I wanted didn't matter here.

Phillip saluted Cassie's guardian with his glass. "Uncle Bertram, you have always felt like a member of the family. Soon, it becomes official."

"Which room is mine?" Bertram winked at Sebastian's parents.

Laughter cascaded through the room.

"Everyone, please raise your glasses and toast to many, many years of happiness for Cassie and Sebastian." Phillip gulped his champagne and returned to his seat.

Toria caught him glancing at Cassie, anxious for her approval. He only relaxed when he saw her smile. Phillip would do the honorable thing and hide his feelings, of course, but Toria added it to her vault of Radcliffe family secrets.

Beside her, Drew murmured, "It must be hard to see them so happy, when you're not."

"I'm only concerned about Sebastian's happiness," Toria said.

"How long has it been?" he asked.

"I've known him my whole life."

"And been in love with him most of it, I would wager." He spoke so softly she strained to hear him.

"We're friends," she insisted under her breath.

"Yet you're seated at the far end of the table. That must sting."

"My escort made me unpopular with Sebastian and his fiancée." She shot him a warning glance.

He reached over and tucked a stray hair behind her ear. His fingers warmed her skin. "You keep talking of his happiness. When do you get to be happy?"

"I was happy until you started this inquisition." She sipped her champagne.

"Liar."

She watched the bubbles rushing to escape from her glass. "Why did you agree to accompany me?"

"My chivalrous nature."

She threw her head back and laughed. The effect delighted Toria. Cassie chewed her lower lip. Sebastian's brow pinched together. Alistair's eyes fired fury at her.

Drew sliced into his roast. "Care to go riding tomorrow?"

"I planned a walk along the cliffs."

"That sounds delightful. I shall accompany you."

Peals of laughter from the other end of the table drowned out her response.

Toria considered the distance between her place and the head of the table. The distance between her and Sebastian. She had been exiled for the great crime of bringing Drew to the wedding. He had been Cassie's childhood love and a convicted criminal, so she anticipated people being aghast, but to be uncivil to her was quite another thing.

Sebastian had forgotten all the sacrifices she'd made for him. And her most trusted ally? Alistair got on so well with Cassie. She wanted to dunk his head in a pot of gravy. Once she removed Cassie from their lives, Sebastian would see the error of his ways. Everything would be as it should.

When Toria reached her room, I almost emerged. Then her maid entered. Toria remained firmly in control while her evening clothes were removed and replaced with a nightgown and wrapper. She sat at her vanity so her maid could methodically unpin her curls and gently tie back her hair.

After the maid left, I tugged on the velvet curtain that kept me offstage. Because of my experience with Leanna, I figured that taking control of Toria's body would get easier over time. That didn't seem to be the case. But I finally found my way through.

I needed to talk to Evan. I scoured Toria's memory so that I could open the secret passageway.

Gulliver's Travels had to be switched with *Shakespeare's Tragedies*. I needed to replace *Robinson Crusoe* with *Le Mort d'Arthur*. Each volume slid into its new location with a delicate click.

Fingers crossed, I scurried back from the bookcase as it swung open. I grabbed the candelabrum and plunged into the passage. The flames jittered around the wicks, casting eerie shadows on the walls. The wind howled through the stones. The air in the passage dropped several degrees. The hairs at the nape of my neck stood on end like porcupine quills. A ghost was near.

"Who are you and what do you want?" I asked.

A woman's laugh echoed in the passage. Freezer-chilled air wafted around me. The tips of my nose and fingers ached from the sudden blast of winter in July. The shadows thickened and the darkness shimmered.

"What do you want?" I asked again.

From the darkness, white smoke escaped. It thickened into a semi-transparent woman with pale skin and grey-green eyes. Her hair shined like a raven's wings. She couldn't be more than five feet tall, but she looked regal in her tunic dress with a simple cord tied around her waist. Silver rings encircled a few of her toes. "I am not here to harm you." Her voice carried a lilting Scottish brogue.

I believed her. Because she felt safe. The same way Toria's ghost had all those years ago.

"They called me Lorelei." She stared at me. "You know what I am."

"A ghost."

She hesitated. "Do you know what you are?"

"A time traveler."

"That's part of it," she said. "But not the important part. You're a dislocated soul. But, for the time being, your soul has taken this body for a home—even if it's not your own. And your soul is still intact."

"Am I hurting Toria?"

She smiled sadly. "You are snatching time from Toria, but you are not a ghost. You're still anchored to your own body. The longer you stay away from your body, the weaker your soul becomes. You cannot draw energy from Toria's body or soul like Leanna's ghost did from you."

"How much time do I have?"

"That is up to you," she said. "Time means nothing to us and everything to you." Her gaze dropped to my ring. She stared intently at it.

"Why are you staring at my ring?" I asked.

"It's not yours yet. In this lifetime, it belongs to Toria, and only she can wield its power."

"Power?" I asked.

"You've felt it. Every time you twist it, you call on its power."

Was that why it always calmed me? I figured it was just an obsessive-compulsive quirk. But if it was magic, I wouldn't have wanted to know. I was too busy blocking out the unbelievables to see what was right on my hand.

The ghost flickered. She was growing weaker.

Before she disappeared, I rushed to ask, "How do I get home?"

"The same way you got here. That mirror was made for you."

"By who?"

Her image dissolved into the shadows and her voice faded away. "By me."

Chapter 17

I trudged along the passageway, skimming my hand over the rock wall and praying I didn't miss the stone outcropping by Alistair's room. The ghost's words tumbled around in my mind. *Made for me.* My mind ached at the meaning of those three words. How could she have made the mirror for me? How would she have known about me? Was I supposed to come here?

And then the rest of her words walloped me. I couldn't destroy Toria the way Leanna had tried to destroy me. My momentary relief gave way to the fear that I would disappear forever if I didn't get back to my own body. The time I had left depended on the strength of my soul, which I had no way to calculate. I had no idea how many days I could exist outside my body and inside Toria's. And it all came back to that mirror. With no clue how it transported us here, I had to get it to take us home.

My hand bumped against the stone outcropping. It pulled me out of my thoughts. I brought the candelabrum closer to the wall and mined Toria's memories. My hand shook. I counted wrong. It took four tries to open the entrance to Alistair's room.

When the wall finally slid aside, I saw Alistair sleeping. Peacefully. A wave of envy foamed around me. Evan got to be normal in this body, while I got to deal with ghosts and psychic visions and our impending disappearance.

I stepped into the room and closed the entrance to the passage. Shadows filled the room. I didn't see the desk until I bumped into it. *That's going to*

112

leave a mark. A mark Toria won't be able to explain.

I needed more light. I used one of my candles to light the kerosene lamp on the desk.

The room was hunter green with mahogany furniture. Very masculine. Very Alistair. His sleigh bed was pushed against the far wall. I padded past the fireplace and put my candelabrum on the dresser beside his bed.

"Evan, wake up. It's Kat."

No response. *Great, a sound sleeper.* I tapped his shoulder. He rolled away from me, forcing me to lean over the bed and hiss in his ear, "Evan, I need to talk to you. Wake up!" When that didn't work, I used both hands to shake him.

My feet left the ground. Half asleep, he dragged me into his arms.

"Evan, let go of me. You idiot, it's Kat." Too late. He'd already pulled me onto the bed. Every inch of him pressed against Toria's petite form through a thin blanket. My face burned with embarrassment. It wasn't Evan; it was Alistair. Either way, I didn't want to know him this well. I tried to twist away, but only succeeded in hiking up my nightgown.

I freed a hand and swiped at his face. "Evan, let go!"

"Kat…what…why are you in my bed?" His voice was slurred with dreams.

"Because you pulled me in. Now. Let. Me. Go." I squirmed away from him.

He released me and rubbed his eyes. "What are you doing here?"

Scrambling off the bed, I pushed my nightgown back over my knees. "Oh you know me, I like to wander into men's rooms at night."

Up went his eyebrow. "And you're mad because?"

I threw the nearest pillow at his head.

Evan ducked and put up his hands. "Kidding. Calm down."

"I should've stayed in my room." I grabbed the candelabrum and stomped toward the secret passage. I wasn't going to leave until we talked, but I hoped the threat of leaving would make him focus.

Evan leapt out of bed and threw his dressing robe on. "Stay. We need to talk."

I pressed the first stone and paused.

He stood beside me. "Why'd you come here in the middle of the night?"

"To finish our conversation." It was so hard to snatch moments alone together. I stopped fiddling with the stones. "Dinner was exasperating."

"Bloody awful."

Seeing Evan in a silk dressing robe was weird. Scratch that. Seeing Evan in Alistair's body in a silk dressing robe. And for me to be wearing a calico-print wrapper over a nightgown. I'd always thought Victorian clothes were romantic, but wearing them now, I'd kill for some twenty-first-century boxers and a T-shirt.

Evan raked a hand through his hair. "There's so much we need to figure out. Like your ring. How does Toria have it?"

I shrugged. "I have no idea."

"Was it a gift?"

"Yes." My voice sounded so calm. So detached from the emotions inside me.

"Who gave it to you?"

"My father." The two words singed my throat.

"Family heirloom?"

"I don't know."

"What do you mean?"

"I never met my dad or his family." That simple fact had shaped my childhood. I had been the girl without a dad. Not even a part-time dad. Mom tried to be there. My grandparents did everything they could to distract me from the void, but it remained—the space my father never wanted to fill in my life.

"I don't mean to bring up the past, but your ring may be related to our time travel." He sounded so scientific, dissecting my existence.

"Evan, I get it." I watched the candles' flames convulse around the wicks as I tried to control the emotions rising up in me.

"Is Preston your dad's last name?"

"My mom's." She didn't want me to have his name. Not after he left us. I was hers. Not his.

He waited for an explanation.

My chest constricted. Ghosts, time-travel, our impending oblivion—those things were easy, compared to talking about my father.

"I don't know anything about my dad." He started to ask another question, but I shook my head. "Not his last name. Not his face. Not his birth date." I repeated the only thing my mom ever said about their relationship. "They loved each other but couldn't be together."

"Why?"

"Mom never said," I replied.

"You asked?"

"Of course." I remembered the way my mother's face looked when I asked about my father—all that hurt and longing. By the time I was six, I had learned to stop asking. "She doesn't like to talk about him. I try to respect that."

"Did you ever look for him?" Evan asked.

"No." I could have gotten my birth certificate or asked my grandparents. But I didn't. Because I was afraid. Afraid of what I'd find. Afraid I'd discover that he'd never wanted me. Afraid that seeing how little I mattered to him would destroy me. I had run from my father like I had run from the ghosts.

Tears filled my eyes. I tried to blink them away, but I couldn't. They coursed down my cheeks. "I never tried."

You'd think that after seventeen years without him, I'd be used to it. Or at least have accepted it. But every time I talked about it, I realized I'd never be okay with it.

Evan took a step toward me and rubbed my shoulder. "Must have been hard not knowing your dad."

The pity in his eyes slashed through me. I'd seen it so many times over the years. I hated it. And I couldn't take it from him. "My mom and my grandparents are great. We have an awesome life. Every family's different."

"And unhappy in their very own way." He paused. "How'd you end up with the ring?"

I told him how the ring had shown up on my desk with a note from my dad on my seventeenth birthday.

Evan cleared his throat. "So we have no idea how the ring made its way from Toria to your father."

We needed more information. I peeked into Toria's memories. An avalanche of images buried me. I focused on the ring. It took a couple minutes to sort through everything I was seeing and feeling.

"Toria's had the ring since she was fifteen. It's been in her family for generations," I said.

"You sure?"

"Check Alistair's memories."

Evan's forehead wrinkled up in concentration. "You're right. And she wasn't happy about getting it."

I could sense that he was right. "But why did I end up with it?"

"I'm Alistair's third cousin four times removed. Maybe you're related to her? Your dad could be a Langley. That might be the link between our investigating Cassie's disappearance and ending up here."

I swallowed. "There's more. Something happened in the passageway..."

I told him about Lorelei. That the mirror was our way home and that it had been made for me. How we would disappear if we stayed here.

The shock in his expression lasted a few moments. "We can't end like that."

"We've got to figure this out fast."

"We need more time with that mirror. We'll sneak into Cassie's room tomorrow afternoon."

"Toria and Drew have a date to go walking after breakfast."

Evan's brow knit together. He had to be sifting through information in Alistair's brain. "Just do what you can to keep it short. Everyone's going to be out riding at midday. We'll have the whole castle to ourselves."

"Sure. I'll just take control of Toria's body, make some excuse to get away from Drew, and keep Toria in the background long enough for us to examine the mirror. No problem. Would you like me to summon a unicorn as well? Maybe a leprechaun?"

Alistair's face looked a lot like Evan's when it scowled. He went to the desk, wrote a few lines, and handed me a folded piece of paper. "Use this. It's a note from Alistair to Toria, begging her to help him search Cassie's room. She won't be able to resist."

"That might work," I said.

"Put it on her vanity. That way she'll see it first thing in the morning." I nodded.

"It seems like it's easier for us to emerge when Toria and Alistair are together and no one else is around. Let's plan to meet here again tomorrow night."

"Agreed."

I retrieved my candelabrum, reopened the passage, and headed in.

"See you tomorrow," Evan said.

"Tomorrow," I promised.

Chapter 18

I didn't plan to make any stops on my way back to Toria's room. I wasn't exactly eager to meet another ghost with a dire message for me. But the muffled "Damnation!" from the other side of the wall stopped me. I searched Toria's memories and realized that the room belonged to Bertram and there was a peephole. I found the ladybug-sized button disguised as a stone and pressed it. I peeked into his room.

Bertram sat at his desk with a half-empty brandy decanter. He pushed his journal to the side.

The pain in his voice spilled into the passageway. "William, why did you leave her to me? You knew I had other obligations to fulfill."

Who was William? Toria's memory filled the void. Cassie's father and Bertram's younger brother. He had died ten years ago.

"She deserved better. I left a child to fend for herself," Bertram said.

He leapt up and his chair toppled over. He stalked toward the fireplace. Resting his left arm on the mantle, he clenched the brandy glass in his hand. He buried his face in his other hand. When it dropped away, his blue eyes were soaked in anguish.

"Damn you, William. Damn you for leaving us. You were the perfect father. It wasn't in me." His body hunched forward. "There's nothing I can do to prevent it."

He threw the rest of his drink into the empty fireplace. As if everything were settled, he returned the chair to its upright position and sat down. Then he refilled his glass and went back to writing.

Could Bertram be involved in Cassie's death? Or did he sense something evil was coming for her? Whatever it was, it was tearing him apart.

I lingered, hoping he would reveal more, but he didn't. When he started to get ready for bed, I gave up. I pressed the button to close the peephole and scampered back to my room. To Toria's room. To our room.

Standing on the cliff's edge with Drew, Toria gazed at the ocean and fumed. The entire walk from the castle to her favorite spot had yielded nothing of value. Drew sidestepped her questions about Cassie. He refused to open up to her. She didn't have time to unravel his mysteries. She needed to be back at the castle soon, helping Alistair search Cassie's room.

Inhaling the ocean's salt-tinged breath, she tried to relax. Drew needed more coaxing. He needed to know he could trust her. Surely, she could manage that.

But this place distracted her. Standing here, looking out over the Atlantic, she could almost see Sebastian, Alistair, and herself as children playing here. They had been warriors back then, with wooden swords to fight back imaginary invaders.

She would never forget the time Sebastian's pocket watch fell over the side of the cliff and landed on a ledge. Sebastian intended to climb down and retrieve it. Alistair tried to discourage him, but Sebastian refused to listen. Her premonitions told her the ledge would give way. Being younger and smaller, she had a better chance.

Summoning up all her strength, she knocked Sebastian down. Before he got up, she scrambled over the side of the cliff and eased herself onto the ledge. She picked up the watch and safely tucked it inside her pocket right before the ledge crumbled beneath her feet. She screamed and clung to the rocks. Her feet scraped the air.

Alistair hauled her back up over the side of the cliff and berated her for being foolish. She reached into her pocket and pulled out the watch. Sebastian swooped her up in his arms and swung her around.

Drew's voice wrenched Toria back to the present. "What brought that smile to your face?"

"This place," she said.

"Good memories?"

Her throat constricted around four years of pain. She forced out her words. "The best."

"Sebastian?"

She almost denied it. But his sympathetic tone made her share the story of Sebastian's pocket watch. When she finished, the only sound was the waves smashing themselves against the rocks below.

His face softened. "I had that once. A girl I would do anything for."

"Before you went to jail?" she asked. He'd never lied about his past. He'd never explained it either.

He wiped his hand over his eyes as if clearing the image from his mind. "By the time I was released, she'd grown up and was promised to another."

"What did you do?"

"I shot a man."

"Why?"

"It was an accident," he said tersely.

Something told her otherwise.

He had killed for Cassie. Or he had taken the blame for her. This was why she wanted him here. His secret was Cassie's secret. Toria already knew that Cassie was wrong for Sebastian. She just needed something she could show Sebastian. Some kind of proof.

Toria moistened her lips. "Sebastian and I used to be that close."

"What happened?"

"Life." The explanation spilled from her mouth. "His father had a hunting accident, and Sebastian was summoned home. I wanted to go with him, but my aunt passed away." Toria gazed down at her ring. The minute she had inherited her aunt's ring, her life stopped being hers. She became the sworn protector of the Radcliffes. Someone who could never be Sebastian's wife. "We became different people. No longer free to be together."

"The thought of Cassie is what kept me going in prison." Drew's voice was so low, Toria barely heard the words.

"You should have confided in me sooner," she said.

"Last night was the first time I saw that you're as opposed to this wedding as I am. Sebastian hates you being with me." His palm slid down her arm. His fingers caressed hers.

"Cassie dislikes me being with you." She laced her fingers through his. In that moment of understanding, their bargain was struck.

Chapter 19

Fifteen minutes staring into a mirror did not make me vain. It made me frustrated. I'd racked my brain for a way to reopen the portal. I re-enacted everything I did the night Evan and I had passed through it. Touching the mirror and its frame until my fingers felt bruised.

I scoured Toria's memories. Didn't find anything remotely related to time travel, but I did trip over an old memory of her practicing scrying. She'd been looking for a glimpse of her future husband. The face she saw wasn't Sebastian's.

"Stupid useless mirror," Toria had said as she stomped out of her room at the castle. And now that room and that mirror were Cassie's.

It felt wrong. Why didn't they move the mirror to Toria's new room?

I hit a rock wall in Toria's memory. I couldn't go any further. I stumbled backward, and Evan caught me.

"Everything okay?"

In the mirror, concern wrinkled the corners of his eyes.

"Fine," I lied.

His hands dropped away. "My turn." He moved toward the mirror. Ran his fingers over the entire frame. Pressed on the glass from every angle. It remained solid. He stepped back to survey it. "Conceptually, I get it. But actually opening a portal is quite difficult."

"Maybe we should go?" Cassie wasn't due back for a while, but we didn't seem to be getting anywhere. And I was concerned about what might happen if Alistair and Toria were caught in Cassie's room again.

121

"After all the trouble we went through to get here? I'm not leaving until we learn something new. Something that will help us get back to our own time."

I kept poking and prodding at the mirror while Evan searched the room.

He was rifling through the nightstand when I heard him gasp.

"What is it?" I asked as I rounded the bed.

"Cassie's journal."

He flipped it open and I read over his shoulder.

Last night I dreamt of it again. A necklace more beautiful than anything I have ever seen. Four large rubies, like flower petals, reaching in four directions. A compass rose. A circle of diamonds touched the middle of the stones and studded the chain to its clasp. The necklace lay there in its black velvet box. I could not help myself. I reached for it. The rubies begged to be around my neck. Nothing else mattered. I undid the clasp and started to put the necklace on. I woke up certain everyone in the castle could hear the pounding of my heart. Each dream brings me closer and closer to wearing this necklace.

Evan turned the page, but it was blank. He flipped to the entry from a few days before we'd arrived.

Why did Toria bring Drew to my wedding? Every time I see him, I am reminded of how much I betrayed him. He saved me. But gratitude and friendship are not enough to build a life together. Years ago, I felt so much more, but now there is Sebastian. Drew will always be dear to me, but his presence here makes me nervous. Why would he come to my wedding?

Evan flipped to the beginning of the journal. I couldn't believe what this entry said. I had to read it twice.

He came to see me today. Four years had made him stronger and rougher. His eyes more guarded. Still my Drew. I never expected to see him again. We lost touch a while ago. No, that is not true. There is no point in keeping a journal if I fill it with lies. Every time a letter arrived from Drew, I took sick. Uncle Bertram ordered me to stop writing Drew. And I did.

I hated thinking of that day. Each letter reminded me that Drew was in jail for my sins. I wanted to forget what happened. Drew, my Drew, was a living reminder.

If only I had not been alone in the house.

Drew found me curled up against the desk. Lost in my mind. Reliving the events of that afternoon. Unable to escape any of it.

On the floor in front of me lay Pastor Fitzgerald with a bullet buried in his chest. I didn't not know how many hours he lay there, but his blood saturated Uncle Bertram's oriental rug.

Looking up, I saw someone move toward me. I raised the gun. It shook in my hands. He stopped and slowly lowered himself to the floor.

He kept saying, "It's Drew" and "You're safe now." Over and over, he told me that he would not let anyone hurt me.

It felt like days passed before his words reached me. This was Drew. I was safe with him. I lowered the gun and collapsed into his arms.

I told him how the Pastor attacked me…hurt me. The Pastor had punched me so hard that he knocked me to the floor. When I tried to get up, he kicked me back down. Then he climbed on top of me, his face twisted with rage. My struggling excited him. He tore the front of my dress. His hands grabbed everywhere. I screamed and he hurt me more.

When he was done, he left me lying there.

I saw death in the Pastor's eyes. It hurt to move, but Pastor Fitzgerald came after me. He taunted me. Said he was not finished with me. I remembered where we kept Papa's gun. The Pastor said he would kill me. He told me that I did not have the nerve to shoot him. I begged him to stay back, but he refused. I pulled the trigger. The gun roared. Shock registered slowly in his eyes. Then he crumpled to the floor in front of me.

I was only thirteen. I did not know what to do. Drew did. He sent *me to change and wash up. He burned what was left of my dress. Then he summoned the local magistrate and confessed to shooting the Pastor in "a terrible accident." He went to jail to protect me.*

I should have confessed. Drew says he does not blame me, but I do. He sacrificed himself for me and what did I do? I fell in love with another man. Unforgivable.

I wanted to keep reading, but Cassie's and Leanna's voices wound their way up the stairwell. They'd cut their afternoon ride short, which meant Sebastian was probably on his way back to his room. Evan and I rushed toward the secret passageway's entrance, hoping to get back to Sebastian's room before he ever knew we were there.

"Should we take the journal?" Evan whispered.

Would it matter if we borrowed it for a few days? I decided that it wouldn't. We skedaddled into the secret passageway.

I reached under a diamond-shaped stone in the passageway's wall and pressed a tiny lever. It opened a peephole into Sebastian's room. The crimson and gold furnishings befit a king. I looked left. No one sat in the chocolate brown leather chairs facing the marble fireplace. Then straight ahead to the vacant hand-carved desk and chair. A glance to the right told me no one was on the canopy bed. "All clear."

"Let's go," Evan said.

Relying on Toria's memories, I opened the passageway.

A section of the wall swung back toward us.

"Nice work." Evan stepped into Sebastian's room.

Pulling back the tapestry on the wall, I skated my finger along the bottom section of a row of stones until I felt the tiny lever. After I pressed it, the wall moved back into place. Evan crossed Sebastian's room in several strides and overtook me. While I struggled with the weight of Toria's bustle and underskirts, he rounded the bed and reached for the door handle.

Before he could get out of the way, the door careened into his face and sent him flailing backward. I dove under the bed, fighting with my skirts until they were out of sight. Poor Evan lay sprawled on the floor. I clamped my hand over my mouth to keep from laughing. As soon as he looked into Sebastian's eyes, Evan vanished. I made the same mistake.

Chapter 20

"**G**ood God, are you alright?" Sebastian asked.

Alistair nodded but made no effort to get up.

"What are you doing in here?" Sebastian asked.

Alistair pinched his nostrils together to keep from bleeding all over his shirt and waistcoat. "Getting my nose bloodied by you." With his free hand, he searched his pockets and found a handkerchief to staunch the bleeding.

Sebastian gripped Alistair's hand and pulled him to his feet. "A fitting punishment for sneaking into my room."

"I don't sneak. I came to see you."

"And stayed when I wasn't here because?" Sebastian asked.

"I wanted to borrow a book." Alistair's voice jumped two octaves.

Toria held her face in her hands. Alistair had always been a terrible liar, but, at the moment, he was more inept than usual.

She and Alistair were off somehow. She didn't quite remember how they got to Sebastian's room, but she knew they had planned to search Cassie's room again.

Sebastian looked at Alistair's empty hands. "Did you find a book?"

"Ah, no." Alistair paused to check his nose. The bleeding had slowed. "How was your ride?"

"Short. Leanna is no horsewoman." Sebastian dropped his riding gloves on the dresser. "You're a terrible liar. You need Toria to pull off these stunts."

Sebastian strolled past the bed and toward the leather chairs facing the fireplace. He threw himself into one.

Alistair's eyes darted around in search of Toria.

She waved a hand from under the bed.

He coughed to cover his surprise. "You caught me." He walked over and took the chair beside Sebastian's. "I'm worried about Toria. She's not handling your impending nuptials well."

"She invited Drew to cause trouble." Irritation inflamed Sebastian's words. "That's why I've been keeping my distance."

"Your...intimate connection was severed four years ago. Do you really think she's still nursing a broken heart?"

"I fancied myself in love with her. But at fifteen and nineteen, what did we know?" Sebastian asked.

She knew she would have given up everything for him. All he had to do was ask.

"You know the rules. The Langley heir and the Radcliffe heir can never be together. It doesn't matter what we wanted. She accepted our fate. Until she met Cassie," Sebastian said.

"Toria hates to lose. She takes it very personally," Alistair said.

"You see her more clearly than I ever did," Sebastian said. "Why not do something about it?"

"I, well, she's one of my closest friends. It's not like that between us. She's my cousin."

"Our parents may be blinded by that excuse, but fourth cousins don't count," Sebastian said. "By the time you screw up your courage, Drew may steal her away."

Alistair leapt from the chair and paced around the room. His eyes sought hers. "She's too smart to be taken in by Drew. She creates uncomfortable situations when she's unhappy about something."

Toria scowled up at Alistair.

Alistair clenched his fists. "What? You know I'm right."

"Why are you yelling at my bed?" Sebastian asked.

Alistair grimaced. "Sorry. I got carried away." He lowered his voice. "She doesn't care about him. She's using him to get back at you."

Sebastian stood to face Alistair, forcing Toria to worm farther under the bed.

Sebastian ran his hand through his hair. "You two are perfect for one another."

It took everything she had not to crawl out from under the bed and clap Sebastian on the ears.

"She only has eyes for you." Alistair didn't glance in her direction. He hesitated before he asked, "How did you know with Cassie?"

Sebastian walked over to the mantle. He stared at the picture of Cassie sitting on a swing surrounded by lilac bushes. "Women have been fun, exciting, pleasurable…but never nerve wracking."

"All you had to do was crook a finger. They came willingly. Gave you whatever you wanted."

"Not Cassie." Sebastian touched the picture. "I wish Toria understood."

Oh, she understood. Sebastian always wanted what was beyond his reach.

"Give her time. She loves you. She'll come around," Alistair said.

"I'm not so sure."

Alistair's voice thickened, cushioning his words. "Her premonitions make her suspicious of everyone."

Sebastian grunted.

"Have you thought about how she must feel?" Alistair asked.

She'd given up more than she dreamed possible for Sebastian and he'd bruised her heart more than anyone should. Sometimes, she came close to hating him.

"I should have realized this wedding would be hard on her." The weight of another obligation flattened Sebastian's voice. "The premonitions are worse?"

"More frequent and more vivid. She never lets on how much they affect her," Alistair said.

"Her feelings are clouding her judgment."

"Possibly. But if she's right, you're in serious trouble."

"We all are," Sebastian said. "Which is why we need to wring whatever happiness we can out of the present."

The warm summer night provided the perfect setting for Toria and Drew's tryst. The weather pulled everyone to the courtyard after dinner. They gathered around Cassie and Sebastian, dispensing advice about marriage and asking questions about the honeymoon.

Drew and Toria huddled together on the edge of the courtyard.

I hated being a part of their manipulations. Mostly because I was afraid what they were doing would lead to the murders. Stirring up jealousy and playing on people's fears could only make things worse for everyone. But I had zero say in what she did. With each day, I grew weaker and had to conserve what was left of my energy. I couldn't afford to get angry or upset. I had to be a neutral observer.

Drew leaned close to her ear. "Alistair can't take his eyes off us."

"And Sebastian?" Toria asked.

"If looks could kill, I would be in a casket."

She reached up and adjusted his necktie, making sure her fingers lingered longer than necessary. Drew caught her hand and pressed his lips to her gloved knuckles.

"And Cassie?" he asked.

She pretended to brush something off his shoulder and glanced at Cassie. "The girl is three shades paler than normal."

"Ready?"

She took his arm. They lingered long enough for Sebastian to notice their departure, without drawing the attention of his parents. As they entered the labyrinth, Drew's arm glided around her waist.

"You have no trouble getting into character," she said.

"I have a wonderful leading lady." His voice stroked her skin.

She led Drew to a secluded spot, where Sebastian could stumble upon them. Come to think of it, Sebastian had kissed her here once.

Drew pulled her toward him. She closed her eyes, trying to remember what a passionate embrace felt like. She expected to strain her acting abilities.

His lips swept over her jaw on their way to kiss her. Then his mouth came down on hers. It had been so long since someone held her, touched her, kissed her.

It was an intoxicating experience—for all three of us.

Chapter 21

"Perhaps you should save something for your wedding night." Sebastian's voice scalded Toria's skin.

Her eyes never left Sebastian's face while she disentangled herself from Drew, adjusted her dress, fixed her tousled hair, and tried not to gloat. At least, not openly.

"Radcliffe." Drew nodded a greeting. "Why are you roaming around the maze alone?" He slid his arm around Toria's waist and pulled her to his side.

Sebastian glared at her. "Toria, go back to the castle."

"I'm not a child." She stamped her foot, but her soft-soled slippers made no sound.

"I won't allow you to ruin your reputation on someone like him. If need be, my parents will chaperone you." Sebastian said.

"Like they did four years ago?" She and Sebastian had gone beyond the bounds of propriety right there on the castle grounds while under his parents' careful supervision.

Sebastian's nostrils flared. "Don't test me, Toria."

She promised Drew, "Later."

He spoke to her, but he stared at Sebastian. "I look forward to it."

Sebastian stepped toward them.

Toria raised her hand to ward him off. "I'm going." With that, she skipped around a corner of the labyrinth.

Once she was out of sight, she peered through the thick hedges, watching what unfolded between Sebastian and Drew.

"Stay away from her, Nolan," Sebastian said. "Toria is not the kind of woman you dally with."

Drew folded him arms. "It's true that she can be a tigress, but she deserves a little happiness."

Toria stifled a gasp. She had been trying so hard to learn Drew's secrets. She hadn't meant to share any of her own.

"I have no idea how you wheedled your way into her good graces, but I will not allow you any closer." Sebastian's voice was thick with emotion.

"Planning to have a sweet wife and keep the tigress on the side?"

Sebastian's fist flew at Drew's jaw. Drew stumbled backward, but recovered in time to block Sebastian's next blow. Drew made a few quick, sharp jabs to Sebastian's belly.

"What are you up to now?" Alistair demanded from behind her.

He startled her. She released the branches so that the hedge hid what was happening with Sebastian and Drew. Then she turned around to face him. "Nothing. Nothing at all."

He paused. Then he cocked his head to the side, listening. The sound of scuffling and the occasional grunt penetrated the hedge maze.

"Your doing, I assume?" He yanked the hedges back and saw Sebastian and Drew fighting.

She tapped her fan to her lips. "Care to make a wager? My money is on Drew. He has no problem fighting dirty."

"Get back to the castle," Alistair said.

She ignored his order while he dashed around the corner of the maze and waded into the fight. He pulled Sebastian off Drew.

How disappointing. Sebastian's split lip might require some explanation, but she'd wanted a bit more bruising and bleeding. She'd wanted an injury that Sebastian would have to explain to Cassie.

"Go. Now," Alistair shouted at Drew as he struggled to hold Sebastian back.

Drew's fingers splayed over the ripped shoulder seam in his tailcoat. He turned to Alistair. "I expect you will replace this."

Alistair nodded curtly. Sebastian gathered himself together.

Rounding the hedge's corner, Drew found Toria. "Enjoy the fight?"

"I wish you'd landed a couple more blows to his face." Her gaze traveled from his bloodied knuckles to his disheveled hair. The beginnings of a bruise shaded his jaw.

"You said not to hurt him," he said.

"You could have returned what he gave." She ran her gloved fingertips over his jaw. "Does it hurt?" She resisted the urge to heal him. She wanted Cassie to know about this fight.

"I've had worse." He rested his hands on her shoulders.

She whispered, "Go."

He leaned in and whispered, "Until tomorrow." His breath was hot against her neck.

Then he kissed her. Again.

After Toria prepared for bed, I fought to surface. It was harder than last time. I was terrified by how quickly my soul was weakening.

I needed more time with the mirror. I needed to figure out how it worked. But Cassie was in her room. I couldn't use the secret passageway until I knew that she and Sebastian were both out of their rooms. I had an hour to kill before I met with Evan. I paced around my room, needing something to do.

I still had Cassie's journal.

I grabbed it and curled up on Toria's bed.

> *Leanna's parents expect so much of her. When I asked how she manages their expectations, she said nothing more than that family is an unbreakable bond. We have been friends for years, but she holds so much inside.*
>
> *Can you ever truly know another person? You only know what they let you see. And they usually hide the worst of it.*
>
> *Last time I visited my parents' graves, I found her at the edge of the cemetery. She stood in a circle of candles, speaking to a gravestone in a language I had never heard. Tears filled her eyes, but she did not let them fall. I did not disturb her, but later when I asked her about it, I cannot forget the words she said, "A promise made must*

be kept. No matter what the cost."

I flipped through the pages and stumbled upon another passage involving the ruby necklace. It was a recurring dream for Cassie. But the necklace seemed familiar to me—no, to Toria.

Toria had been fifteen. Sebastian almost nineteen. They were in his father's study. Sebastian opened a black velvet box. Inside was a necklace. Four marquise-cut rubies set in a compass rose shape. A circle of diamonds intersected the middle of each ruby. The pendant hung on a rope of smaller diamonds. This necklace had been in Sebastian's family for generations.

As I watched Toria's memory unfold, I thought of the knot design on the magic mirror. They were similar to the shape of the necklace. There had to be a connection between this necklace and that portal.

Sebastian's fingers grazed the ruby pendant. "My wife will be the next woman to wear this."

Toria was afraid to speak.

"Father says the family's fate is forever entwined with these rubies."

"Can I try it on?" She looked up at him, unleashing the full power of her green eyes.

Sebastian grinned. "Feeling confident today?"

Toria came around the desk and perched on his lap. His arms wrapped securely around her.

She snuggled into him. "Accepting the inevitable."

Sebastian laughed and dropped a kiss on the back of her neck. She sat up and lifted her curly hair out of his way. He fastened the clasp around her neck. The stones cooled her skin. She twisted around and buried her face in the crook of his neck. She breathed in the ocean-breeze scent that clung to him. *Sebastian.* He was more essential to her than the blood simmering in her veins.

He leaned back to admire the necklace. "It suits you."

Toria caressed the rubies. "I suit you."

Sebastian traced his thumb along her lower lip. "It's only a matter of time, my love."

It hurt to go there. To see them so in love and know it ended. I brushed the tears from my cheeks, blew my nose into Toria's hankie, and reminded myself that these were her feelings not mine. Not mine.

Observe, Kat, observe.

I'd have to tell Evan about that necklace. *The Wright Chronicle* never mentioned it being stolen, but something like that could definitely be a motive for murder.

I pushed myself to keep reading. Flipping through the journal, I came to Cassie's entry about the day we'd arrived:

> *I cannot understand what Alistair and Sebastian see in Toria. And why in God's name did she bring Drew to the wedding? Leanna and I try to stay away from her and ignore Drew. Difficult to do when we are all in the same castle.*
>
> *Toria and Sebastian have a friendship that spans their entire lives. He wants me to have her as a bridesmaid. I cannot say no, but I loathe saying yes. No matter how badly or outrageously she behaves, he stands by her. It makes no sense to me.*
>
> *I am so afraid he will find out about what happened to me. What I did. I could not survive losing him.*

Chapter 22

"Kat, snap out of it. You have to fight harder!"

I recognized Evan's voice through the haze of sleep.

"Kat, fight her. Please, we have to talk."

Something in his voice yanked me to the surface. I opened my eyes.

"Kat, is it you?" His nose was inches from mine. I could see every green fleck in his eyes. I'd never seen so much fear there.

"It's me. What's going on?" I asked.

"I couldn't get you to come out."

"I was going to meet you in your room later. I must have nodded off," I said.

"That was last night."

A wave of nausea washed over me. *Last night.* "No."

"It's true." He ran his hand through his hair. "I've been trying to talk to you all day. Toria and Drew were inseparable. When I came in here tonight, Toria almost pulled Alistair to the surface."

I staggered and fell back into the chair at the vanity, barely able to ask, "I missed a day?"

He nodded. "Why didn't you come out?"

An entire day gone. I had no sense of the time passing. I was lucky to be here now. I started shaking.

Evan grabbed the blanket from the bed and draped it over me. He pulled a chair over and sat in front of me, chafing my hands.

"It's happening. I'm fading away. Just like Lorelei said. I'm going to disappear forever." My teeth chattered.

"We seem to help each other stay in control. We'll just spend more time together. And if you slip away again, I'll pull you back. Just like I did tonight." There was no hesitation or doubt in his voice. He rested his hands on my shoulders and stared into my eyes. "As long as we keep fighting, there's a chance."

Warmth trickled over me. My body stopped shaking. Maybe it was the blanket. Or maybe it was Evan.

"There's something I need to ask you." He cleared his throat. "What's going on with Toria and Drew?"

"They're pretending to be lovers to break up Cassie and Sebastian," I said.

"Alistair and Sebastian are all worked up over it."

"That was kind of the point."

Evan's lips started to form words before he pressed them together. "What?"

"Does Toria like Drew?" he asked.

"She likes kissing him."

"Oh." Evan frowned. "So what's the last thing you remember?"

"After the fight in the labyrinth, Toria went back to her room. I emerged and read some of Cassie's journal."

"Hmmm."

Not exactly a comforting response. "What's Toria been doing?"

"She fawned over Drew throughout breakfast. They spent the day together, reappearing at dinner. They're inseparable."

"Sounds like a tough day. I'm sorry."

"You had no control over any of it. It's bloody difficult to open the secret passageway. Then I see Toria sitting at the vanity, fixing her hair without a care in the world. That worried me. I called your name, but Toria remained in control." He smacked his palms on his thighs. "Let's concentrate on the present, okay?"

I choked back a giggle. "Hard to do when we're trapped in the past."

His lips verged on a smile.

"What did you do today?" I asked.

"I found a book in the library called *British Lore*."

"Navy leather, gold lettering?" I asked.

"How did you know?"

I told him about my trip to the library during our first night at the castle. The same book popped out at me and refused to go back on the shelf. Now he'd stumbled across it. Clearly, the ghosts wanted us to have that book.

He scratched his head. "I wasn't sure if the book caught my interest or Alistair's."

I touched his hand. "But you kept it together. You're a lot stronger than I am."

"Maybe Alistair's a lamb and Toria's a tiger?"

"Or maybe I'm a lamb and you're a tiger?"

"Doubtful." Evan chuckled. "Anyway, in the chapter on curses, someone wrote in the book's margins. Alistair couldn't place the terrible handwriting. It was quite difficult to decipher, mixing four branches of the Celtic language."

"Did you figure anything out?"

"Some of the words. *Disappear, heir, death, pain, suffering.*"

The Radcliffe Curse...

Before I could say a word, he added, "I saw the similarities."

"So what does this tell us?" I asked.

He shrugged. "It's hard to say. Our theory is that the curse triggered both the wedding night disappearances and the heirs' deaths."

"And we have one person behind everything that happened," I said.

"Given the pattern of the curse, we can assume the curse caster wanted to harm all first-born sons in the Radcliffe family."

"It's rare that a parent would wish death on their child or their child's child," I said.

"Rare, but not impossible," Evan reminded me.

"But probability says parents usually don't kill their kids. So if we continue that thought, then Phillip wouldn't create a curse that harmed his offspring. And Leanna probably wouldn't marry into a family she'd cursed, knowing her kids would suffer under the curse, right?"

"It makes sense." Evan puzzled over the logic. "Unless the curse had unintentional consequences. Then again, maybe it's a ghost?"

"Only the living can cast curses."

"Are you sure?" he asked.

"Trust me. It's something that infuriates ghosts."

"But a ghost could form an alliance with the living?" he asked.

"Yes. Or force a living person to do their bidding. Being haunted can make a person desperate."

"So the person may be an unwilling accomplice?" Evan asked.

I nodded. "A ghost can possess someone if it's strong enough," I said. We might be dealing with a living being as well as a supernatural one. This gave me a glimmer of hope. Toria wasn't alone in this. Maybe Alistair could help her.

I thought about the rest of what Evan had told me. "I wonder why the curse is written in multiple languages."

"Here's the interesting thing, on the next page of the book, someone circled a section. It talked about a Celtic tribe that believed the most effective way to curse an enemy was in his own language."

"So someone casting a curse could use four languages if he wasn't sure of his victim's ancestry?" I asked.

The world of unbelievables collided in my head. My understanding of things slammed into Toria's memories. Toria's Aunt Julia telling her curses were real and explaining the power of four in their magic. It was a strong, balanced number. It was why they used it in the passageways and why the Radcliffes, Langleys, Kingsleys, and Mallorys united. She taught Toria how to defend against curses. The funeral. Her aunt's star sapphire ring weighed heavily upon Toria's finger. She twisted it, calling on its power to help her through that day.

I probed the memory further. Instead of being bounced away, I slipped through. A little deeper into Toria's inner world. She went away to her grandmother's cabin in Maine, where she trained for the role she never wanted. Her grandmother called it the Langley legacy. The ring had chosen her to be the spiritual guardian of the Radcliffes. Alistair provided physical protection, but only a Langley could protect the Radcliffes from the things that went unseen and unheard. The unbelievables that only a Langley could sense.

Sometimes Toria wished she'd been born a Mallory. They were the watchers. They never had to fight. They were loyal chroniclers of what happened to the families.

The memory stuttered and halted, leaving a dull ache in my right temple.

"You alright?" Evan stared at me.

"Migraine. Toria gets them a lot." I rubbed my temple. "I should probably head to bed."

"Right." He went to my door and locked it.

"What are you doing?"

"Staying here."

"All night?"

"I want to make sure you wake up as you in the morning. I'll slip out through the secret passageway before anyone knows I've been here." In the candlelight, his eyes were that unnatural color again. Out of nowhere, I thought of a cat we took in years ago. I ended up liking the cat, in spite of him constantly scratching my legs.

Chapter 23

The smell of death clung to the air. Panic welled up in Toria, threatening to choke off all rational thought. She bit the inside of her mouth until she tasted the familiar metallic liquid. Blood brought her back from the edge. She needed to find Sebastian. Could he…? No, he had to be alive.

Her shoes clacked through the castle's corridors as she hurried to check each room. No signs of life on the first floor. Not even a servant. Warning bells sounded in her head. She raised her skirts and raced upstairs to the bedrooms.

She threw open the door to Sebastian's room. Empty. *Cassie.* She dashed up the spiral stairwell, lost her footing, and fell up the steps. The stone stairs scraped across her palms. She forced herself to get up. To go up the stairs.

Another deserted room.

She turned her ring three times, calling on its power. The star sapphire glinted back at her in the mirror. That horrid mirror started shimmering, beckoning her closer. The shimmering faded and an image formed. It came into focus and a scene played out before her eyes.

She saw a version of herself in a wedding dress. Blood covered her hands.

Toria screamed. She looked down at her bright blue morning dress. She turned her hands over and saw scraped palms but no blood. Her gaze darted back to the mirror.

She watched in horror as her double tried to wipe the blood off her hands, smearing crimson all over her dress. No matter how hard she pressed her hands against the fabric, they remained coated in blood.

Collapsing on the floor, her double sobbed, "Sebastian." She sat in a pool of blood. Red tears began to trickle down her face.

Awareness struck her. The mirror was never wrong. This was a glimpse of the future. What was she going to do?

Anguish ate away at her. Everything closed in. She cried out for Alistair, but he did not come. She was the only one left.

Toria awoke to the final notes of her own scream. Darkness. Confusion. Her heart thrummed in her ears. The room came into focus.

It was a dream. A dream that worsened each night. Death stalked this castle. She didn't know how to protect Sebastian. Powerlessness crushed her. Reassuring arms enveloped her. She smelled sandalwood and soap. *Alistair.*

His voice rumbled in her ear. "Everything will be all right."

The terror ebbed, but she was left with chilling certainty. The wedding would be the end of someone. She had seen herself covered in blood. Did that mean that she was going to kill someone? Was she going mad? No. Something vital lay beyond her reach. Resting her cheek against Alistair's chest, she swore his heart thumped, *I am here, I am here.*

"Tell me about the dream," he said.

She told him everything. Tears coursed down her cheeks and wet his shirt. Toria wanted to believe he would always be there. She had no idea how or why he was in her room, but she was too thankful to care. When the nightmares intensified, she had begun dosing herself with laudanum. She couldn't control the panic and the headache that followed without it. But this morning, she borrowed Alistair's strength instead.

He broke into her thoughts, murmuring, "The wedding is taking such a toll on you."

"They cannot get married." She willed him to understand. "Someone will die. It may be Cassie, Sebastian," her voice broke, "or you."

"It will not be Sebastian."

Alistair still didn't understand. He hadn't felt the despair. He hadn't seen the blood on Toria's hands. The blood all around her. Agitated, she lifted her head to look into his eyes. "Our oaths to Sebastian will be broken.

Every time I close my eyes, I'm haunted by what I see. That's why I cannot let this wedding go forward."

He waited until she laid her head back on his chest to continue. "Let's entertain another theory."

She tensed at his words.

"What if these visions are simply nightmares, a reaction to losing Sebastian to Cassie?"

"My feelings never interfere with my abilities."

His voice was rough with emotion. "Toria, you're losing the most important man in your life."

An uncomfortable silence stretched between them until she said, "I love Sebastian, but I've always put his happiness first." She paused, hoping it would lend more credence to her words. "My feelings are an afterthought."

"Your entire future is at stake."

The bleakness of his words tore through her. She pulled away from him and stood up.

"How dare you. I've protected Sebastian my entire life."

Alistair was too stubborn to ever see things from her perspective.

He rose to leave. And then he swiveled around. Evan's eyes bore into hers. "Kat, you're stronger than her. Come back. I need your help."

A tiny sliver of light was all I needed. I darted toward it. "I'm here, Evan."

"Do you remember what happened?"

I rubbed my forehead. "Bits and pieces. Toria was drowning in her loneliness and guilt."

"What about her conversation with Alistair?"

"He doesn't believe her."

"Good. You keep holding on."

I swallowed. He had no idea how hard it was. Even with him here, the desire to let go and disappear was so strong. I was tired of fighting her. Of trying to steal moments in her body so I could exist. I didn't know how much longer I could hold on.

"There's something I want to show you." He turned on the kerosene lamp beside Toria's bed and pulled a folded piece of paper out of his pocket and handed it to me.

I scrutinized the diagram. Names of people at the castle were underlined or encircled with arrows pointing to Cassie's and Sebastian's names. "What's this?"

"Alistair started mapping out the potential threats to Sebastian. See how he underlined Drew and Cassie? They're the main suspects."

"And the circles around Sebastian, Bertram, and Leanna?" I asked.

"I made them. Those are our suspects."

"When I saw the photo of Leanna in Astor's office, I thought it might be her. That she killed Cassie. But I'm having trouble believing she would sentence her first-born son to death," I said.

"I kept her there because I've been rethinking our theory," Evan said. "We don't know if the murders were part of the curse or if they triggered the curse. Was everything the work of one person or multiple people? We've grown attached to the idea that it was all related, but we may need to treat them as separate phenomena."

"So if Sebastian killed Cassie, Drew could have cursed him," I said. "Doesn't that give us more suspects?"

"It does." Evan frowned. "Today, Alistair caught Leanna and Drew talking. They immediately separated, but it struck him as weird."

"What do you think they were up to?" I asked.

"Maybe Drew was trying to get her to talk to Cassie for him?"

"He and Toria have been conspiring to break up Sebastian and Cassie. He's desperate enough to make a last ditch appeal to Leanna." I rubbed my temple. "The wedding is coming up so soon and we're no closer to figuring out who's behind the murders and the curse."

"And I don't think we can go home until we do."

A few hours later, Toria was tending to a sick Alistair. Or rather, I found myself in Alistair's bedroom with Evan yelling and shaking me.

I fought to bring myself to the surface. "What's going on?"

"Alistair sunk to Toria's level and played sick to get her to stay with him."

That explained his dressing gown in the middle of the day. "I don't see Toria as the Florence Nightingale type."

"She's jolly good with herbal remedies." Evan removed the robe and tossed it on the bed, revealing a full set of morning clothes. "I think she's a witch."

I bristled at the term in a way only Toria would. "She's a priestess."

He laughed. "How is that different from a witch?"

Toria's memory filled in the blanks. "A witch is a low-level magic worker. Anyone can become a witch. But becoming a priestess takes discipline, and much more skill." Toria and I both wore the same ring. Was that a sign? A status symbol? Was I supposed to become a priestess, too? I didn't want to think about that question, so I switched topics. "Have you noticed how edgy Cassie's been? Do you think it's just wedding jitters?"

"Maybe she's panicking over her missing journal." He tsked. "I know you think that the universe can handle small disruptions in the space-time continuum, but maybe taking Cassie's journal was too much."

"Maybe Cassie will freak out so much that she calls off the wedding. Maybe, with no wedding night, there won't be any wedding night murders."

"Maybe more people will die. Maybe Toria and Alistair." He added, "I think we need to return it."

"Then I need to finish reading it."

I snuck back to Toria's room and retrieved the diary. Then I made my way back to Alistair's room and sat on his bed, reading. Evan worked at Alistair's desk, translating the phrases he'd found inscribed in *British Lore*.

One journal entry stuck out, so I read it to him.

> *I must pay for what I did. I had no choice. I defended myself. He destroyed my innocence. But I took his life.*
>
> *Since I accepted Sebastian's proposal, I have been plagued by dreams of the pastor. He stands before me, his dark eyes piercing. The crimson stain on his shirt grows as he says, "God will punish the wicked." I want to believe that I'm haunted by guilt for taking a man's life, but I'm not certain. Could it be the pastor's ghost haunting me?*

"Could Pastor Fitzgerald's ghost have caused the murders? Maybe he found a way to set the curse in motion?" I asked.

"Have you sensed his ghost?" Evan asked.

"It's really weird. I expected to encounter more ghosts after I started believing again. This place felt like it was crawling with ghosts back in our time. But besides Lorelei, I haven't sensed any at all."

"Do you think your powers are affected by being in Toria's body?"

That would be the only perk of this situation—except that I needed to be able to sniff out the unbelievables now more than I ever had before. So far, they were playing a nasty game of hide-and-seek with me. A game that could doom Evan and me to nonexistence.

Chapter 24

Probability requires that every run of good luck be met with some bad. When it came time to return the journal, no one caught us in the hallway. Sebastian wasn't in his room. I got the passageway open on the first try. But the voices coming from Cassie's room stalled our adventure. Toria's memories helped me locate and open the peephole into Cassie's room.

Cassie fidgeted with her engagement ring, while Drew asked, "Put aside your obligations and listen to me."

"Please, it's unseemly for you to be in my room." Her eyes flittered to the door.

"No need to worry, pet. Sebastian's out riding."

"I have to meet Leanna."

"Cassie, I'm still your friend. Hear me out," Drew said.

She turned away from him. Her hands shook as she fiddled with the perfume bottles on her vanity. "I don't deserve your friendship."

"I only wish I'd gotten there earlier." His voice was heavy with bitterness and regret.

"Before I shot a man?" She squeezed her eyes shut.

Drew gently turned her around to face him. "You defended yourself against someone who hurt you in the worst way possible."

She studied the floorboards and half-whispered, "Why are you doing this?"

"Because I need you to know: You did nothing wrong. You were protecting yourself. If you only believe one thing I say today, believe this: It wasn't your fault."

Her voice quaked with unshed tears. "I took a life and let you sacrifice four years of your own for me. I can never forgive myself."

Tilting her chin up, he forced her to meet his eyes. "*Je ne regrette rien.* You're everything to me."

She swept her palms over her wet cheeks. "What about Toria?"

"I'm taking comfort in someone who understands my pain."

"You haven't told her about our past?" She clutched the lapels of his morning coat. "You didn't help her steal my diary, did you?"

"I told her nothing. You know I keep my promises, Cassie." He squinted at her. "You weren't foolish enough to write about it in your diary?"

She raked her teeth over her bottom lip. "I never let it out of my sight."

"Yet it's gone missing."

She let go of his coat. "It disappeared a few days ago."

"If Toria stole it, she'd have taken it straight to Sebastian," he said.

"Maybe she's waiting for the wedding?"

"She does enjoy a good show," he mused.

"Are you sure you didn't tell her anything?"

"Have you so little faith in me?"

Cassie ran her knuckles over her lips. "I'm sorry. I haven't slept well lately."

"Nightmares?"

The dark circles and tiny bags under her eyes confirmed it, but she nodded softly.

"Have you ever considered that everything feels wrong because you're making the wrong choice? Since accepting Sebastian's proposal, you've become a shadow of the girl I knew."

Her words ran together in their rush to be spoken. "I'm just overwrought, what with the missing diary and my impending wedding."

"You're overwrought because you're trying so hard at something that shouldn't require work." He gritted his teeth.

"Everything worth having requires effort."

He took her hand in his. "Remember how easy it's always been between us? I know everything, and I'm still here for you. Do you have that with Sebastian?"

"Sebastian makes me happy."

"Cassie, please. There's still time for us."

She withdrew her hand from his. "I cannot leave Sebastian. I love him."

"And me?"

She blurted out, "Sebastian makes me forget what happened. But I see it all again when I look at you."

He flinched. "I didn't realize. My apologies. I won't trouble you further." He started to leave.

Grabbing his hand, she pulled him toward her. "You remind me of the girl I was. Of the tender feelings I had for you." Tentatively, she stood on tiptoes and brushed her lips across his. "But that love must remain in the past."

He touched his lips. "I hope you find happiness. But, mark my words, this wedding is a mistake." Drew slammed the door behind him.

Cassie dropped into the chair at her vanity. Her shoulders slumped forward, and her face fell into her hands. She cried as though her heart had shattered.

Maybe it had. How could she choose between her best friend and her future husband?

A half hour passed before she looked up, her eyes barely able to contain her sadness. Her fingers fumbled through the top drawer of the vanity. She found a handkerchief, mopped her face, and blew her nose. Reaching into the lower vanity drawer, she pulled out a photo. Her fingers stroked it. She slouched into a sigh before she put it back in the drawer.

As soon as Cassie left, we charged into her room. Evan and I stashed her journal between the nightstand and the bed underneath layers of gloves and lace. On the way out, I stopped to open the bottom drawer of Cassie's vanity and see what she'd been caressing. Inside lay the hand-painted picture of Cassie and Leanna. The same one I saw that stormy night when all this madness began.

I pushed it aside. There was another photo beneath it. I'd swear the kids in it were Cassie and Drew. "All those brave words to Drew, yet this,"

I held the picture up, "hints at another truth."

"Maybe Cassie realized her mistake and was driven to kill again?" Evan grabbed the picture. "Drew spent the rest of his days in town, swearing to avenge her."

"Maybe she did try to kill Sebastian, and it went terribly wrong. That might explain all the blood in the room."

"Maybe Drew's the killer? Maybe he swore revenge to cover his guilt?" Evan tucked the picture back in the drawer.

Muffled footsteps climbed the turret staircase and voices cascaded up to us. We scurried into the passageway. The armoire slid back into place against the wall. Reopening the small peephole, I watched the bedroom door fly open.

The room buzzed with Cassie's nervous energy. "Sorry to drag you up here. I'm such a dolt."

"With the wedding so close, you have more important things on your mind than remembering your shawl. But with your delicate constitution, we can't be too careful." Leanna sounded positively maternal.

While Cassie pawed through her armoire, Leanna dug through the pile of gloves and found what we'd left behind. She held it up. "Is this the diary you were looking for?"

The tension drained from Cassie's posture. "Where did you find it?"

"By the bed."

"I checked there."

Leanna eyed the clothes and accessories scattered about the room. "Maybe you missed it."

Cassie grabbed the diary and gave Leanna a quick hug. "This is the best wedding present in the world."

"It was nothing. Now let's find your shawl and get back to our picnic."

"Just a moment." Cassie locked her diary in the top drawer of the vanity. She tucked the key securely into her pocket.

Leanna watched her. "What do you keep in there?"

"More than I should." Cassie shuddered. "I hated the idea of someone reading my private thoughts."

"Must have been awful." Leanna knelt on the floor to sort through the hatboxes and fabric sticking out from under the bed.

Cassie gave a cry of delight and toppled into the armoire. She tumbled out, waving the shawl around.

Leanna helped her up. "This room is in shambles. You really need a better maid."

"She does her best. But I'm forever making messes," Cassie said.

Leanna laughed.

After they left, I shut the peephole. Evan and I trudged back to Sebastian's room.

"The pieces aren't fitting together," he said.

My head ached with possibilities. So many suspects. My mind flashed back to the first night at dinner. Phillip had so many repressed feelings for Cassie. "Could Phillip lash out at Sebastian and Cassie?"

"At this point, anything is possible."

The more we saw, the less sense things made. There were too many motives. Motives we saw and motives that remained a mystery to us. Time was running out for Sebastian and Cassie. And for us.

Chapter 25

Toria flirted with Drew and watched Alistair squirm. Frustration flamed in Sebastian's eyes. He wouldn't admit that he still wanted her, but his eyes told her he couldn't stand the idea of her with Drew. And Cassie, poor simpleton Cassie. She had no idea how fragile her world was. Or that Toria was determined to unbalance everything.

Toria glided around the drawing room, champagne flute in hand. Drew followed her with his gaze, just like they'd planned. Neither Alistair nor Sebastian could take his eyes off her, either—except to note Drew's unconcealed admiration. Her green dress, crafted from the finest silk she could find, fit her to perfection. She caught a glimpse of herself in the mirror, and she liked what she saw.

Toria wove a path toward the adjacent turret room. It housed Mrs. Radcliffe's study, but she had retired hours ago. It was the closest room and would give Toria just enough privacy. Toria beckoned Drew with her eyes. She was forcing Alistair and Sebastian to make a move. She saw them silently conferring. Alistair stalled Drew by offering him an after-dinner cigar. Sebastian left Cassie's side and followed Toria into his mother's study. He shut the door behind him.

"What are you thinking?" he demanded.

"More than you are," Toria said.

"Things are so bad that you've chosen Drew?"

She sipped her champagne, letting the liquid roll over her tongue. "So bad? Nooo. I adore nightmares that leave me terrified during my waking hours. I enjoy knowing that I'm fighting forces beyond my control and failing you. I love the fact that no one believes me."

"You aren't failing me, except by getting drunk and mooning over Drew. You deserve better. You have better. Open your eyes."

"I let you go for the sake of our families. And what do I have to show for it?"

"Our love and trust," he said.

"Maybe your friendship, but never your love. And your trust is conditional." She raised her glass in a mock toast and downed the rest of it.

"I'm sorry my wedding upsets you so."

"Don't stand there pitying me, dismissing me as a foolish girl who can't separate her feelings from her intuition," she said.

"No one is infallible."

"Willing to wager your life on that? Because that's what you're risking."

"I won't postpone my wedding."

"Heaven forbid, you make a sacrifice for your own good. Do you know how many times I have sacrificed myself for your safety? You have no idea what I've given up for you." She hurled her champagne glass at him. It flew past his shoulder and smashed against the wall.

She turned away from him, fighting tears. She might have won if the memories hadn't exploded through her mind in a whirling kaleidoscope of emotions and images. The joy of having a family tempered by the sadness of Aunt Julia's death. Her promises to her parents and to the Radcliffes. Being shackled by responsibilities she never wanted. The loneliness and isolation of being *chosen*. The shredding of her heart when she locked away her love for Sebastian. The cruelty of fate. A perfect baby girl stolen from her arms. A bittersweet goodbye captured by the wing of a blue monarch.

Her self-control crumbled. Tears blurred her vision. It didn't matter. None of it mattered. All of it had been for nothing.

Sebastian caught her and pulled her toward him. She would stake her future on what she felt when he touched her. The love they shared wasn't dead. His mouth descended on hers. She hesitated, fearing it would be snatched away again. Her arms wrapped around his neck. Her fingers entwined in his hair. Close enough to breathe him in. The ocean smell that clung to him. How she missed that smell.

She tasted sweetness in the salt of his tears. His arms tightened around her waist. He was searching for something only she could give—forgiveness.

All too soon, he pulled away. She followed. He dropped weightless kisses on her eyelids, but his fingers rested on her lips, stalling their pursuit.

"I shouldn't...I don't want to keep hurting you," he said. "I had no choice. We couldn't live the life we wanted with each other."

She dabbed her cheeks with her gloved palms. "I was beginning to think I imagined us. I needed to know that our time together mattered to you."

"You always mattered." His fingertips stroked her cheek.

She caught his hand and held it to her face, memorizing every detail of him.

"But I had to let you go." Sebastian stepped back, putting space between them.

She tightened her grip on his hand. "I've always loved you. Trust it. Trust me."

"I do."

"Please, delay this wedding," she said.

"I cannot."

"If I upset Cassie so much, I'll disappear for a while. Just give me some time. A few weeks can't matter to Cassie."

He squeezed her hand. "She's already uncomfortable with our closeness. I won't give her a reason to doubt my affection."

"It's far worse than you imagine." She willed him to believe her. "I can feel its hatred growing. Revenge is only the beginning. It's strong enough to inhibit my visions. It may be powerful enough to tear us all apart."

"Then time is truly precious." Before she could protest, he put up his hand. "Stop playing around with Drew. We're beyond childish antics. Trust me. You risk something valuable by continuing your plan."

"I've already lost you."

"Open your eyes to Alistair. Let him love you." His half-smile apologized for how much the truth hurt.

"Alistair is my dear friend." She touched her ring, summoning calm from it.

His mouth tightened. "He's completely in love with you. He can give you everything I can't."

"You're wrong."

"Toria...I wish things could have been different." His pocket watch's chain caught the candlelight. It was attached to the same watch he'd always had, the one she'd rescued for him. What she hadn't told Drew, when she'd recounted this story for him, was that, even when she'd felt the rock crumbling beneath her feet, she hadn't regretted her choice. She would have died for Sebastian—even then, even when she was just a child, even before protecting him was her sworn responsibility.

She blinked back tears. "We must fulfill our promises." As he turned to leave, she reminded him, "Be vigilant."

"I will. But sometimes, we have to take a blindfolded leap into the unknown. It's your turn to do that." He left the room.

So, this was the end. Sebastian was marrying Cassie, and there was nothing Toria could do to stop him. She would honor her duty as his guardian, but she had to bury her feelings and let him go. She had to walk out of this room looking annoyed, as if she had just endured another of Sebastian's endless lectures. She had no choice.

She yanked the door open and flounced onto the chair beside Alistair. Ignoring him, she glared at Sebastian.

Drew raised his eyebrows to ask, *What happened*?

She couldn't break his heart tonight. Tomorrow, she would tell him that their plan had failed.

Cassie pouted until Sebastian led her off to the piano, cajoling her into playing something for him.

Toria yawned and stood up. "It's past my bedtime."

"I'll escort you upstairs," Alistair said.

"Thank you." She accepted his offer to avoid talking to Drew.

Halfway up the stairs, Alistair asked, "What happened with Sebastian?"

"Nothing."

"He brought that light back into your eyes."

"I can't hide a thing from you."

"Very few things."

"I'm beginning to see that," she murmured.

"Sebastian?"

"Reminded me of what we will always be to each other."

Alistair tensed. "Which is?"

"Friends." The word scraped its way up her throat.

Alistair put his arm around her. "We will do our best to protect him."

"We will fail." She leaned her head on his shoulder.
"Not for lack of trying."
"Never for lack of trying," she said.

Chapter 26

I tried to concentrate on what Toria was doing, but staying aware without
Evan around exhausted me. Especially when Toria's actions creeped
me out and my instincts urged me to run and hide.

She was kneeling on the floor in her nightgown. A bloodied knife lay
beside her. She had wrapped her palm in strips of muslin, but the white fabric
was already stained crimson. It burned where she had sliced her hand open.

She was speaking in a language I didn't recognize, but I had a sense
of the ritual she was performing. She was seeking insight into the danger
threatening Sebastian. Imploring her ancestors to reveal her enemy, she
sprinkled vervain and yew into the mortar that already held her blood. A
lump of frankincense. Strands of Sebastian's hair. She ground everything
together with a pestle as she chanted.

All of her energy focused on opening a gateway to her ancestors. To
their ghosts. Concentrating on her words, she closed her eyes.

When she opened them, she was no longer in her room.

Neither was I.

We stood in the middle of a cave. The rocks smelled of earth and
endings. Her ancestors encircled us. They varied in age from a child to an
old woman. I'd never seen more fully-formed ghosts, but their solidness just
made their blue-gray skin seem more awful. They looked more alive and
more dead than any ghosts I'd known. Their eyes were all shades of green.

Toria remained composed, as if she'd simply taken the secret passage
to Alistair's room. I, however, was freaked out. I did not want to be here.

Toria faced a brown-haired woman. Her Aunt Julia. She listened to her words.

Her voice reminded me of a bird singing. It was beautiful, but I couldn't understand anything she said.

When Julia finished speaking, Toria whirled to face the woman behind her.

A woman with raven hair and gray-green eyes. *Lorelei.*

Toria begged, "Please, give me my enemy's name."

Lorelei looked directly at her, but refused to answer.

Toria pleaded with each ancestor in the circle for help. One by one, they refused to answer. Then a little girl skipped forward. Toria dropped to her knees and the little girl bounded into her arms. She whispered something in a language I'd never heard.

Toria understood, though. They couldn't—or wouldn't—help her. Disappointment seeped through Toria and into me. Tears burned her eyes and ran down her face. The little girl kissed her. An oddly human gesture until she licked the tears from Toria's cheeks.

I didn't hear the little girl's words so much as I felt them. *You should not be here.*

Toria closed her eyes. When she opened them, she was back in her room again. She cried, "Pain, loss, despair. But who causes it? Who?!"

She stalked to the fireplace and slammed her hand on the mantle.

"Why are the answers I need hidden from me?" She threw the contents of the mortar into the flames and hoped for a sign. Nothing. Lost in her own misery, she didn't notice him until he was just a few steps away. She spun toward him, prepared to wield the mortar as a weapon. He caught her arm before the heavy marble dish made contact with his head.

Alistair.

She relaxed, and he pulled her close.

"Stop pushing yourself so hard," he said.

"It doesn't make sense. I called to my ancestors, but they won't answer my questions. They gave me this task, but they won't help me. And I don't know what to do next," she raged, her face buried in his shoulder. "I was convinced it was Cassie, but now…I'm not sure…it could be a ghost. Or maybe it's something I've never encountered before." This thought unsettled Toria. And me.

"And when I talk to Sebastian, he makes me feel like I'm losing my mind." She clung to Alistair. "Do you think, I mean, could the threat to his happiness be me?"

"Absolutely not."

"There are gaps in my memory. Time I can't account for. I could be doing anything then," she said.

That was my fault. All the time I had stolen from her. I was making her doubt herself.

Alistair's face paled. "I didn't want to say anything. You have enough worries right now, but I've been having the same experience. Something is interfering with our abilities. Interfering with us."

Her breath hitched in her throat. Her words tumbled out, "I don't trust myself anymore."

"I trust you. Sebastian trusts you. Julia trusted you."

"We only have one day until the wedding and we're no closer to saving Sebastian." She laughed as the horror of her words hit her.

"When did you last sleep, Toria?"

"Last night. No, the night before. I'm not sure. It's not important. I have to..."

"Get some rest," he finished her sentence.

"I can't."

He picked her up and carried her to her bed. "Consider it a direct order."

He noticed her hand. It had been a careless cut, deeper than she had intended. The wound still bled.

He went over to her vanity and grabbed extra strips of muslin and healing ointment. He tended to her hand. "I hate what the spells demand from you."

"Blood fuels the magic." She tried to brush him off, but he ignored her. "And blood calls to blood—to my ancestors."

"And they came, but they wouldn't tell you what you need to know?"

"Wouldn't, or couldn't. The force we're fighting against is so strong." She tried to rise, but the bed swayed beneath her.

He pulled the armchair closer to her bed. "Sleep. I'll think for both of us tonight."

She shook her head. A few seconds later her eyelids slipped shut. The oblivion of sleep claimed her.

Chapter 27

"What will you do?" Alistair rested his head against the back of the armchair and closed his eyes.

Toria hadn't intended to wake him, but her nervous pacing had done it. "We will stay close to Sebastian on his wedding day. When the worst happens, we have to be there to help."

"That might ruin his wedding night."

"And save his life," she snapped.

"I doubt Sebastian will see it from your perspective." He pinched the bridge of his nose.

"Has he ever?" She paced the radius of her room again.

"Is the laudanum helping?"

The pain in her head had settled to a dull ache. "Always does."

Under his breath, he asked, "Why can't you let him go?"

"We've loved and protected him all our lives." She sat on the bed. "I can't let him go, any more than I can let you go."

His eyes searched hers. "I mean that much to you?"

Her first instinct was to deny it. But every once in a while, it felt good to tell the truth. Deep down, she prayed it mattered. "I wouldn't be here without you. When Sebastian left me, I felt dead inside. Your letters brought me back to life." She took his hand in hers. "You're more than my closest friend. You're my savior."

"Your courage is an admirable trait—even when it seems like pure obstinacy." He flashed his dimples at her.

She wrinkled her nose. "I thought I drove you to distraction?"

"Your schemes add a certain excitement to my existence." His eyes glowed in the candlelight.

She was mesmerized by what she saw there. Such tenderness and affection. Sebastian was right. Alistair loved her. Tentatively, he leaned toward her. His lips touched hers. She froze. Then she remembered this was Alistair, the only man she could count on.

When he started to pull back, she softened her lips. He tasted of life. She clutched at his shirt. Leaning back on the bed, she dragged him toward her. She never thought she could feel this again. She didn't want to stop touching him. He saw every gray speck on her soul. Knew every devious plot she concocted. And he still wanted her.

"Sebastian and I weren't meant to be." She kissed the tip of his nose. "I can let him go. But I still have a job to do. Everything in me is screaming that this wedding will destroy the Radcliffe family."

He rolled onto his side and looked down at her. "You and Sebastian have a long history."

"As do you and I." She pushed a stray lock off his forehead.

"True." He opened his mouth and closed it again.

"And?" She tapped his chin.

"And Drew?"

"A ruse to cause problems between Cassie and Sebastian." No sense in admitting to the ephemeral attraction.

"I see." He hesitated. "What caused your epiphany about Sebastian?"

Her fingers tiptoed along his collarbone. "The ability to see the future is no guarantee against a blind spot. I knew Sebastian and I weren't meant to be. But I never accepted it in here." She pointed to her heart. "And then two nights ago…" She decided not to mention Sebastian's kiss. "It was like walking in a thick fog, headed the wrong way the entire time, but not knowing it. When the fog lifted, I saw everything clearly and had to admit my mistake."

"That must have been quite a conversation with Sebastian," he said.

"It was long past due."

"I agree." He smiled down at her, and his dimple emerged again.

Toria traced her fingertips over his forehead and trailed them down his cheeks. Kissing him had awakened something deep inside her. She hungered for more.

All these years thinking Sebastian was the one...

First love was a powerful thing. It had blinded her to true love—love that kept its promises, love that endured, love that sustained you a lifetime.

Laying her head on Alistair's chest, she finally understood where her home resided. She used to think it was at Castle Creighton with Sebastian or Dumbarton with her parents, but now she understood. It was wherever Alistair was. He was everything she needed. She inhaled his sandalwood cologne blended with his own earthy scent. He always reminded her of an exhilarating autumn day. Her hands trailed down his chest. Only a thin layer of cotton separated her from his warm skin.

But not for long.

Chapter 28

Standing by the window, Toria ignored the lush greenery that crept toward the bright blue sky. She was watching ravens fly, looking for signs, hoping that a fresh omen would contradict everything she knew. But all she saw was death and misery. The lump in her throat expanded, threatening to block her airway.

"Worse than physical death, this death entraps the soul," she whispered to herself.

The fate she saw for Sebastian sounded like what would happen to Evan and me if we didn't get home soon.

She turned away from the window. "What are we going to do?" she asked Alistair.

A mischievous light filled his eyes. "After the wedding, I shall pay a visit to Dumbarton and speak to your father." He sat in the armchair beside her bed, flipping through a book.

She strode over to him and flung the book on the bed. "Not about us. Sebastian." Hurt passed over his features and she hastened to add, "Of course my parents will be overjoyed to see you when they return from London. They've always adored you."

"I'm lucky their daughter finally came around."

She leaned in to pinch his arm.

"Manhandling me again?" He pulled her into his lap.

"Be serious." She tried to wiggle out of his grasp, but he held her in place.

She scowled up at him.

He puckered his lips and made kissing noises at her.

She tried to look stern, but a giggle escaped her mouth. "Can we focus on Sebastian and Cassie?"

"If we must." Alistair kissed her neck. "As best man, I'll be with him all day."

"And I'll be with Cassie. I wasn't happy when Sebastian insisted that I be a bridesmaid, but now I'm glad. Hurting her would be an easy way to hurt him."

"You're going to protect Cassie?" Alistair sounded incredulous.

"Don't look at me that way." She never flinched when the impossible presented itself. "I can do this for Sebastian."

"Of course, dear." The corners of his mouth twitched.

She chose to ignore him. "Sebastian will be in the greatest danger at night. Away from the crowds of well wishers. Distracted by his first night with Cassie. And we won't be nearby."

Alistair cleared his throat. "He and Cassie will be in her room…"

Toria knew what they would be doing; there was no need to finish the sentence. "He'll be distracted."

Alistair peered into her eyes. Whatever he saw there made him able to concentrate on their plan. "Our best option is to hide in the passageway and keep watch."

"I would sooner lose an eye than watch that. But we have to be there when he needs us."

"It's just one night. And it's the only way to make sure Sebastian has many more nights. Then we can focus on us." He leaned in to kiss Toria. She let him.

It was some time before Sebastian intruded upon her thoughts again. She pulled back from Alistair. "I can't stop something I can't sense." All her frustration came rushing out. "How can I fight something if I don't know what it is?"

"You've encountered so many spectral beings. It must remind you of one of them?"

She shook her head. "That's the problem. It reminds me of a few of them. But it's more than each one and less than all of them. It's not just a ghost. It's something different. Something I don't know."

Alistair's silence meant he was preparing to tell her something she wouldn't want to hear. She laid her head on his shoulder, so close that she could feel the vibrations in his throat as he said, "Maybe we've been going about this all wrong."

"What do you mean?" she asked.

"Your visions are usually clearer and easier to interpret."

"So?"

"You were always given the tools and the knowledge to fight and win. You stopped that ghost from haunting him, you protected him from that witch's love spell, your visions have saved his life countless times. What if this time, you can't win? Maybe you aren't supposed to?"

"Hogwash!" In the back of her mind she knew her ancestors would never allow her to be slaughtered, unless her death would save Sebastian's life. Without their help, she couldn't intercede. Were they purposely keeping her out of the fight because it was a fight she couldn't win?

"Maybe Sebastian must face his future alone."

"Are you surrendering?" She slipped off his lap.

He made no effort to stop her. "Simply pondering our powerlessness."

"So we stand by and do nothing?" Was this retribution for all the years that Sebastian had stood between them? She squashed the thought like a mosquito that dared to pierce her skin. If she began to doubt Alistair, she'd be lost.

"Of course we'll do all that we can." He sounded resigned. "But it may not be enough this time."

"We took an oath. A blood oath. An unbreakable promise."

"But you're not infallible, and I'm not invincible."

"We're close enough."

He sighed. "You can't control the future, Toria."

"I don't mean to." She folded her arms across her chest. "I only need to control tomorrow here on the Isle of Acacia. A small slice of the future."

He stopped arguing and rose from the armchair. Without another word, he closed the distance between them and succeeded in tearing her thoughts away from the horrors that awaited them.

The setting sun burned such intense colors into the sky. Reds and oranges like none Toria had seen before. She had always loved the view from atop Castle Creighton. But tonight, the brilliant sky did nothing to lessen her sense of hopelessness. Twilight faded into darkness, and she felt her enemy rise.

She took refuge in a memory, gathering her strength. She remembered chasing Sebastian around the rampart, how their laughter filled the air as their shoes slapped against the stone rooftop. She almost saw the children they had been.

I remembered being overtaken by this same memory the first time I climbed the heights of Castle Creighton.

Time folded in on itself.

Time was what Toria needed. Time for all of them.

Time she was afraid they didn't have.

Time was what we needed, too. Evan and me. And, like Toria, I was afraid we didn't have it.

Toria's worst fear echoed in her mind, *There is no more time for Sebastian.* She couldn't admit it to anyone, but she sensed it and she would extract a brutal retribution.

Chapter 29

Evan turned down the kerosene lamp and settled into bed beside me. Now that Toria and Alistair were a couple, it was easier for them to explain away Alistair's constant presence in her room.

"You and Toria are the key to unlocking the portal and getting us home," he said.

"Agreed. But it's not like I can talk to her about it." Even though I shared her body, I'd never found a way to directly talk to her. And I hadn't been able to find anything in her memories to help us out.

"Toria pulled you through the mirror the first time." He dragged the covers toward him.

I tugged at the blankets and stuffed them under me on my side of the bed. Alistair and Evan were both blanket hoarders. "So you think she has to shove me through to get back home?"

"You two were in Cassie's room for a reason. Maybe you both need to decide to be there again?" He punched the pillow and rolled over.

"We were both there when we took Cassie's journal. Toria didn't send us back home then."

My mind went there—to what would happen if we couldn't open a portal to our time. We would never get back to our own bodies. Our souls would fade into oblivion. I stared up at the ceiling, watching the darkness pixelate into multi-colored webs of light. Migraine aura. Toria's migraines coming for me.

Evan cleared his throat. "Maybe we aren't meant to leave yet. Maybe we have to find out what happens on the wedding night. Maybe the portal won't re-open until we do."

"I can't just watch people die," I said.

"We may not have a choice."

"Toria and Alistair might find a way to save them."

"What if that means we never get back to our own bodies?"

I took a deep breath. "Let's try and get the mirror open tomorrow." I wanted to be one of the good guys. I wanted to save Cassie and Sebastian.

But I wanted to save me and Evan, too.

Chapter 30

As a member of the bridal party, Toria stayed close to Cassie the entire morning of her wedding day. Leanna regarded her with open suspicion, but Toria didn't care. She had more pressing concerns. While Cassie and Leanna primped and preened, Toria watched for anything untoward. Hours passed. And now, the wedding was here.

Leanna fussed with Cassie's train. Bertram stood beside his niece, looking proud.

Phillip stepped next to Toria. She slipped her hand into the crook of his arm and peered into the ballroom. The crystal chandelier caught the afternoon sun and refracted it. There were pink roses everywhere. Rows of Louis XIV chairs formed two long columns with a central walkway for Cassie's wedding procession.

She whispered, "Everything looks lovely."

Phillip ran a finger under his collar. "I shall be glad when tomorrow's morning breakfast is over."

The morning breakfast was a useful wedding tradition to extend the wedding celebration into the morning since the castle could not accommodate all the guests. Once low tide came, they would return to the mainland on horseback.

She pointed to the wooden archway with hundreds of flowers woven through it. Today, it served as the altar. "Interesting addition to the ceremony."

"Cassie's request," Phillip said.

"Why was she so opposed to a religious ceremony?" Cassie had insisted the wedding be held at the castle with a justice of the peace.

Phillip shrugged. "More convenient than going to the church in Wright."

Four generations of Radcliffes had been married in that church. Toria had almost been married in that church. "Forget about family tradition," she muttered. It irked Toria that she remained bound by traditions, but Cassie was allowed to change them.

She wished her family were here, but her parents had gone to see their new grandson in London. The newest Langley. She prayed he'd been blessed with brown eyes and marked for a happy life.

The violins started up. The flower girl made her way down the aisle. Dressed in pale pink, she tossed pink and white rose petals along her path. Toria and Phillip were next. Her gaze went to Sebastian. This was what she had once dreamed of. Walking down the aisle toward him. Except now, she had a new dream. A dream where Alistair greeted her at the end of the aisle. She smiled at him. He winked at her.

Once she and Phillip took their places, the maid of honor, Leanna, glided toward them in a pink dress. Cassie had a fondness for pastels. Toria adjusted the skirt of her peach gown.

Cassie floated down the aisle on Bertram's arm. The cream-colored dress highlighted her pallid skin. It fit snugly to her waist. The skirt gathered over a bustle in the back, cascading into a long train. Lace surrounded her throat and puffy shoulders burst from tight sleeves. A crown of orange blossoms sat atop the veil.

When Sebastian took Cassie's hand in his and pledged his life to her, Toria wanted to be happy for him. But seeing Sebastian in his wedding suit and gloves gave her a twinge of what-could-have-been. It hurt to let go of a dream. Even one she had outgrown. Her eyes drifted to Alistair. The heat in his eyes melted everything inside her.

The moment passed and her mind quickly returned to the threat Sebastian faced. She still had no idea who or what was behind it. She glanced around the room. So many faces. So many possible enemies.

Her gaze settled on Drew. His expression was dark. The look in his eyes. So much anger and hurt. She could almost feel it emanating out at Cassie. Toria had tried to convince him that there was life after Cassie, but he refused to listen. There was only Cassie for him. She didn't know why he stayed to watch the wedding. It had to be torture for him. Seeing the one you love commit to someone else could drive a person to do something horrible.

Could he be behind the threat to Cassie and Sebastian? She shuddered. To attack an enemy was one thing; to betray a loved one was an entirely different matter. It required a malevolence of the soul that she hoped never to encounter.

During the reception in the courtyard, Toria exchanged pleasantries, munched on hors d'oeuvres, sipped champagne, and watched out for expected evil. The day progressed without incident. Sunset surrendered to darkness.

Alistair whirled her around the courtyard while a waltz played. She closed her eyes, sinking into the pleasure of having him so near. All she wanted was to disappear with him, but tonight she had to protect Sebastian and Cassie. Alistair would be hers soon enough.

The music faded. She opened her eyes. Alistair had waltzed her into the castle's front gardens, without a single soul to disturb them. She started to ask why they had left the reception, but he kissed the words right out of her mouth.

Too quickly, his warm lips abandoned hers. His voice changed. "Kat, fight her. We have to go home. I can't do it without you."

"Alistair, what are you talking about with that silly British accent? Did you have too much champagne?"

I heard Evan's words from deep within Toria's mind. I didn't think I had it in me to make it back to him.

"It's now or never. Help me find the way back. Professor Astor is counting on us. Don't you want to see Morgan and your mom again?"

Toria's body trembled. Exhaustion snaked around my ankles, threatening to drag me back to the depths of Toria.

"Kat, get your bum up here now. There's no time to spare." There was a note of panic in Evan's voice.

I kicked and paddled—my final spurt of energy. I broke through the surface and clutched at his arm. "I thought I was trapped inside her forever."

"A Kingsley never breaks a promise."

I released him and stepped back. "How are we getting into the castle?"

"Through the front door."

"Cocky," I said.

"Everyone's out back at the wedding reception."

"And if someone isn't? The minute they talk to us, Toria and Alistair will emerge." Toria would reclaim her body. My future would disappear. I would be gone. Maybe, this time, forever.

He handed me two small clumps of wax. "Plug up your ears. If we can't hear anyone, we can probably remain in control."

It made sense. "It's not just being near people, but having them interact with us that makes us disappear."

"And the wax stops them from interacting with us."

"Clever."

He smiled.

We slipped through the front door with ease, but hit a major snag getting upstairs. A maid offered her assistance. Evan gave her a knowing look and signaled that Toria had had a bit too much to drink. I feigned drunkenness, Toria-style, which meant leaning heavily on his arm and stringing swear words together in the longest, most creative phrases imaginable. The maid gave him a sympathetic smile and scurried off.

We headed straight to Sebastian's room. I opened the secret passage. We bounded down the passageway, burst into Cassie's room, and headed straight for the mirror. Toria knew how to open the portal, but I had no idea.

Still, I went over every inch of the mirror. Touching. Stroking. Pressing. The glass surface remained solid, reflecting Toria's image back at me. I tried probing Toria's memories. Nothing. But Lorelei had said the mirror was made for me.

The sound of approaching footsteps sent me into a panic. I dashed toward the passageway, forgetting we'd already closed it. Evan grabbed me and shoved me inside the armoire. He jumped in behind me and closed the doors.

Peering out the tiny windows in the armoire, we watched the bedroom door swing open. Leanna walked across the room and Drew skulked after her.

"Leanna, we need to talk," Drew said.

She jumped and whirled to face him. "What are you doing up here?"

"I haven't been able to get a moment with you all day. When I saw you break away from the festivities, I followed you."

"I'm preparing the room for Cassie's wedding night," Leanna said.

Drew winced. "Do what you need to do. But I need to get out of here. Seeing Cassie with Sebastian is too hard. As soon as that sandbar appears tomorrow, I'm gone."

"It's horrible to watch the person you love with another," Leanna murmured.

"That's why I need my cut of the jewels tonight." The pain in his eyes was so raw.

"Alright. There's no need to panic. I will bring it by your room tonight," she said.

He paused. "You took things too far yesterday. You promised Cassie wouldn't be harmed."

"Her collapse was the only thing that would distract Sebastian from the rubies. It gave me enough time to sneak into his study and replace his family heirloom with my replica. We have the rubies and she's fine."

"I wish I had never agreed to keep watch." Drew rubbed the back of his neck.

"You need the money to start over. Far away from Cassie. Sebastian stole the love of your life, you're just taking something equally precious in return."

Drew nodded. "He had it coming."

"My family needs the money. You said you understood. You said you'd help me. Please, don't back out on me now," Leanna begged him.

He rubbed his face. "This has to end tonight. Bring my share of the jewels to my room. I need to leave before Sebastian realizes his priceless heirloom has been replaced with a counterfeit."

"No one will be able to tell the difference," she said.

"Sebastian will."

"Not with all his attention on Cassie tonight."

Pain slashed across his face. "He will notice the fake eventually."

"By the time he does, there will be so many suspects and they will all be far from the castle. Trust me, we'll be safe."

Drew's eyes glazed over like he was in a trance. "We'll be safe."

Leanna touched his arm. "And you can never speak of this to anyone, but you will always remember what you did."

"I'll never speak of this to anyone, but I'll always remember what I did," Drew murmured.

She cast some sort of spell over him.

Leanna withdrew her hand. "I'll come by your room later."

Drew's eyes sharpened. "The sooner the better."

She smiled. "I understand. Just let me finish up in here."

After he left, Leanna carefully closed and locked the door behind him. She leaned against it, took a deep breath, and strode across the room.

She paused before the black velvet box on Cassie's vanity. "This is for you, Uncle Patrick. For what they did to you." She added, "Drew will lose her and know he helped bring about her downfall. But he will never be able to tell anyone. It will eat away at him. Just like you wanted. I hope it's enough."

Opening the black velvet box, she reached inside with gloved hands, removed the ruby necklace, and placed it on the vanity. From the folds of her skirts, she retrieved a small bundle. Carefully unwrapping the fabric, she pulled out an exact replica of the ruby necklace and put it into the velvet box.

From this far away, I had no idea which was the real necklace and which was the fake. But if what Leanna said was true, she had stolen the real necklace last night and was now returning it to Cassie.

"Such a beautiful necklace must unleash a world of pain." She closed the box. "*Muintir thar gach ní i gcónaí.*"

Evan whispered, "It's Gaelic for 'Family above all else.'"

Coldness nipped at my nose. The air beside Leanna darkened and shimmered. Dark gray tendrils coalesced into something I'd never seen before. It was the silhouette of a man, outlined in blue. But inside this outline, it was mostly shadows. Dark writhing shadows. At the core, light flickered—a tiny remnant of his soul. Not a typical ghost. Malevolence rolled off of him.

His voice was a whisper. "Getting Drew to turn on Cassie. Making sure everyone suffers for what they did to me. You've been very busy, my dear."

Leanna shrank back. "I've done all that you asked, Uncle. Please leave me and my brother in peace now," she pleaded.

"I will be gone when everything is done," he said.

"And my brother, he'll recover?" she whispered.

"It will take him a few days."

She nodded. "Then everything will be done tonight."

"Tonight." He dissipated into the shadows.

Working with exquisite care, Leanna removed her gloves and wrapped them in the fabric that had concealed the necklace. Then she returned to the vanity, slipped the other ruby necklace into a pouch, and hid it underneath her skirts. She glanced at the closed velvet box and left the room.

I struggled to understand what I'd seen and heard. Ghosts could drive you mad with their hauntings. And they'd do it too, just to get their reckoning. But this wasn't a ghost haunting Leanna. It was something beyond a ghost. And it was threatening her and her brother. What was it? Who was it? What uncle had Cassie and Drew harmed?

I couldn't make sense of it. Then there was Drew. What was his part in all this?

And why would Leanna steal the ruby necklace, promise to split the jewels with Drew, then return it to the velvet box a few moments ago?

More than anything, though, I wanted to know how what Evan and I had just seen might affect our return to our time.

I tried to open the armoire doors, but they refused to budge.

"The doors are stuck," I hissed.

Evan pushed against them, but they didn't move. My stomach did a back flip into my lungs. I shoved him aside and pounded on the doors. I clawed at them with my fingers. Nothing worked. My mind shouted one word over and over, *Trapped.*

He grabbed me. "We're stuck in here. There's nothing we can do about it. If we call for help, we'll revert back to Toria and Alistair when it arrives. We'll never get home."

We were trapped inside a box. A small box. And the wooden panels seemed to be getting closer. My breath came in short gasps. "I…can't… breathe."

"Calm down. The doors aren't airtight. Look at them."

A sliver of light trickled through the crack between the armoire doors. We had air. My pulse throbbed in my ears, but the tightness in my chest eased.

He let me go and swept a bunch of Cassie's dresses to the floor, giving us a little more space. My mind understood, but my body wouldn't stop shaking.

Evan pulled me into his arms. He stroked my hair. "I think this is why we came back. Not to prevent it from happening, but to watch it unfold."

"I don't want to watch. Please, get me out of here," I said.

"Don't you want to know the truth? This is exactly where Alistair and Toria planned to be. Now, we're here. This is where our lives converge and diverge again. We need to be here."

"Promise we'll get out of this box."

"I'll rip the armoire to pieces if need be," he said.

When he released me, the panic swarmed around me. Without thinking, I grabbed his hand. "It helps to hold on to something."

He squeezed my hand. "Yes, it does."

Chapter 31

Minutes dragged their feet, refusing to shuffle forward.

I gnawed at my cuticles. "I don't want to watch Cassie die."

Evan rammed his shoulder into the armoire doors. They rattled on their hinges but remained shut. "Looks like we don't have a choice. We aren't meant to stop it from happening."

Back to our biggest argument. One of those can't-agree-to-disagree situations. If I sided with Evan, we did nothing and let people die so that our own world remained undisturbed.

I couldn't. I had to believe the universe could auto-correct the deviations we'd caused—not just little things like stealing Cassie's journal, but big things too. Things like preventing a double homicide. Maybe I was idealistic, but someone had to be in the face of Mr. Doomsday.

I was about to say this again when the bedroom door opened and Cassie danced into the room, humming the Wedding March. Leanna trailed behind her.

Cassie twirled around to face her best friend. "Sorry for taking you away from the reception, but I need help preparing for tonight." Pink spread like wildfire from the tip of Cassie's nose to each ear.

Leanna spun Cassie around and set to work on the line of pearl buttons stretching from Cassie's neck to her bustle. "The way your uncle is carrying on, the celebration will still be in full swing tomorrow afternoon."

"Uncle Bertram never behaves this way. I worry about him, all alone in that big house."

"With a dozen servants." Leanna didn't try to disguise the wryness in her tone.

Cassie's expression melted into a puddle of embarrassment. "I'm being silly, aren't I?"

Cassie twisted around to look at her and Leanna frowned. "Stand still or I'll never get these buttons undone."

Leanna's voice echoed in my head, *This is for you Uncle...*

It was like Evan could read my mind. He murmured, "She's taking revenge on Cassie and Drew." He thought for a moment. "Pastor Fitzgerald. What if the pastor Cassie killed is Uncle Patrick? Leanna isn't targeting Sebastian at all."

Suddenly, I understood. This was why Toria couldn't see the threat. Her powers were tied to Sebastian. He was caught in whatever Leanna was doing, but he wasn't her primary focus. He was collateral damage.

I didn't want to see what was going to happen to them tonight. But we were sealed inside the armoire. We couldn't do anything but watch.

As Leanna came toward the armoire to hang up Cassie's dress, Evan and I froze in place. If she discovered us, Toria and Alistair would take control and Evan and I would disappear.

"Please hang it outside the armoire. My maid can pack it away tomorrow," Cassie asked.

"Why?" Leanna asked.

"I want to see it. I still can't believe this is really happening."

"It's really happening," Leanna murmured.

After Leanna helped Cassie into a lacy nightgown and wrapper, Cassie perched on the bed. Leanna removed Cassie's hairpins and brushed her hair. Leanna stepped back to admire her work before kissing the top of her friend's head. "I will miss our afternoons together."

Cassie sounded perplexed. "You're my best friend. My getting married won't change that. Picnics and needlepoint."

"Picnics and needlepoint." Leanna's eyes glistened.

She didn't want to do this. What had that thing, who had once been

Pastor Fitzgerald, done to her?

"Now, who's being a silly goose?" Cassie coaxed a smile out of Leanna. "Promise me something."

"What?"

"Give Phillip a chance." Cassie laced her fingers together in a mock prayer.

Leanna pursed her lips like a mother with a difficult child.

"It's my wedding day." Cassie's lower lip jutted out, progressing into a full pout.

"I'll do everything possible to win Phillip's affections. Happy?"

Cassie smiled. "Ask him to help you find your gloves. Men love to fix things."

Leanna looked at her bare hands. "I shall."

"Time for you to get back to the party." Cassie made a shooing motion. "I have to wait for my husband."

"Cassie...I..." Leanna hesitated. "Enjoy every moment."

"I will." She sounded giddy. "Now go before some girl makes eyes at Phillip."

Leanna lingered a moment before the shadows in the stairwell swallowed her.

Cassie hopped off the bed. She fiddled with the tie on her wrapper until she had the perfect bow. She picked up a book only to discard it after reading a page. She moved toward her wedding gown and fondled the lace on the sleeve.

"I'm Mrs. Sebastian Radcliffe," she breathed.

Finally, she ended up in front of her vanity for some final primping. She reached for her perfume bottle, saw the black velvet box, and gasped.

Her fingers trembled as she lifted the lid. Her eyes widened. It took a few seconds for her to decide. Necklace in hand, she pranced toward the full-length mirror. Placing the rubies around her neck, she secured the clasp. The ruby and diamond pendant nestled between her breasts and the diamond-studded chain disappeared under her golden hair. She spun around in front of the mirror, watching how the stones glowed in the candlelight.

Moments later, everything changed. Anxiety stole across her face. Her fingers worked frantically on the clasp, but it refused to come undone. She tried to pull the stones away from her skin, but they burrowed into her flesh. Tiny droplets of blood beaded up around the edges of the stones. The drops turned to rivulets.

She fell onto the bed, gasping for air. She lunged for the door, but didn't make it. She slid back toward the mirror. A trail of blood darkened the white bedding. Collapsing onto the floor, she clawed at the necklace.

Watching her struggle, I forgot about my future. I pounded and kicked at the armoire doors. I bloodied my knuckles, but the doors remained sealed shut. "Leanna must have cursed the necklace," I whispered. That was my only explanation for how a necklace could attack someone.

"And laced it with something deadly." Evan said. "That's why she never touched it with bare fingers."

"We can't help?"

He kicked at the doors, but they still wouldn't budge.

It felt like a century before someone knocked on the bedroom door. Cassie opened her mouth, but no sound came out. She fell onto her side. Her jaw clenched against the pain. Tears coursed down her cheeks. Her eyelids twitched. Then she was still.

I shuddered. Evan wrapped his arm around me.

Another knock at the door.

I shouted, "Come in," but the person didn't. Cassie was dying and the only person who could possibly help was caught up in social niceties.

Slowly, the bedroom door swung inward. Sebastian stood in the doorway. "Cassie, do you need a few more minutes, love?" Her silence galvanized him to enter the room. He caught sight of the blood-covered sheets and charged around the bed.

Cassie lay in a pool of her own blood.

He dropped to his knees beside her. Horror widened his eyes. He took a stilted breath. "Sweetheart, what happened?"

Blood gushed from the large wounds inflicted by the pendant. The tiny cuts made by the chain of diamonds widened, connecting into a deep slash around her neck. Sebastian reached for the rubies. He grimaced in pain and drew back. Red blisters covered his fingers.

"So much blood." He seized the necklace again, but the clasp refused to come undone.

Cassie convulsed. Sebastian gathered her in his arms.

She whispered, "Sorry."

"Hush, darling." Sebastian rocked her.

"Forgive me."

"You did nothing wrong."

Her eyelids fluttered open. She stared at him with such wonder. "My husband."

He squeezed her hand. "Cassie, stay with me."

Her eyes lost all focus.

A growl of agony tore through Sebastian. He yanked at the necklace until the clasp snapped. The necklace fell to the floor, glittering against her blood. He cradled Cassie in his arms. The mirror shimmered behind Sebastian, but all he saw was Cassie.

He placed her on the bed and tried to find a pulse. A sign that she wasn't gone. His face contorted with grief. He sagged under the weight of what he had lost. When he picked her up, he caught sight of the liquefying mirror. He tilted his head like he heard a voice we couldn't, then he nodded.

He kissed her forehead. "There's only one place we can be together now," he whispered. He carried her across the mirror's threshold and disappeared from sight.

I pressed my face into Evan's shoulder, trying to shut out the images. My muscles twitched in terror.

Through the haze, I heard Toria's voice say, *Get the rubies.*

Evan pushed against the armoire doors. The doors shuddered and gave way. Whatever had held us inside the armoire was gone.

He dragged me toward the mirror as it started to solidify.

Evan yelled, "Hurry up."

Toria's voice was in my mind, louder than ever. *Use my shawl—don't touch it—but get the necklace.*

I pulled out of Evan's grasp and bent down to scoop up the necklace. Recoiling from the blood, I fumbled with the shawl.

In those few seconds, the mirror hardened.

Evan screamed, "Kat."

His words blurred together. I couldn't understand what he was saying with Toria's voice echoing in my head, *You can do this. Touch the mirror. The magic is in us—it's in your blood.*

I stuffed the bundle under my arm. I reached for the mirror and pressed my bloodied knuckles against it. The mirror softened. Like a single teardrop rippling across a cup of coffee, the surface melted outward. As soon as it all liquefied, I grabbed Evan's hand and pulled him into the mirror. We sank into the gelatinous substance. I twined my fingers through his, praying we'd make it home.

We free-fell through darkness. I fought against exhaustion, but my senses began shutting down. My vision pitch-blacked. My skin deadened. I tried to call Evan's name, but no sound came out. Uncertainty drowned me. I had to find him, but the darkness sucked me under.

Chapter 32

I awoke, a prisoner inside my own mind again. Zero control over my body. If it was my body. My thoughts pin-wheeled, reliving everything I'd seen. Cassie's blood soaked into the hardwood floor. Her eyes frozen in death. The bleak expression on Sebastian's face. I'd give anything to open my eyes and escape the images my brain had on replay.

All I could do was force my thoughts to the next fear. Where was I? Please let it be 2015.

Tingling. Scorching. Like blood rushing to my feet after two hours of kneeling. Except it was everywhere. Impossible to figure out what it meant. Pain rushed over me, short-circuiting my brain. My thoughts bounced around. I couldn't stay in a memory. I leapt through years of me. Morgan. Mom. Professor Astor. Evan. Always back to Evan.

Eventually, sensations started slipping through. It took me a while to put it together. And then I knew that I was lying on a hard surface. Something poked at my ribs.

Wait, warmth and comfort were so close. I puzzled over what I was feeling: heat and calloused softness. The connection between my body and mind rebooted.

A hand held onto mine.

I opened my eyes, but all I could see was vague shapes. When things came into focus, I saw Evan's dark brown hair and golden skin. I let out the breath I'd been holding.

Evan was in his own body again. He was next to me on the floor, but he lay motionless. His stillness frightened me. I let go of his hand. My muscles burned and spasmed as I crawled closer to him. "Evan, you okay?"

He didn't move. I couldn't lose him. Not after everything he'd done to save me.

I placed two fingers on his wrist, pleading for a pulse. I went from wrist to elbow four times before I found it. "I can't do this without you. Please, wake up."

His eyes didn't open.

I leaned in. If he wasn't breathing, I would start CPR. I wouldn't let him go. No matter what.

As my face descended toward his, Evan rasped, "Stealing a kiss?"

Relief washed over me. "Making sure you were breathing."

"I am." He sat up and looked around. "Cassie's room?"

"Are we back in our world?" My voice teetered.

"I think so." He frowned. "You okay?"

"I don't know." I didn't know what to do with everything we'd seen. Where to put it so it couldn't keep ripping into me. The more I tried to ignore the images, the faster they rose up: the pool of blood, Cassie's death gaze, Sebastian's hopelessness. "I'm not myself right now."

"But you are." He touched my cheek. "Finally."

My gaze trailed over my body. My clothes, my hands, my feet. It was me again. But my face. I couldn't see my face. Not without a mirror. My gaze flew to my reflection—long blonde hair and glasses. My fingers touched each feature to be sure.

My heart thumped so hard, joy bruised the inside of my chest.

Cassie's bedroom door flew open, slamming against the wall. Joshua filled the doorway. Behind him, I glimpsed salt and pepper hair and a tweed jacket. *Professor Astor.*

"What was that racket?" Professor Astor asked.

"It's them!" Joshua advanced upon us like a betrayed husband. "Where have you two been?"

Evan went with the truth. "We never left the castle."

Joshua stopped. "Impossible." His nostrils flared. "We've been searching for days, from towers to catacombs. All we found were Kat's notebook and a couple flashlights in here."

They'd have missed us by 129 years.

Professor Astor stepped forward and rested his hand on Joshua's shoulder. "I know that you've been worried, but there's no need to berate them. Let's see what they have to say."

"How long have we been gone?" I asked.

"Four and a half days," the professor said.

But we'd spent six days in 1886. It was too much to process. The time gone. What had happened to us—to our bodies?

Feet pounded up the stairwell. A five-second warning before Morgan and Adam appeared in the doorway. Morgan sprinted across the room to hug me. Her freesia perfume enveloped me. I held on tight. I couldn't believe I was back here with her. Fear. Sadness. Happiness. They all whirled inside me. I squeezed my eyes shut. If I started crying now, I'd never be able to stop.

Morgan pulled back. She gripped my arms, while her gaze trailed over me. "Where have you been? Are you okay? Don't ever disappear without texting. Do you know how scared I was?"

"I missed you too," I said.

"I'm glad you're back," Morgan sounded relieved, but her eyes narrowed. "What happened?"

How could I explain everything? I didn't have it in me to make them believe in all the unbelievables we'd encountered. Not right now.

Everyone crowded into the room, expecting an explanation. Waiting for our story.

Seth came over to Evan, shaking his head. "What were you thinking? Disappearing with a minor."

Olivia clutched at Joshua's arm. Adam leaned against the wall, watching Morgan.

It was too much for my fritzed-out senses. Too many questions. Too many people. All at once. I needed it to stop.

And then Morgan reached for the bundle at my feet.

"Don't touch that!" I pushed Morgan away and grabbed Toria's shawl, careful not to spill its contents.

Adam's expression darkened and he came closer.

"What's wrong with you?" Morgan's shock morphed into anger.

"Do. Not. Ever. Touch. This." I knew it was the wrong thing to say the second the words left my mouth, but it was too late to suck them back in.

"I gave her strict orders to guard the shawl. It's critical to our research." Evan covered for me. He was the only one who knew how dangerous the rubies were.

Morgan shook her head. "You must be exhausted. About as tired as I am after four and a half days of constant worry."

Guilt walloped me. I looked at Evan and twisted my ring three times. The way Toria did when she called on its power. I needed his help.

"Professor, we really need to speak with you privately," Evan said.

"Of course," Professor Astor replied. He turned to the others and said, "Joshua and I would appreciate a little time to sort things out with Kat and Evan."

"We'll keep waiting for information to trickle down. Astornomics." Seth gave Evan a mocking wave. "Next time you and Kat run off together, leave a note so we know where to send the cops."

Morgan lingered nearby like she wasn't ready to leave, but finally let Adam coax her from the room.

Olivia trailed out. "You'll fill me in later?" she asked Joshua.

He nodded.

As the room emptied, I felt a mix of relief and fear. They had almost distracted me from what had happened here. It came back. Memories I would never be able to escape. Pain that could never be undone. Suffering that was unstoppable.

I clutched the bundle. My world tilted again.

Chapter 33

Evan caught me and steered me to Cassie's old bed. "Sit down." He knelt in front of me and peered into my eyes. "Are you okay?"

"Not really," I whispered.

"Me neither," he muttered. "Coming back is harder than I thought it would be."

"Our souls are depleted." All that time living inside another body had drained mine of its energy.

"Just try to breathe. We'll get through this." He sat next to me.

His nearness helped.

Professor Astor turned the vanity chair toward us and sat down. "Kat, everything is going to be fine."

"Not for Cassie and Sebastian," I said.

Joshua stood beside the professor with arms crossed and an intense expression on his face. "What are you talking about?"

Professor Astor frowned. "Perhaps, we should let them rest before we interrogate them."

I shook my head. "Let's get this over with."

"Under the circumstances, we're doing quite well," Evan said. "Professor, what are you doing here?"

Joshua was the one who answered. "When you went missing, I called him." He started to ask, "Where were..."

But the professor interrupted him. "Can you tell us what's in the shawl?"

"You're not going to believe it," Evan said.

"Show me," Professor Astor replied.

"No." Terror gripped my heart. "No one can touch it."

Professor Astor furrowed his brow. "Why?"

"The rubies killed Cassie," I mumbled.

"And they're in the shawl?" Professor Astor leaned toward me.

"Yes," I said.

"That's a priceless family heirloom. It disappeared the night of the murders." Joshua reached for the bundle.

I tucked the bundle closer to me.

Evan moved quickly. He grabbed Joshua's arm and didn't let him touch it or me. "Let her finish."

"Joshua, you're not helping," Professor Astor said.

Joshua shook off Evan's grip and stepped back. He didn't take his eyes off the bundle.

"How did you get it?" Professor Astor asked.

"I took the necklace after Cassie died," I said.

Joshua's tan skin lost its glow.

"I presume you were there, as well?" Professor Astor asked Evan.

"May we start from the beginning?" Evan asked.

"Please do." Professor Astor acted like we were discussing Evan's reasons for being late to a meeting, not time travel and deadly heirlooms.

Evan rubbed his chin and asked Joshua, "When did you realize we were missing?"

"The day you missed every meal—July first," Joshua said.

"The night before, when the big storm was about to hit, Kat and I searched this room." The rest of Evan's explanation covered everything that had happened to us since then. Falling into Toria's and Alistair's bodies where we were in danger of disappearing forever. Me seeing ghosts and whatever Pastor Fitzgerald had become. Toria's spell-casting. Leanna cursing the necklace. The wedding night horror. He finished by admitting, "If I hadn't experienced it myself, I wouldn't believe it."

The professor walked over to the mirror. He pressed his palms against the glass. "How'd it feel?"

"What?" That was his first question? He couldn't possibly believe us. It couldn't be that easy.

Professor Astor's eyes were gentle when he looked at me. "Our work is unorthodox. When I heard you'd disappeared, I knew I'd have to suspend disbelief to find you." He wrapped his knuckles against the glass. "It must have been befuddling."

"Falling through the mirror was like moving through mud without getting wet," Evan said. "Kat equates it to swimming through Jell-O. Then you spiral into darkness until you lose consciousness." He looked at me for confirmation.

"Followed by the terror of trying to figure out where you are and who you are. The most frightening part is not being able to move." I shivered.

"The physical doesn't always take well to the metaphysical. There are some uncomfortable adjustments." Professor Astor stared at his reflection, as if he were waiting for it to change.

"Have you time traveled before?" Evan asked.

"Unfortunately, no. Are you offering?" The professor sounded excited.

"It wasn't me. It was Kat," Evan said.

"How did you do it?" Joshua asked.

"It's in my blood." That's what Toria had said. My blood activated the mirror.

Joshua didn't look very surprised by any of this. As if I were confirming things he'd suspected all along.

Astor's expression filled with excitement. "Can you do it again? Can you open the portal?"

"No!" I wasn't planning to touch that mirror again—not for him, not for anybody.

The professor looked abashed. "Sorry, I got lost in the moment. We can try it another time."

Like five minutes after never.

I stared at Joshua. He was way too calm about all this. "You knew this might happen to us, didn't you?"

Joshua stared right back at me. "With your connections to the Langleys and Kingsleys, I expected that something would happen. Your families have always protected mine."

"You knew I was a Langley?" I asked. Evan and I suspected it, but this was the first time anyone confirmed it. I was a Langley. My dad was a Langley.

"Our families have been friends for ages. But you're part of the most elusive branch of the Langleys. I wasn't positive until I saw your ring. It's a Langley family heirloom," Joshua said.

I rubbed my right temple, feeling the sharp contraction of a soon-to-be-born migraine.

"What do you know about the ring?" Professor Astor asked him.

"The Langley Sapphire is as legendary as the Radcliffe Rubies," Joshua said. "Family lore says that our strength lay in our stones. Only one person in each generation can tap into the power of the stones, though. The Langley Sapphire wasn't that hard to track, but the Radcliffe Rubies disappeared without a trace on Sebastian's wedding night."

The pounding in my temple morphed into a relentless throb. "That's why you wanted to look at my ring in your study. You wanted to make sure. Why didn't you say anything then?"

"I couldn't risk scaring you away," Joshua's voice deepened. "I couldn't trust that you'd be willing to take on the responsibility that the ring entails."

The migraine retreated as my anger surged. "So much better for me to accidentally time travel, get trapped in my ancestor's body, and watch a horrible murder. Thanks, Joshua."

He looked confounded. "I had no idea any of that would happen. The prophecy..."

"The prophecy?" I asked.

"About the Langley family," Joshua said.

A prophecy. About the Langleys. My family. Me. My sense of outrage grew. "And what does this prophecy say?"

Joshua began, "I never really believed it..."

Evan's brow furrowed. "I wish you'd told us, Professor."

"He didn't know," Joshua said. "I only told him about it after you disappeared."

Evan turned his annoyance on Joshua. "What does the prophecy say?"

Joshua said, "She who controls the stars twinkling in the night sky will restore the family. She will return to places others cannot and bring justice to those who have been wronged. She alone can bring peace back to the isle."

Was it my destiny to be dragged back in time? Lorelei said she'd made the mirror for me. She was Toria's ancestor. My ancestor. From my father's side. A part of the missing half of my existence. I stared down at my ring.

Pain pulverized my right temple. Wetness trickled out of the corner of my right eye. I brushed it aside and took a few shallow breaths. I twisted my ring and begged for calm.

It lapped around me. My emotions stilled. I could think clearly. Sharply.

"Did you plan this entire project to lure me out here?" I demanded.

"I funded the professor's research, hoping you could make a difference." Joshua's chin lifted. "My life was at stake."

"So you risked mine? And Evan's?" I asked. How did he rationalize swapping us for himself?

"You're both fine now," Joshua said.

"That doesn't make it all right," Evan said.

Joshua started to defend himself, but the professor interrupted him. "Joshua was wrong to risk your lives like he did. I'm sorry that I trusted him, because you two put your trust in me and that put you in danger. This isn't what I wanted for either of you." He sighed. "You have every right to be angry and upset."

Joshua cleared his throat. "I'm sorry for everything that happened to you. I should have been honest with you when you arrived, but I was desperate. I feared you wouldn't help me. Still, it was wrong of me to keep this from you." He looked down at his hands. "You can leave as soon as the tides allow it."

If we left, the curse would claim its last victim. Joshua would die. We hadn't been able to save Cassie and Sebastian, but we couldn't abandon Joshua to a similar fate.

I swallowed. I didn't want to feel this sympathy. This guilt. This responsibility.

I glanced at Evan. He gave me a half-smile.

I nodded.

Evan said, "We're not leaving yet. We have a curse to undo."

Joshua's eyes filled with gratitude. "Thank you."

Professor Astor sighed. "If the kids are helping, so will I. Evan, can you tell me more about the book you found with the Celtic curses scribbled in it?"

Evan sounded like a British GPS navigator. "*British Lore* has a navy leather spine that's about five inches thick with gold lettering."

I jumped in with, "I borrowed it my first night at the castle. It should be on my nightstand."

"I hope it's there." Joshua moved toward the door, eager to find it. He paused, and turned back toward us. "I need to see the rubies."

He'd gone from contrite to commanding in 10 seconds. It startled me. Still, part of me wanted to give in. His voice had power over me, probably because he was a Radcliffe and I was a Langley. But that meant I needed to protect him, and the rubies were deadly. "No," I said.

"Patience, Joshua," Professor Astor said. "She's convinced they are dangerous."

"She's a child," Joshua replied.

A child who was right here while the adults who'd put me in danger talked over me.

"A child who did the impossible." Professor Astor was using his professor voice now. "She opened the portal. She traveled through time and shared a body with an ancestor. She brought the necklace back. She risked her life without knowing why. She may be the only one who can save you. You owe her your trust."

"You're asking me to rest all my hopes on this girl's shoulders?" Joshua asked.

"You already did," I reminded him.

Joshua looked from me to Professor Astor. The professor remained silent. Then the Radcliffe heir clenched his fists and stormed out of the turret room.

"I'm sorry about that. He's been growing more and more volatile as his birthday approaches." Professor Astor adjusted his glasses and returned his attention to us. "You must be exhausted."

"And hungry," Evan added.

"Yeah," I said. I hadn't realized it until he mentioned it, but I was starving.

The professor led us to the door. "I'll have something sent up for you. Try to get some rest."

Evan said, "Thanks."

"I'm sorry for all the pain this has caused you." Professor Astor's face filled with regret. "That was never my intention."

I nodded. I didn't trust myself to speak. I feared spewing venom on Evan and the professor when it should be directed at Joshua. And the

Langleys. And fate. I was furious at the universe right now.

By the time we got to my room, my migraine had destroyed my appetite. I put the necklace in my armoire and collapsed onto the bed. I was out before I knew it.

The creak of my door opening brought me back to consciousness. I rolled over.

Evan hovered in the doorway. "I woke you. I'm sorry. I'll go."

"No, stay. I could use the company."

After he closed the door, he sat on the edge of my bed. "I'll keep watch over the necklace while you rest."

"We can't let anyone touch it." I felt lines of worry take their place on my forehead.

Evan smoothed them away with his fingers. "I know. It's deadly."

I bit my lip. "Do you think we were destined to go back in time?"

"The prophecy said you were, at least."

I stared into his eyes, remembering all that we'd been through. How he'd stayed with me and kept me from disappearing. "What about you?"

"An accident." His gaze didn't waver.

"There are no accidents in a perfect universe."

He chuckled. "The universe is far from perfect."

"Mine is. It auto-corrects."

He chuckled. "I was wondering when you were going to mention that."

"That being?"

"That you were right," he whispered.

I murmured, "Glad I didn't go it alone."

"Me, too." He was the last thing I saw before my eyes drifted shut again.

Chapter 34

I couldn't see five inches beyond the tip of my nose. Fog swirled around me. The humid air clutched at my skin. Damp grass swallowed my bare feet. I stubbed my toe and hissed as the pain shot into my ankle. Last I remembered, I was in my room with Evan. So how did I end up outside, banging my foot against the stone wall surrounding Castle Creighton?

Sleepwalking. I must be sleepwalking. I should go back to my bed. My feet, however, refused to budge, like they were keeping an appointment I didn't know I had. A hand reached out and grabbed me. My arm went all cold and tingly at the touch. I screamed until I noticed my ring glowing on the stranger's hand. The fog parted. My eyes trailed up the sleeve of her electric blue evening dress, all the way to her face.

Toria.

"I need to talk to you." She squeezed my arm.

Before she could say another word, all the questions that I had tumbled out of my mouth. "Why couldn't I make a difference? Where did Sebastian and Cassie go? How did you pull me through that mirror?"

"You did make a difference, Kat." She conspicuously avoided my other questions.

"Cassie and Sebastian died. I didn't change anything."

"You brought the ruby necklace back to the Radcliffes. That counts."

"Could I have saved Cassie and Sebastian if I'd tried harder?" I asked.

She wouldn't look at me. "You did what you could."

I was afraid that if I pushed her further, I wouldn't like her answer, so I changed the subject. "Was that mirror really made for me?" I asked.

"Lorelei made it for all of her descendants. It responds to the magic in our blood. For each of us, it does something different. You're the first to time travel through it."

"You saw the future in it?" I asked.

"That's how I could see you. You reached out to the past and I reached out to the future at the same moment."

"So how did Sebastian use the mirror?" I asked.

Toria frowned. "I haven't been able to figure that out. Only Langley blood awakens the mirror."

"Are Cassie and Sebastian still inside it—or in limbo or something?"

Toria nodded, her eyes grave.

"Are they suffering?" I asked, knowing that they must be.

Tears welled up in her eyes. "It's a brutal way to spend eternity."

"Can we help them?" I asked.

She nodded. "But first, I need to apologize."

"For what?"

"For letting Leanna frighten you while you were studying."

It took me a moment to understand what Toria was talking about. That night in Gilman Library felt like a million years ago.

"That was Leanna?" I asked.

"Some of it. Your research was dissolving the barrier we'd worked so hard to create. I tried to get your attention with the books. But that put you in even greater danger. Leanna was always there, watching and waiting. I gave her a chance to break through. I'm sorry."

"You were trying to stop me?"

She nodded.

"But the Radcliffes needed me. Joshua needed me. I'm a Langley. I have the ring. I had to help."

She gave me the saddest smile. "I've always tried to protect you from this. I never wanted any of this for you."

"Why?" I asked.

"I wanted you to have a life of your own. I wanted you to live the life you wanted. Not the one you were obligated to live. I didn't want you to have the kind of life I had."

I heard the regret in her voice. And my thoughts turned to Leanna, driven by the specter of her uncle. I was vulnerable to her again. "Is Leanna still here?"

"She lingers, yes. But I think you're safe from her now. She wanted to possess you so that she could compel you to save her descendants. I believe she understands now that she doesn't need to force you."

I was confused. "But she's the one who cursed her descendants."

"She didn't know what she was doing. None of us did," Toria said.

I didn't know what to say to that. My gaze slid back to her ring. The exact same one I wore now. "You and me—we're related."

She sighed. "More than you realize. I'm not just your ancestor's ghost. I'm a piece of the soul that eventually reincarnated in you."

My jaw dropped. "I'm you?"

"Lorelei is much better at explaining this sort of thing," she grumbled. She took a deep breath and tried again. "When a person dies, her soul shatters. The ghost is a small piece that breaks away and remains behind. The largest piece of the soul progresses onward. The wheel of life keeps turning for the soul and it reincarnates. In the next life, the soul gathers more knowledge and experience. It grows and changes over each lifetime. I am not you and you are not me. But our connection goes beyond blood."

I stared at her. She was more human than any ghost I'd ever met. "You need me to break the curse, too, don't you?"

Regret filled her voice. "Long ago, I resigned myself to never having my reckoning, but now..."

"What can I do?" I whispered.

"You don't have much time. Joshua's twenty-third birthday is three weeks away. He will die on that day unless you help him."

"But what can I do to help *you*?"

Toria smiled. "You can help me by helping Joshua."

I couldn't say no to her. Not to a lost piece of my soul.

The mist thickened and she became translucent. She rushed to explain. "Don't touch the rubies. They're coated in a deadly poison. You must bathe the stones in the hot spring near the ruins."

She faded into the fog. Her voice threaded through the air, weaving its way to me. "But even after you cleanse them of the poison, they will remain cursed."

"What do I do about the curse? I can't do this alone."

Her voice became a mere whisper. "I will be with you when you need me."

"How? Toria, please tell me how." I'd never learned how to summon a ghost, just how to send them away. And she was already gone.

I still had so many questions. I should have asked about Pastor Fitzgerald. What he'd become. When I thought about him, my teeth chattered as if I'd been dunked in an ice pond. The fog closed in on me, and everything faded to white.

I sat up in bed, rubbed my eyes, and groped for my glasses. It couldn't have been a dream. I still had goose bumps where Toria had touched my arm. I squinted against the bright light from the lamp. Evan was hunched over my desk, snoring.

Toria's words echoed in my mind. *The hot spring near the ruins.* I didn't remember seeing it during Olivia's tour. Something tugged at the back of my mind. *Wait, Joshua mentioned it.*

The clock on my nightstand read 3:26 a.m. Not the best time for a hike, but time wasn't something we could waste.

I bundled up the shawl, shoved it in my backpack, grabbed my flashlight, and crept out of the castle. Ducking through the front gate, I trained my flashlight's beam on the ground. I paused when I saw four faint depressions in the ground—like angel footprints. Exactly where Toria and I were standing in my dream. I didn't have time to linger on that. I had to find the path to the ruins. It was just a matter of tapping into those shared memories from when Toria took Drew there.

The inky darkness and tall grass obscured my view. The ferocious roar of the ocean warned that the cliff's edge was close. I inched along the path, taking an hour to reach the ruins.

I bent down, examining the ground for signs of a trail to the hot spring. I didn't find any. I got frustrated. Swore a lot. Right up until my flashlight illuminated two flat stones covered in creeping grass. I swept the grass and dirt aside with my hand, uncovering Ogham symbols carved into the rock.

I almost wished Evan were here with me to translate. Maybe I should have woke him up. He'd have come with me. But I wasn't sure what would happen at the hot spring. What I'd have to do to remove the poison.

When my foot touched the second stone, the undergrowth parted—all by itself—to reveal the next stone in front of me. Freaky squared. This continued until the stone path ended at a pit of steam surrounded by giant boulders. I eyed them, trying to figure out which ones I might be able to climb. Luckily, no one was there to witness how many times I lost my footing or my grip.

When I finally reached the top, I found a pool of water surrounded by a circle of rocks. Kneeling, I braced one hand on the rock and cautiously dunked the other into the water. Bathwater warm.

I pulled the bundle out of my backpack and dropped the shawl and ruby necklace into the pool. The fabric unfurled and released the necklace. Both sank to the bottom.

What am I doing here? Blind faith was not one of my strong points. I needed Toria's help. I hoped this worked. I closed my eyes, twisted my ring, and called out to her.

"A cleansing spell," Toria whispered. Her ghost sat beside me. She was almost solid in the predawn moments. Still slightly faded and not quite alive, but much more present than she'd been in my dream.

"Wow, you're here."

She smiled. "The ring. Our ring. It gives you the ability to summon ghosts—among other powers."

"Really?"

"Be careful what you ask for."

There was so much I wanted to know about the ring and the Langleys. "Why didn't anyone tell me about this?"

She smiled. "The Langleys have been trying to protect you. The longer you went without using the ring, the longer you remained safe."

"So why did my dad send me the ring without any explanation?" I demanded.

"He didn't have a choice. The ring chooses its wearer."

My voice rose with my frustration. "But he could have warned me. He could have explained what the ring meant."

"I've never met your father. I can't imagine what he felt when he found out you were the heir." Toria looked down. "I wanted you to have a life of your own. I never wanted you to have this ring, but it wasn't in my power to prevent it."

"Am I in danger?" I asked.

"We're all in danger," Toria said.

"From who?" I asked.

"It's more of a what."

I thought for a moment. "Pastor Fitzgerald?"

She nodded. "Not him, but what he's become. What you saw...it's so much worse now. He's become a new unbelievable. Completely devoid of light. Pure darkness."

"How?"

"He gave the last of his soul to the shadows." She said it with such distaste. "The shadows are how we emerge into your world, but we don't trust the shadows. We don't ally with the shadows. Because they are pure darkness."

"And ghosts still have some light in them?"

She smiled. "That piece of soul that forms a ghost—that's the light in them. It's not much. Just enough to let us remember our lives, just enough to keep us from the darkness."

"What are we going to do about Pastor Fitzgerald?" I asked.

"Right now? Nothing. We have to focus on Joshua. You need to do a cleansing spell."

This was my first spell ever. "What do we need?"

"Your blood."

The sight of my own blood freaked me out. And it made me lightheaded and nauseous. "Can we substitute someone else's?"

She shook her head. "Our magic requires our blood."

My stomach churned. "How much?"

She pointed to a sharp rock lying next to me. "Cut your palm and let your blood flow into the water. When there is enough, you will stop bleeding."

I wasn't willing to bleed out for a spell. "How much is enough?"

She laughed. "A few drops should do it."

She made it sound like we were adding oil to a cake, not casting spells with my blood.

I swallowed. "There's no other way?"

She shook her head.

I reached for the rock and pressed it against my palm. But I didn't break the skin. I was afraid of the pain. Of the blood.

"Do it quickly, it hurts less," she said.

I closed my eyes and slashed at my palm with the rock. She was wrong. It stung like every cut does. My blood bubbled to the surface. I swayed.

"Close your eyes," she whispered.

I did as she said. I still smelled iron. It turned my stomach. Sweat beaded across my forehead and brow.

"Good girl. Now lean forward a little more and drip it into the pool," she said.

I kept my eyes shut. Her strength washed over my skin. She whispered words I didn't know. Words I found myself repeating.

I peeked through one lid. The necklace remained at the bottom of the pool.

"It's not working," I said.

"Patience, Kat." She peered into the water. Waiting.

I didn't want to see the blood trickling from my palm. I looked up and caught the sun sneaking above the horizon. I closed my eyes and took a few deep, calming breaths.

When I opened them again, Toria was semi-transparent. She sounded weaker when she said, "The poison is gone. Retrieve the necklace."

The necklace swam up to me. I caught the diamond chain as it broke through the water's surface. The stones warmed my hand. When the shawl spiraled up, I expected to wring out a sopping wet mess. Instead, it felt fresh from the dryer.

I looked at Toria. "Are we done here?"

She smiled. "With this part." She disappeared before I could ask her what she meant. I wanted to call her back, but I was so tired. The aftereffects of a ghost visit and my first spell crawled over me. My head drooped.

A loud sneeze startled me.

My adrenalin kicked in. I flattened myself against the boulder, scanning the area. "Who's there? Show yourself, you coward!"

Evan sniffled as he stepped out from the cover of the tall grass.

"What are you doing here?" I asked as I sat back on my heels.

He sneezed again. "Discovering an allergy to the isle's plant life."

"Why did you follow me?"

He used his hand to shield his eyes from the morning rays. "I've never known you to venture out before daylight without good reason."

I shoved the Radcliffe Rubies and the shawl into my backpack, slipped it onto my shoulders, and started to climb down the rocks. I tried to baby my injured palm, but it split open. The cut burned and throbbed. I gritted my teeth.

"How long have you been here?" I asked.

"A while," he said.

"So you heard..."

"You casting a spell with Toria? Yes."

"You saw her?" I asked.

"I'm a believer now," he reminded me.

 "Why didn't you say something?"

"You left without waking me. I assumed that you wanted to be alone."

I lost my grip and skidded the last two feet to the ground. Evan caught me. Steadied me. His hands were warm on my waist.

"But you're here," I said.

He started to release me. My head spun.

Evan caught me again and lowered me to the ground. "Are you okay?"

"Spells and ghosts take so much energy. I just need a few minutes." I curled up and rested my forehead on my knees, waiting for the world to stop spinning.

He sat next to me and rubbed my back. "I couldn't let you wander off alone in the dark."

I was glad that he'd followed me. "I can't believe we're both a part of all this."

He shifted closer and I rested my head on his shoulder. I watched the sun take its place in the sky. Morning was still morning. The sun still rose. The sky still turned blue. The earth still sat below us. But my world would never be the same. This was the beginning of my life as a Langley, tied to the Radcliffes and the Kingsleys. Back in a world filled with unbelievables.

Chapter 35

By the time Evan and I made it back to the castle, all I wanted was a nap. Instead, I was summoned to the library without breakfast.

Professor Astor's "How are you feeling?" barely penetrated my thoughts. He followed up with "Trouble sleeping?"

I nodded.

"What happened to your hand?" Joshua asked.

I'd wrapped it in the shawl. "I cut it."

Professor Astor's brow knit together. "Let me take a look."

I pulled my injured hand closer to my body. "It's fine."

Evan leaned against the wall of books. "It's a rather long story. Food and coffee would help us tell it."

Joshua called the kitchen and ten minutes later the food arrived. I was on my fourth piece of bacon, second serving of eggs, and third cup of coffee before I felt like myself again.

Professor Astor cleared his throat. "What took you both out of the castle so early?"

I told them about my dream and how I'd gone to the hot spring to get rid of the poison on the rubies. What I'd had to do to cleanse them.

Joshua said, "It must be nice to be able to talk to an ancestor."

I wrinkled my nose up. "It's kind of creepy, but cool."

He smiled. "All of this is."

I nodded. It was good to not be alone with the unbelievables anymore.

Joshua's voice swathed me in velvet. "Show me the necklace."

Sure. No wait. It was so hard to say no to him. I didn't like it.

Toria had told me the rubies were safe now. The necklace belonged to his family. He had a right to see it. "It's still cursed," I warned as I handed it to him.

"My grandfather told me, until the rubies are returned to us, we will have no peace." He stared at the pendant. "I never understood what his words meant."

The night the rubies went missing, the Radcliffe family's fate was sealed. But now we had a chance to change things.

It was as if Professor Astor read my mind. He put *British Lore* in the middle of the table.

"When did you get it from my room?" I asked.

Joshua said, "I grabbed it after I left the turret room yesterday. I wanted Astor to look it over as soon as possible."

The professor pursed his lips. "I've never broken a curse before." He flipped to the page with the scribbling on it.

"Are you sure you're up for this?" Evan's eyes locked on mine. I'd swear he would stop this from happening if I said no.

I swallowed. I was still recovering from the first spell I'd cast, and I wasn't looking forward to shedding more blood—but that was how Langleys worked their magic. And I was a Langley. I had to break the curse. I had to save Joshua. I had to help Toria. "I can do this."

In my head, I said a silent prayer that I was right.

Chapter 36

I trudged through the castle, searching for Morgan. She wasn't in her room or on the terrace. I had to tell her all the things that happened and why I was so mean about the shawl.

I stumbled upon her and Adam in the private movie theater. Every inch of her was pressed against him.

I retreated several feet and then stomped back to the door. I wanted to give them a heads up about my arrival. They stopped kissing, but they didn't disentangle.

I blanked out for a second. Like couldn't form one syllable. I rubbed my lips together. "Can I talk to you?"

"Sure." She shifted to face me from the circle of Adam's arms. Her necklace caught the light. Something about that blue butterfly wing pendant reminded me of Toria, but I couldn't place it.

I said, "It's girl stuff."

She smiled at Adam. "Can you go get us some snacks?"

He got up. "Anything special you want, sweetie?"

Sweetie. If I were a cartoon character, my eyes would have popped out of my head, bounced around the room, and gotten tangled up in each other.

Adam shut the door, leaving me alone with Morgan. I ran my tongue over the back of my teeth. "I'm sorry about yesterday."

Morgan got up from the couch and hugged me. "Kitty Kat, don't you get how worried I've been about you? I don't care that you snapped at me. I care about what happened to you." She pulled me back to the couch. Her face scrunched up. "How bad is it?"

I bit my lip. My world wasn't the same as Morgan's world anymore. "You wouldn't believe me."

"Of course I'll believe you," Morgan said.

"Really?" Part of me wished she wouldn't. Her disbelief would make our friendship complicated—if not impossible—but it would keep her safe. "Maybe you shouldn't."

"You're my best friend. I'll totally believe you. Unless, you tell me you see ghosts or something."

I opened my mouth to respond, but the words wouldn't come, so I closed my mouth again.

Morgan laughed and gave me a gentle shove. "I already believe. Professor Astor sat us down last night and explained everything. Adam and Seth need more convincing, but I believe. There's no way you were on the island the past four days. We searched everywhere, and I know you wouldn't have let us worry about you if you could have helped it."

She believed. I didn't have to explain myself. I wasn't going to lose Morgan. But Morgan was going to be at risk now.

"Thanks for not letting me near the rubies." She shuddered. "I wouldn't want to end up another victim of their poison."

"Aren't you scared?" I asked.

"Absolutely. But life is all one big scary uncertainty," she said.

Only Morgan could be so fearless in the face of the unbelievables. It was so good to be back with her again.

"So are there really ghosts at Gilman Library?"

I nodded. "Toria and Leanna both came to visit me there."

"Are there others? Like, fulltime?"

"Probably. Ghosts love old buildings. Cemeteries. Even old churches. They're drawn to historic places. Or at least have an easier time breaking through there."

"Freaky!" She sounded excited. "I can't believe you never told me any of this!"

"I had to stop believing," I said.

She waved her hand around. "I get it. But still, this was a major secret you were sitting on, Kitty Kat."

"I'm sorry I couldn't tell you." I never wanted to keep things from

Morgan. But I didn't have a choice. The secret kept me safe.

"I understand, but I tell you everything. Besties shouldn't keep secrets." She touched my hand. "I feel like I get so much more now. You hate parties but force yourself to go to them—it's to keep the ghosts away, right?"

I nodded.

She assumed her thoughtful pose, tucking her feet under her and biting on her pointer finger. "What I can't figure out is why you?"

I filled her in on how Toria was my ancestor and a piece of my soul that had broken away lifetimes ago. My father was a Langley and my ring was a family heirloom. I ended with the Langley prophecy.

"Wow. This is crazy. You're a Langley." Morgan threaded her necklace between her lips and ran the pendant back and forth on her chain.

I stared at it. I'd seen it on someone else. In another lifetime. Toria's lifetime. "Where did you get that necklace?"

"It was my mom's. Passed down to the first-born daughter." She held it up for me to see.

The blue butterfly wing. Images from Toria's life flashed before me. Her belly growing big with Sebastian's child. Her pregnancy a secret from everyone. Her only companion a blue monarch butterfly. The butterfly dying. Tears nearly blinding her as she crafted a necklace from its beautiful wings. Her blood used for the protection spell on that necklace. Right before she gave it to her infant daughter.

Everything fell into place. Toria's heart-wrenching goodbye to Sebastian. The emotions that had overwhelmed me, the memories that refused to fit together. They were about the child that tied her to Sebastian. The child she longed for…the child he never knew about. No wonder it took her so long to let go of him. It meant saying goodbye to her daughter's father.

Toria's feelings bled into mine. Warm tears wet my cheeks. I brushed them aside with the back of my hand. Morgan wasn't just my best friend. Morgan was family. We were both related to Toria. This was so weird.

"What's wrong?" Morgan asked.

Staring into her blue-green eyes, for a second I felt like I was looking into Sebastian's eyes. As if I glimpsed a bit of his soul in her. I blinked and it was just Morgan in front of me.

I told her everything I knew. Everything I'd seen in the past, and everything I'd seen in my mind just now.

"That's creepy. I mean, that's way too many coincidences," she said.

"I don't think any of this is coincidence. There are ghosts working to break the curse, and men like Joshua have the money and the power to make impossible things happen."

The realization dawned on her face. "Is that why he picked me as the Radcliffe Scholar? To put us in each other's path? Has he been pulling our strings for years?"

"I think so. He definitely wanted you and me here—Evan, too. I'm sure he knows that you're related to Toria." I understood why Joshua did what he did. But a part of me still didn't like the idea of him orchestrating our lives. Pushing us together. Even if I loved being Morgan's bestie, I didn't like thinking it wasn't completely my choice.

Morgan crossed her arms. "Why would anyone care that much about my long dead great-great grandmother?"

"Because you're a part of this, too. Somehow."

Morgan was still processing my first revelation. "*Ay Dios mío*! Can you imagine my family at the next Radcliffe reunion? A touch of brown in that sea of white."

Only Morgan would be able to find the humor in this mess.

I was working on a different problem. "What about Seth. Why is he here?" Then it came to me. His last name was Fitzgerald. "Seth is descended from the pastor."

"But how would Joshua know about Pastor Fitzgerald? Didn't you just find out about him when you traveled back to the past?"

She was right. "The ghosts. They must have somehow sent Seth our way. And Adam too."

She wrapped her arms around herself. "Think about it. Without Joshua, I wouldn't have gotten the scholarship and we'd have never met. Without the ghosts, Adam and I wouldn't have reconnected out here. Whatever is happening, I got a best friend and boyfriend out it."

A chill crept up my spine. "Maybe we were all meant to be here. Wait, boyfriend? What happened between you and Adam while I was gone?"

"Seth was no help. He kept saying you'd turn up. He was too busy flirting with Olivia to care about Evan."

"Typical." I rolled my eyes.

"I didn't have anyone else to turn to. Our cell phones don't work out here. The landlines were down for a day too. All I had was Adam. He started pointing out the holes in Joshua and Olivia's stories." She grabbed my arm. "They had you stuck out in some remote building on the isle during the first day. Then, get this, they said you returned while we were asleep and snuck into the catacombs below the castle. I'm sure they were trying to keep us calm while they scrambled to find you, but still."

"They get points for creativity."

"I saw your face when they announced our fieldtrip to the submarine last year. You and underground tunnels—never going to happen."

She was right. I faked a sick day to get out of that fieldtrip. "What did Adam do?" I tried to picture the series of incidents that pushed them back together.

"He kept coming up with excuses to check the phone lines. The minute we knew they were working, we made sure Joshua called Professor Astor." Morgan added, "When Astor heard that you'd gone missing, he raced out here. He was really worried about you. I knew he wouldn't rest until you were found."

"And Adam was there for you?" I asked.

Morgan nodded. "The whole time. He promised we'd find you. I saw the old Adam again. Now that he knows Sebastian had nothing to do with Cassie's death, we can finally move forward." Hope threaded through her words.

They were a *we*. Morgan dated, but she never got into relationships. She refused to be a couple. Now, they were a we.

"So was all that time with Evan the Terrible like a root canal without Novocain?" she asked.

I squirmed. "He's not that bad when you get to know him."

"Tell me about the Antichrist's redeeming qualities."

I winced. "I called him that?"

"With a few modifiers."

"He's a jerk, sometimes."

Morgan raised both eyebrows.

"Okay, a lot of the time. But I'd never have survived without him."

When I entered the library to check on Professor Astor and Evan's progress translating the curse, they were sitting behind their laptops. Dictionaries and assorted papers littered the long table.

"Professor, how are you translating Cumbric? The entire language became extinct in the Middle Ages," Evan said.

"Just because no one speaks a language, doesn't mean it's completely gone." Professor Astor kept his eyes trained on his laptop.

"Seriously?" Evan glanced at me.

I shrugged. Professor Astor was a cornucopia of secrets lately.

"Some languages live on in magical texts." Professor Astor scribbled something on his notepad. "Bits of it remain in spells and curses." He thumbed through *British Lore*, then consulted something on his screen and frowned.

Every once in a while, they bent over the text, muttering half sentences to each other before returning to their computer screens. I watched and waited. Neither of which I'm good at. Minutes bundled into hours.

I picked up the ruby necklace. Running my fingers over the stones, I remembered Cassie's excitement when she touched them. The reel of film played over in my mind with no way to stop the memory from reaching its bloody conclusion.

A bang jerked me back to the present as Evan's fist hit the table.

Professor Astor looked up. "Take a break, Evan."

"But we have two more phrases to translate," Evan said.

"Yes, we do," the professor said. "And we aren't going to be able to do that unless you have a clear head. Take a break."

I saw the *No* forming on Evan's lips, but he picked up on the command in Professor Astor's voice.

Evan plunked down next to me on the couch.

Something about his presence soothed me. What a reversal from a few weeks ago.

His knee bounced up and down.

"You seem a little stressed out," I said.

"We've got three weeks to save a man's life by breaking a curse. A phenomenon I didn't believe in until I time traveled and snatched an ancestor's body. I can almost forget while I'm working, but…"

"Do you think you can finish the translation in time?" I asked.

"We don't have another option."

I looked down at my hands and touched my ring. "I could summon Leanna and ask her about the curse." I didn't want to call Leanna's ghost to me. But if they needed me to, I would.

"She's the one who tried to possess you?" he asked.

I nodded.

"And you'd risk that for us?"

I swallowed. "I'm stronger now. I was just a little kid the first time. And I don't think that she'd try to possess me now. All she wants is for the curse to be broken. I want that too."

"It's not worth the risk." He leaned closer. "You don't have to do any of this, you know."

I looked up. "I do. I have to do everything I can to fix what happened."

"You've done more than enough. Let Astor and me do our job. We'll crack that translation soon."

"If you can't?" I asked.

"We will." Evan gave my shoulder a reassuring squeeze. "We promised to see each other through this. And this isn't over."

"Right." His hand was so warm and solid. I didn't want him to let go. I counted to five and forced myself to lean forward because needing him scared me almost as much as the unbelievables.

Chapter 37

Joshua loomed over me. "Any progress?"

I rubbed my eyes and checked my watch. Two hours had passed since I'd drifted off. Professor Astor and Evan hunched over a book, debating the meaning of a word. "They're finishing up the third phrase."

Professor Astor's head popped up. "No, we're working on the last one right now." Then he went back to work.

Joshua sat beside me on the leather couch. His eyes were rimmed in shadows. He looked a decade older than twenty-two. I wanted to comfort him. To promise him that this time the Langleys wouldn't fail the Radcliffes.

I touched his arm. "We'll figure this out in time."

"I hope you're right."

"We'll use every resource we have." I'd summon Leanna if he needed me to.

"I hate thinking about this countdown to my death." He rubbed his hand over his face. He'd let inches of stubble grow over his jaw. He whispered, "Distract me."

I had so many questions I wanted to ask him. "How long has your family been connected with the Langleys?" I asked.

He tilted his head to the side. "I've traced the union between our families back to the Middle Ages. Before that, there aren't any records, but my grandfather told me that we've been allies since our families were tribes."

A thousand years—at least. That was a lot of history. History I knew nothing about and yet I was a key part of.

"Are you in touch with them—the Langleys, I mean?" My voice cracked.

"Some of them. Most are scattered around the globe, but I can help you find them."

I didn't say anything. I wasn't sure how I felt about any of this. Tracking down my long lost family. The father who'd abandoned me. The family who'd never reached out to me. "Thanks. We can talk about it later."

"What if there isn't a later?" he asked.

I shook my head. "There will be."

He ran his hand through his hair. "I understand why some of my ancestors overindulged. Trying to pack a lifetime into twenty-three years."

Professor Astor cried, "Eureka."

Evan shouted, "Bloody Hell."

Our conversation was forgotten. Joshua crossed the room in a few strides. "What does it mean?" He splayed his fingers on the table and leaned over them.

Professor Astor nudged Evan. "Go ahead."

Evan's face glowed like an eight-year-old on Christmas. "This first line is *May the wearer of this necklace feel the pain of those she hurt tenfold.* The second line says *May she and her beloved disappear in an unending death from which they can never return.*"

Professor Astor took over. "The second line explains why Cassie and Sebastian went into the mirror. The portal is a place where time has no meaning. Hence, an unending death."

"But Sebastian chose to go into it," I said.

"Maybe he thought it was the only way he could be with Cassie," Evan said.

I turned to Joshua. "Did your ancestors know about the mirror's magical properties?"

"It's very possible. I heard stories about how it was a portal to magical lands. I figured it was a fun story, but I'm sure Sebastian heard about it in his time too."

Professor Astor's glasses slipped down his nose. He pushed them back up. "The last two lines were harder to translate. Leanna used some very archaic language." Professor Astor launched into a short lecture about how impressed he was with her grasp of Cumbric and how seamlessly she switched between the languages.

Joshua growled, "The curse."

"Yes, of course," the professor hastened to explain, "The third line translates as *May the legacy of pain and loss be felt by every generation descended from my uncle's murderers.* The last line reads *May none find peace until the wrongs done by their ancestors are righted.*"

Evan said, "The third line curses Cassie and Drew for covering up Cassie's role in Pastor Fitzgerald's murder. But it doesn't stop there. Generations of the Mallory and Nolan families are sentenced to continual pain and loss for the pastor's death."

Joshua murmured. "The Mallorys lost their fortune three generations ago. Every time their finances started to improve, something horrible befell the family."

I remembered what Morgan said about Adam being an orphan. "Adam faced so much death at such a young age."

Professor Astor took off his glasses, fogged up the lenses with his breath, and wiped them on his pants. "The last line makes this a reversible curse."

"Why would anyone write a reversible curse?" Joshua demanded.

"Because she didn't want to do it," I said softly. "Pastor Fitzgerald forced her to curse them, but she wouldn't sentence everyone to misery for eternity. That last line was her way of helping."

Professor Astor murmured. "What a clever girl, but she masked the loophole by extending the curse to every family involved. At first glance, it looks like none of the families can ever find peace."

Joshua's stance radiated tension. "So how do we reverse it?"

Professor Astor frowned at his lenses and wiped them again. When he put them back on, the smudges were worse. "By undoing the wrongs done 129 years ago."

"Everyone is dead. The curse is irreversible." Joshua's word rang out with finality.

"Don't be so literal. The current generation can make amends," Professor Astor said.

"But how will we find them in time?" Evan asked.

"They're all here," I said. "Isn't it a lucky coincidence?" I asked Joshua.

"Very lucky." Joshua's eyes gleamed.

Evan quirked an eyebrow.

I ticked each one off on my fingers. "Adam is the descendant of Drew Nolan. Evan's descended from Alistair Kingsley. I'm related to Toria Langley. Seth's a Fitzgerald. Joshua's ancestors are Leanna and Phillip. All we're missing is a Mallory."

"Olivia's a Mallory from her mother's side," Joshua said.

"Your girlfriend's a Mallory?" I asked.

Joshua explained. "We've known each other since we were children. Her name has nothing to do with why I fell in love with her."

Professor Astor's lips thinned. "Joshua is a mix of the Radcliffe and the Burnsby bloodlines."

Wasn't sure why, but I got the feeling this was bad.

"And?" I asked.

"He can stand in for Phillip or Leanna, but not for Sebastian," the professor said.

"What does it matter if he's a direct or indirect descendant?" My gaze ping-ponged from the professor to Evan.

"It doesn't," Professor Astor said. "But Leanna's curse harmed Sebastian. Her descendant cannot stand in for Sebastian." Professor Astor raised his hands. "Magic has rules. It's all about symbolism. *As above so below*. A descendant of a killer can't stand in for the victim. Symbolically, it doesn't work."

"Sebastian's line ended with him." Evan's lips compressed to white.

"Not exactly," Joshua said. He explained about Toria and Sebastian's illegitimate daughter.

"That means everyone affected by what happened 129 years ago has a descendant here at the castle," the professor said. "The Kingsleys and the Langleys who tried to protect the Radcliffes and failed. The Fitzgeralds who tried to harm the Mallorys and succeeded. Even the Nolans and the Burnsbys who were forced or tricked into helping harm the Mallorys and the Radcliffes. All of them have representatives here."

Something was off. I toyed with my ring, trying to shake the feeling. Then I realized the source. "The curse extended to all the families, but there's no mention of the Radcliffe heir suffering a fate like Sebastian's. The bizarre deaths of the first-born sons don't fit the curse."

Evan rolled his pen on the table. "Leanna married Phillip a year after the murders. She cast that curse. She knew exactly what it would do."

"It's hard to imagine she'd knowingly marry into the family and let her children suffer the Radcliffe Curse." I still couldn't wrap my mind around it.

"Unless she was forced to by Pastor Fitzgerald," Evan said.

The shadow creature I'd seen was definitely twisted enough to punish generations of his own family in avenging himself. "Maybe he realized what she did with the last line of the curse and wanted to punish her for creating that loophole?"

"We translated and retranslated each word. Frankly, I am at a loss to explain it," Professor Astor said. "There is nothing about the first-born sons in this curse."

"Breaking the curse might not prevent my death?" Joshua asked.

"Unfortunately, you may be right," the professor said.

Joshua slammed his hand on the table. "What's behind my death sentence?"

My head throbbed. Floating shadow worms and sparkly particles clouded my vision. Separated me from the rest of the room. I fumbled into the nearest chair, throwing my hands over my eyes to block out the unbearable brightness of the lights. After everything we'd been through, how could it end like this?

I twisted my ring. What was I missing?

The voices quieted and the library melted away.

I was Toria standing on the rampart, watching the sun drop below the horizon. As the sky darkened, I worried about the future of the Radcliffes.

If I cannot prevent the pain and suffering that is coming, I will make sure it is returned in kind. I stood in the middle of the turret sprinkling my blood over Sebastian's pocket watch. Casting a protection spell over him.

But that wasn't enough. I used a yew branch and my own blood to cast a spell that would doom the first-born sons of anyone who harmed Sebastian. Those sons would only enjoy as much happiness as Sebastian knew, and they would endure sorrows equal to his. The spell's permanence depended on the safety of the yew branch, so I hid it inside the stonework in the western turret. I used more blood to seal it away forever.

The vision ended abruptly, thrusting me back into the library. I held my head in my hands and whispered, "There's a retribution spell."

"What?" Evan sounded so close. He had to be kneeling in front of me.

"Leanna's curse isn't what killed the first-born sons," I said.

"How do you know?" Professor Astor asked.

Evan tugged my hands away and held them in his.

There was so much acceptance in those hazel eyes. "I was there when Toria cast the retribution spell. I was Toria."

"A Langley cursed the Radcliffes?" Joshua asked.

I gripped Evan's hands. "Toria wasn't trying to hurt the Radcliffes. She didn't know who—or what—threatened Sebastian. She was trying to protect him. If she couldn't, she wanted vengeance against anyone who succeeded in hurting him. She had no idea what she was doing, and she's been trying to make things right ever since."

I shared the memory with them.

"Toria caused the near extinction of the Radcliffe family." Professor Astor sounded dazed.

"She didn't mean to. She thought she was protecting them."

"How do we fix it?" Joshua asked.

I let go of Evan's hands and twisted my ring. *Toria how do we fix this?*

The shadow cast by my chair darkened. The air shimmered. From the darkness, white smoke curled and weaved into a woman. A semi-solid woman. Like a faded photograph, Toria stood beside me.

Evan said, "Hello, again."

Professor Astor smiled and Joshua paled.

"You see Toria?" I asked.

Professor Astor bowed. "It's a pleasure to meet you."

Toria acknowledged the professor and Joshua with a nod. "I'm sorry we must meet under these circumstances. I never wanted any harm to come to the Radcliffes. I didn't know Leanna was behind the curse when I cast my retribution spell. By the time I figured it out, it was too late to undo it."

"Is that why she wanted to take me over? To break her curse and undo your spell?" I asked.

"We've both spent ages trying to fix our mistakes. But we need you to do it," Toria explained.

"How?" I asked.

"You must destroy the branch, but only after Leanna's curse is broken. It must happen on the evening of the balsamic moon. My spell can be undone the next morning."

"Is that all?" Joshua asked.

Toria ignored him. "Please Kat, you have to do this for me—for all of us."

"We will. I promise," I said.

"Why is this happening now? After 129 years?" Evan asked.

Toria said. "This is the first time all the necessary souls have reincarnated in the same lifetime. We have never been reborn together before. This may be our only chance to fix everything we broke."

"Evan is Alistair's reincarnation?" I asked.

"Just as you are mine and more than mine." Toria smiled.

"But what about Cassie's and Sebastian's souls? Aren't they trapped in the mirror?" I asked.

"Cassie's the only one who couldn't reincarnate." She asked, "Haven't you ever heard how the eyes are the windows to the soul? Didn't you notice how perfectly Morgan's matched Sebastian's? She's only a tiny piece of his soul, but it's the best piece of it—born from first love. His love for me."

"But this isn't just about our ancestors. This curse is about all of us."

Toria nodded. "My retribution spell will end the Radcliffes. Leanna's curse will continue to harm the Mallorys and Nolans. Although the last line makes it reversible, it also stretches the curse across all the families who committed any wrongs, even unintentional ones. It hangs over the Langleys and the Kingsleys as well. All the future generations will remain under it, too."

Joshua's face hardened like a terracotta soldier. "What's the likelihood of accomplishing all this before my birthday?"

It was only three weeks away.

"There is only one balsamic moon between then and now," Toria said.

One chance to fix everything.

Chapter 38

After Toria helped me retrieve the yew branch from the castle wall, we took it to the library, where Evan, Professor Astor, and Joshua were waiting for us. It was strange for me to be interacting with a ghost that everyone around me could see. But after the initial weirdness, Toria just became part of the team. We would have been lost without her. By evening, we had a plan.

Most of us were feeling optimistic, but Joshua slumped in his chair. "We're never going to be able to do all this in time." He sounded exhausted. And afraid.

"Yes, we will," Professor Astor assured him. "Much of what we need to do has already been set in motion."

"That's right," Evan said. "Seth and Olivia have forged a friendship. That's a step toward making amends for Pastor Fitzgerald's attack on Cassie. "Joshua has brought the descendant of Sebastian's illegitimate daughter back into the family. He even made it possible for her to go to one of the best private schools in the country."

"You're right," I said

Evan's lips curled up. "I've lost count of how many times you've said those words to me."

"Really? I thought you could count to three," I said.

He laughed. The professor looked bemused. Toria smiled. And Joshua still seemed defeated.

Professor Astor slapped his hands on the table. "Let's break for dinner, shall we?"

If the professor had hoped to cheer us up with food and conversation, he must have been terribly disappointed. Joshua's mood infected the room. Adam opened his mouth to speak, but Morgan elbowed him in the ribs, and he shut it again. Olivia rearranged the food on her plate, but very little made it to her mouth. Evan's expression was guarded.

Then there was Seth.

He seemed to thoroughly enjoy his beef bourguignon. When he was done eating, he laid his fork on his plate, leaned back in his chair, and linked his fingers behind his head in a display of after-dinner relaxation. "All right, Evan. Let's have it."

Almost everyone at the table stopped in mid-bite and stared at Seth. Professor Astor continued eating. I admired his commitment to a good meal.

"Have what, Seth?" Evan's eyebrows leapt up.

"What really happened to you and Kat?" Seth asked.

"Seth, we agreed not to put Evan on the spot," Professor Astor chided from the other end of the table.

"No offense, professor, but I want to hear from Evan, not you," Seth said.

"Insane as it sounds, everything Professor Astor told you is true," Evan said.

"Time travel and a curse? Seriously?" Before Evan could answer, Seth burst out, "You don't even believe in curses."

"I do now." Evan ate a piece of mushroom.

"You're way too calm about this," Seth said.

"Traveling back in time through a magical mirror and watching a woman die from a curse will do that to a man." Evan stared Seth straight in the eye.

Seth looked momentarily baffled.

"All those experiences changed my perspective," Evan said.

Seth studied Evan's face as if trying to discern how genuine his words were. Finally, he raised his water glass to Evan and said, "To new experiences."

Evan returned the salute and that was that.

The mood in the room lifted a bit. Adam took advantage of the shift to ask me, "Can you contact Drew?"

"You can't ask her that," Morgan hissed at him.

Adam stared at me. "I want to believe what you and Evan are saying, but this is nuts."

Adam represented the Nolan family. If we were going to defeat this curse, we needed his help. "I might be able to call Drew here, but you're not going to be able to see him unless you believe. Can you?"

Adam looked uncertain.

"Your grandfather believes. I saw Drew whispering in his ear, when we went to interview him," I said.

I'd never actually seen someone's face go white before, but Adam's did right before he said, "I can try to believe."

Evan put his hand on mine. "You don't have to do this."

"But I do." I smiled at him. "It'll be fine."

I twisted my ring and called to Drew. Shadows swirled in the corner of the room. They danced over to me. The air shimmered. White smoke unfurled and coalesced. A semi-transparent Drew Nolan appeared.

"Why am I here?" he asked.

I pointed to Adam. "Your descendant wants to meet you."

Adam had managed to believe and now he was seeing his first ghost. I didn't think it was possible for Adam to get any paler, but he did. "It's you." His voice was a whisper.

"Has Cassie's death been avenged?" Drew asked.

Adam's lips moved but no words came out. First ghost sightings were like that.

"Leanna was behind it," I said. "Pastor Fitzgerald made her help him. I think she put a spell on you to keep silent."

"I thought Sebastian killed Cassie because of me. Because of what I did." Drew's fists clenched and his voice sounded choked. "They used me to hurt Cassie."

"We're going to set things right," I said.

He turned to Adam. "A Nolan keeps his word."

Then Drew faded away.

The shadows shimmered again. Someone else was coming through. Someone I hadn't invited. She stepped into the room in full ghost form. Nothing translucent about her. Gray eyes and brown hair and a pale blue dress. *Leanna.*

The room spun. I clutched at the table to stay upright.

Evan grabbed me. "This is too much for you."

"I'll be okay," I lied and gritted my teeth.

"I left *British Lore* in the library, praying someone would find it and break this curse." She looked at me. "I pushed it into your hands that night. I'm sorry it had to be you. He's going to be angry."

"Who?"

She looked back into the shimmering darkness and whispered. "My uncle. He wants the curse to continue. He'll come for you."

"What is he?" I asked.

She shuddered. "I don't know what he became when he gave himself to the shadows. He's something even ghosts fear."

A tremor ran through me.

"I don't have much time here," she continued. "I didn't want to cast that curse. I never wanted any of this." Then she turned to me. "I didn't mean to scare you. I've tried for so long to fix things and I got desperate. I'm sorry."

I didn't say anything. I couldn't say anything.

The darkness seemed to grow and reach for her.

"He's coming," she whispered.

And then she was gone.

Chapter 39

Two weeks flew by in a fever of activity with Professor Astor, Evan, and me crafting a ritual that would end Leanna's curse. I tried summoning her—twice—to see if she could help us, but she never appeared. I worried about what her uncle might have done to her.

Toria stayed with me. She promised we would end the curse. And find a way to deal with whatever Pastor Fitzgerald tried to bring down on us. I wanted to believe her, but she had failed to overcome him in her lifetime. How could she beat him in mine?

I buried my fear with work. Researching pagan texts about creating sacred space for spell-casting and learning the meaning behind different herbs and oils. Formulas calmed me. Recipes were soothing. Something I could measure and practice. Toria nixed several of my suggestions and directed me to something else. Spells came so naturally to her.

I felt lucky to have a project. Joshua had nothing to do but wait. It seemed as if he lost a pound a day. Olivia's beauty faded; worry made her look pinched and pale. Toward the end, even those of us who had something to do felt the toll. Professor Astor's face showed every one of his forty-seven years. Evan snapped at everyone. Anxiety crept over me.

What if we ran out of time? No one dared ask the question. Because the answer was too horrible to speak aloud. Joshua would die. We weren't sure what would happen to the rest of the Radcliffes. If there wasn't a first-born son, would the retribution spell claim the next line of heirs? Regardless, the other families and their descendants would still suffer under Leanna's curse. Pastor Fitzgerald would win. We couldn't let any of that happen.

The night of the balsamic moon arrived faster than I would have liked. I needed more time to practice. More time to prepare. More time to accept all of this.

But the moon didn't care about what I wanted. This was the last sliver of lunar light before the new moon. A time for healing. A time to shape destiny. I had one chance. One night to fix what had been broken. My failure would mean Joshua's death. And a curse that would haunt generations of our families.

I ran the lines over in my head, stumbling through the Scottish Gaelic phrases. I visualized the entire ritual. So much blood. It bothered me, but Toria assured me that it was necessary. We all had to willingly bleed to undo the forced bloodshed of the past. And it was my blood that would activate the magic.

Everyone else was as ready as they could be. Joshua and Olivia had been committed from the beginning. Evan was a believer now, and Morgan would have done this for me even if she hadn't cared about her connection to Sebastian. Adam was on-board as soon as Drew's ghost had appeared. I don't know how Evan convinced Seth to help. Maybe it was seeing Leanna's ghost. Maybe it was the promise of Joshua owing him.

A part of me still couldn't believe any of this was happening.

My hands shook as I laid the ingredients and tools on the table we'd carried up to Cassie's room. Evan followed me, shifting everything around.

"Am I doing anything right?" I asked.

"More than I expected," he said. "This is a complicated ritual."

My shoulders slumped.

Evan's warm breath tickled my ear. "We can do this."

I turned to look at him. He gave me a firm nod, and my spine straightened.

When Professor Astor signaled for the ritual to begin, everyone crowded around the table. Last night, I'd practiced in my room. Today, we'd run through it in the library. Preparation should have eased my nerves, but it hadn't.

It didn't matter that Toria's ghost was beside me, guiding me. I was still nervous. She seemed to sense it.

"Do you want me to join with you for this?" she whispered.

"How?" I asked.

"It's like when I got rid of Leanna's ghost. A temporary possession, except we both remain conscious and we can communicate. You'll have access to some of my knowledge and power."

It was tempting. But I couldn't bear to have a ghost inside my body again. Even Toria's ghost. "Can you just stay with me?"

She nodded.

I began.

I poured a wide circle of salt on the floor, surrounding everyone and everything we needed for the ritual. This would protect us from anything nasty that might try to slip through while we were working.

Evan followed behind me, lighting candles in the east, south, west, and north part of the circle. Then he went to the center of the circle and lit the oil burner on the table. The scent of sandalwood filled the room. It reminded me of Alistair. Of safety. Of strength.

I went to each candle, invoking the guardian at each cardinal point. This sealed the circle so our energy built inside it and powered the ritual. Evan laid the ruby necklace on the table.

Everyone tightened around the table. On the tabletop lay a large stone bowl, seven knives, an assortment of herbs and oils. Everything we needed to complete the ritual. Olivia, Evan, Morgan, Joshua, Adam, Seth and I simultaneously spoke the same incantation, calling the Mallory, Kingsley, Radcliffe, Nolan, Fitzgerald, and Langley ancestors to us.

Olivia used the words of Cumbric that we'd cobbled together for her. Evan spoke Irish Gaelic and Joshua used Cornish. Despite Evan's tutoring, Adam still struggled with the Irish Gaelic. Seth's family heritage required him to speak in Cumbric, too. Scottish Gaelic was Toria's ancestral language and tripped over my tongue after a few days of practice. These weren't just our ancestral languages. They were also the four languages Leanna had used in her curse.

One by one, ghosts came to hear us. They manifested outside the circle. Some were just wisps of smoke, others were nearly solid. Some looked like faded photographs, others like pale versions of who they had been. Dozens of ghosts assembled around us. All related to the Fitzgerald, Nolan, Radcliffe, Mallory, Kingsley, and Langley families. Ghosts of everyone who had been affected by this curse.

Leanna was the last to arrive. She flickered weakly. What had Pastor Fitzgerald done to her? And was he here to do it to me? I let my eyes wander around the circle. I didn't see him. I didn't sense him. But, in the past, he had evaded Toria's notice too.

Toria felt my apprehension. "Relax, Alistair is behind us. And nothing can happen to you inside this circle."

Bertram stood beside Olivia. Phillip near Joshua. Ancestors seemed to congregate by their descendant as if they were lending their strength to this moment.

I heard gasps within our circle. Everyone saw the ghosts. We were all believers now.

"We are safe here in the circle," Professor Astor reminded everyone. "They are only here to listen to our words and witness our ritual."

Olivia stepped forward and cut her hand. Her blood dripped into the stone bowl to make amends for Cassie shedding Pastor Fitzgerald's blood. When Olivia finished, Joshua gently bandaged the cut. This was recompense for Leanna's betrayal of Cassie's friendship and her becoming a Radcliffe at Cassie's expense. But there was more to it than that.

After he finished tending to Olivia's wound, Joshua removed a small box from his pocket. He opened it to reveal a diamond large enough to sparkle in the low light. "Olivia, I have loved you since the first time we played at the old fort. I will love you until the day I die. Will you spend the rest of your life with me? Will you marry me?"

Tears streamed down Olivia's cheeks as she nodded. Joshua slipped the ring on her finger.

Oblivious to the rest of us, she grabbed his face in her hands, whispering, "Yes," over and over again until Joshua quieted her with a kiss.

One by one, each of us stepped forward to shed our blood. Joshua. Morgan. Seth. Adam. Evan. Me.

My blood was the last to drip into the stone bowl. The smell of iron and salt cocooned me. Bile burned my throat. I couldn't swallow away the scorching bitterness. I stumbled and gripped the side of the table.

This ritual took more power than anything I'd done before. But it was my blood that activated the magic of our words.

"Toria, I need you," I whispered. "Join with me."

I felt her sliding into my skin. It wasn't cold. It wasn't unpleasant. It was a moreness. As if my soul recognized this broken piece and welcomed it home. I wasn't alone anymore. She knew what to do. And she would help me do it.

I felt stronger. Like I could do this. All of this and more.

Evan handed me the vervain shavings. I sprinkled them into the blood to remove negativity. Pinches of cinnamon and ground cloves for cleansing. Three drops of cedar oil for protection and five drops of eucalyptus oil for healing. Then I stirred the mixture clockwise eight times with a wooden spoon.

Adam cleared his throat. "I am sorry for the lies," was how he began telling the true story of Pastor Fitzgerald's death. His words made amends for Drew Nolan's lie to the Fitzgerald family. But Adam wasn't finished. The ancestors needed to hear the truth about Cassie's death to clear Drew's name and bring peace to the Nolan family. And they did. They heard everything.

Adam finished with an apology. "I'm sorry for all the harm my family caused the Radcliffes. We were seeking vengeance for Cassie and Drew. But we were wrong. I'm sorry." His gaze lingered on Morgan. "I can't believe I get a second chance with the girl I love."

Morgan's smile was a beacon of happiness. "I love you too."

Then it was time. Toria and I had to break the curse on the rubies. Holding the ruby necklace above the stone bowl, I felt her strength rushing through me. My hands trembled as I started to recite the necessary words in Scottish Gaelic.

Toria's voice whispered insistently in my head. Her words became my words. My ring glowed.

Energy vibrated against my skin. Toria was directing the power inside me. I staggered and almost dropped the rubies. Toria kept the rubies in our grasp. She held me upright as the power thrummed through me.

When the light from my ring dimmed, I placed the necklace by the stone bowl on the table.

Adam picked up the necklace and handed it to Morgan. She placed it in a black velvet box.

Morgan handed the box to Joshua. "Full circle, right? Back where it belongs."

Olivia, Evan, Morgan, Joshua, Adam, Seth and I brought the ritual to an end. Toria stayed with me. Between the two of us, we could finish.

As the last words slipped from my lips, Leanna limped toward me. She was almost translucent. She looked so weak.

"Are you all right?" I whispered.

She shook her head. "He's coming for you. I can't stop him. I'm so sorry." And then she dissolved. I'd never seen a ghost dissolve before.

What happened to her? I thought at Toria.

Toria whispered in my head, *I don't know.*

What do you mean?

She came to see the curse removed. This was her reckoning. But more than that, I can't tell you.

Did Pastor Fitzgerald do something to her?

The darkness in the fireplace sparkled. It seemed impenetrable. A darkness that even the darkness would fear. And, as if in answer to my question, I heard a twisted laugh.

I hated him. For what he did to Cassie. For what he'd done to Leanna.

Not now, Toria urged. *Hate has no place in our circle. Focus on what binds us together.*

I swallowed my anger. Looked back at Evan and Morgan. Thought about love and friendship, trust and forgiveness.

A gust of air swirled up from the floorboards, snuffing out all the candles and plunging the room into complete darkness.

The mirror shimmered. Two orbs emerged from its surface. Pure sparkling light, too bright and beautiful to look at directly. The orbs circled around everyone as if to say goodbye. They lingered a moment above my head.

Cassie's and Sebastian's voices said, "Thank you."

I didn't know if they meant me or Toria. But I knew their souls were freed from the mirror's endless death. As the orbs disappeared through the window and across the night sky, the candles came back to life. And all the ghosts were gone. Except Toria.

Chapter 40

I crouched beside the old stone pit, coaxing my first fire to life. I tried to ignore the searing burn in my leg muscles. I got the rowan leaves to catch fire, but the wind kept snuffing out the infant flames. I sighed and switched to kneeling.

I twisted my ring and asked the wind to stop. It slowed to a standstill. Flames leapt up to greedily devour the leaves, licking at the branches. When the fire reached the sides of the blackened pit, I twisted my ring and called out to Toria.

The winds kicked up from the north, whipping my hair away from my face. The air shimmered beside me and Toria appeared. "You really shouldn't play with nature like that."

"I just stopped the breeze," I said.

"And almost triggered a hurricane in the Caribbean."

"What?"

"Every action we take has consequences. Stop something here, start something there."

"I'm sorry. I didn't realize."

"Use the ring when you absolutely need to. But avoid anything weather related until you understand more about how its power works."

I nodded.

"Ready?" she asked.

"Yes." This was it.

I picked up the cursed yew branch and impaled the nearest flame. She touched my other hand. Her words filled my mind. I could feel the power in them. Almost taste the magic in my mouth as I said them. I didn't notice the branch burning beneath my fingertips until the heat singed them.

"Now," she said.

I threw the yew branch into the fire pit.

"Almost done."

I hated the next part. She said I'd get used to it, but using my blood for spells was gross. And it made me really lightheaded to watch my life drip out of me.

I took a deep breath and dragged the blade over my arm. It burned. The blood beaded to the surface. My gag reflex kicked in. I squeezed my eyes shut to stop from throwing up. I lifted my arm above the flames and let my blood drip into the fire.

It felt like hours passed before Toria said, "You can wrap your arm now."

I opened my eyes and sat down on the ground. The bleeding had slowed, like my body knew it had given enough. Nausea rolled over me. I tore open the bandage and stuck it on as fast as I could.

I stayed there, while the blaze consumed everything. Waited for the fire to burn down to embers. Pleaded for it to work. Prodded the ash with a long stick. Nothing solid was left in the pit. Toria's retribution spell should be extinguished.

I followed all of Toria's instructions. Found the fire pit near the ruins and filled it with rowan branches. Set the fire and bled into it. Did everything to free the Radcliffes from the retribution spell.

It had to be enough.

I slid away from the fire pit and leaned my back against the ruins of the rock fort. I had never been this exhausted before. Spells took so much out of me. More than the ghosts ever had. Toria said that was the way with beginners. That I'd get better at this. I didn't want to get better at this. I didn't want any of this.

Tears scalded my eyes and blurred my vision. The muscles around my eyes twitched. I hadn't recovered from removing Leanna's curse last night. This morning, I had to undo Toria's spell. Because if I failed…the cost was Joshua's life.

The time travel, curse, ghosts, spells, and deaths all caught up with me. It was too many unbelievables. The sky tilted. The ground undulated beneath my feet. I felt like someone sucked the bones out of my body, leaving behind a blob of flesh. I buried my face in my hands.

I don't know how long I lost it for. I slapped the ground until my palms stung. Sobs wracked my body. I screamed it all away. The powerlessness and fear.

Eventually, the tears dried up and the sobs quieted to hiccups. I lay on my side in the grass. My head rested on my arm. Watching. Waiting.

Toria leaned over the fire pit, running her almost translucent fingers through the ash. She gazed back at me, and her smile widened.

"You did it." She sounded proud.

"The Radcliffes are safe now?" I stared up at her.

Something flickered in her eyes. "Leanna's curse has been lifted. My spell has been removed."

"Joshua will live?"

"You've saved him from my retribution spell," she said.

The weight of a man's life lifted from my shoulders. I had given him back his future. In the pit of my stomach, I felt a warm lightness. We had saved Joshua.

Toria's reckoning was finished, yet she remained with me. All the other ghosts had left as soon as their reckoning was done. "Why are you still here?"

"There is more work for us," she said. "And your soul calls to mine. We are bound by ancestral magic. Our power is in our family. Besides, there is so much you need to learn still."

I bit my lip. "What about Leanna?" I'd called to her a few times since last night. She never came. "Do you think Pastor Fitzgerald got ahold of her?"

She nodded.

"What's he doing to her?" I asked.

"Punishing her," she whispered.

"Can we help her?" I asked.

"We aren't strong enough to go against him. Not yet," Toria said. "We've done so much. We need to rest." She sounded tired.

So many questions remained about shadows, ghosts, the unbelievables, my ring, and the Langleys.

She read my mind. "Everything you need to learn is at Dumbarton."

"Your family home?"

"Our family home." Her voice grew fainter.

"Where is it?"

"Joshua has let them know what happened. They will find you. They will bring you there." She became a wisp of smoke.

And then she was gone.

I wanted to believe her—to believe that my family wanted me. That all these years with no contact were to protect me. But inside, the fear remained. That I wasn't wanted. Not until I was needed.

I was so lost in my thoughts, I didn't hear Evan walking toward me until he crouched down in front of me.

"Are you okay?" Worry creased his forehead.

My body ached everywhere, but I made myself sit up. "The spell's done. Joshua's safe."

"That's great." He sat next to me. "But I asked about you."

I shrugged. "I don't think this will ever be over for me." Not like it was for Evan. He'd helped me get back to our time and break the curse and undo the retribution spell and save Joshua. "Your work is done. Mine is just beginning."

He put his arm around my shoulder. "We are in this together until the end."

*The Radcliffe Rubies
Design by*

Marina A. Raye

THE GIRL WHO IGNORED GHOSTS

Acknowledgements

My biggest thanks go to Jessica Jernigan for sticking with me and the story through all the hurdles, including a change in publishers. Jessica, you did everything you promised and more—you helped me make my story the best version of itself and you held my hand every step of the way. Thank you for all your feedback and insight. You reined in my love of complications and made sure we told a smooth and focused story. I wouldn't have this book without you.

Mom and Dad, we did it! Thank you so much for listening to every one of my meltdowns and encouraging me to keep going. It's never easy to love a writer, but you always do. I couldn't do what I do without your love and support. Katrina Bender, for being my sounding board, my sanity, my critique partner and my dearest friend. You get this crazy writing life in a way no one else can. And you always pull me back from the edge. Hugs and eternal gratitude.

Anthony Dvarskas, remember the hours we spent in middle school toiling over that notebook, creating the concept and character sketches? Thanks for dreaming up this idea with me and letting me play with it as an adult. Your support has meant so much to me. Many thanks to you and Darren for putting me up every time I needed to be in the city for a conference or appointment. You two always welcome me into your home and make me feel like family. That's a gift I treasure. Brett Helgren, for being a terrific beta reader and always believing in this book even after you read the earliest draft. Thanks for giving me a place to stay in Hell's Kitchen and being such a great friend. You are the best photographer I could ask for. Seriously, photo shoots with you are a dream and I love my new author photos!

Grandma Eileen, for reading an early draft and loving it despite its flaws. You saw the heart of my story and loved it. You always fight for me and my writing. Thanks for being on my side! To Jacqueline McDowell, for letting me pick your brain on all things archaeological. Carina Lau and Carol Beaumier, for reading the first draft and making me believe it had potential. Your words kept me going all these years.

Jennie Bentley, for reading a draft after we met at Killer Nashville and giving me great, honest feedback. You opened doors to agents and you helped a newbie start on her publishing journey. I wouldn't be here without your support and guidance. Paige Shelton, thanks for guiding me along this crazy publishing journey and responding to my panicky emails. I am in awe of everything you have accomplished and you give me lots to strive towards. Gretchen Smith and Chris Holm, I read your emails so many times. They helped me pull myself together when the bad stuff happened. Seeing how much you two have accomplished gave me hope when I'd lost most of mine. Madeline Wynn, thanks for pushing me to stick with this story.

Claire McKinney and Larissa Ackerman—I couldn't launch this book without you. Thank you for being the PR goddesses that you are. Jian Chan for designing my amazing website and fielding my crazy suggestions with absolute calm. Lyndsay Hemphill for believing in me and negotiating a great contract with the first publisher. Victoria Marini, for stepping in when Lyndsay left and keeping things on track until the track ended. Beckett Publishing Group—thank you for keeping the dream alive and bringing this book to print!

The Cheeseheads—your support of my writing and your words of encouragement keep me doing this. Thank you so much for spreading the word about my books! I couldn't ask for a better group of friends or super fans. Abby Brown for being the smartest & coolest intern ever. Thanks for all your insight into the teen market. Gwen, Carrie, JM, Lori, K. Lyn,

Kathryn, Aquileana, Andrea, Sue, Ally, Mayumi, EllaDee, Rhonda, Arlene, Jill, David, Karen, Audrey, Naomi, Jenny, Dianne, Vanessa, Kitt, and the rest of my amazing blog followers, thank you for all your support. You guys celebrate the ups and commiserate over the downs—you keep me going in the whirlwind of publishing.

To Chase Collegiate (St. Margaret's-McTernan when I graduated) and Georgetown University for inspiring the setting and teaching me to never ever give up.

And lastly, a huge, huge thank you to my readers. When you talk to me about my characters like they are real people, you make my heart smile. It's an honor to be a part of your world. Thank you for visiting my story world. You are the best!

The Girl Who Ignored Ghosts

Reader Discussion Questions

1) Morgan and Kat have an interesting dynamic in their friendship. Compare how Morgan wants to stand out to how Kat strives so hard to blend in. Discuss how important it is to find yourself but to also fit in and belong to a group as a teenager. Do you think Kat is hiding from herself or does she already know herself too well?

2) If you had to time travel with one character from the book, who would it be and why?

3) Discuss how the concept of actions having consequences plays out in the story. Identify three instances and explore the meaning within them. Specific characters to look at include: Leanna, Toria, Cassie, Sebastian, and Drew.

4) Discuss the parallels between Kat's relationship with the ghosts and her father.

5) How does the author play with time in the story? Explore the use of seeing the future by Toria and traveling to the past by Kat.

6) Discuss Kat's guilt over sharing a body with Toria. How does it manifest in the story?

7) Have you ever had to keep a secret from everyone around you like Kat did? How did it make you feel? What did it cost you? Discuss how it would impact your relationships with other people.

8) What does the story say about family? How are the concepts of loyalty and responsibility intertwined among the families and across generations?

9) Who was your favorite character? Why? Your least favorite? Why?

10) The series title is The Unbelievables because people need to believe in these things before they can see them. What are the effects of this rule and how do they ripple through the novel?

11) We encounter ghosts, curses, spells, and spirits. We also meet something no one can name. Something that has merged with the shadows. What do you think Pastor Fitzgerald might be?

12) Why did Kat start ignoring ghosts? Why does she stop? Discuss the character's arc from believer to unbeliever to believer again.

13) When Kat stays with Morgan's family, she has mixed emotions. Identify some of the feelings it bring up for Kat. Why do you think it's so hard for her to see a complete family unit interacting?

14) Could anyone have prevented the murders? Think about the domino effect of events: what Pastor Fitzgerald did to Cassie, what Cassie did to protect herself, what Drew did to protect her, what Leanna did in her uncle's name, and what Toria did for Sebastian. Was there any choice that could have stopped things from unfolding as they did?

AN INTERVIEW WITH
K.C. TANSLEY, AUTHOR OF
The Girl Who Ignored Ghosts

YOUR BOOK HAS MANY ELEMENTS: GOTHIC, TIME TRAVEL, AND PARANORMAL, WHICH ALL COME TOGETHER TO MAKE AN EXCITING YA NOVEL. WHERE DID THE IDEA FOR THE GIRL WHO IGNORED GHOSTS COME FROM?

It was a concept my best friend, Anthony, and I dreamed up when we were in 7th grade. The 11-year old me loved the idea of ghosts, curses, spells, castles, time travel, and a murder mystery. I was a huge fan of soap operas like Dark Shadows and Santa Barbara and that's where the romantic thread came in. Back then, I only thought about the story I wanted to tell and this was it.

Anthony and I never got beyond the character sketches and general concept because the original idea had way too many characters. He still has a notebook somewhere filled with dozens of character sketches.

Decades later, when I was working on Wall Street and mourning the end of the Harry Potter series, I thought if I could write my own novel, the characters would always be with me. That was when the 28-year-old me remembered the story the 11-year-old me was dying to tell. I emailed Anthony and he gave me the go ahead to work on it. And then the work truly began.

The Girl Who Ignored Ghosts

THE MAJORITY OF THE BOOK TAKES PLACE AT CASTLE CREIGHTON IN CONNECTICUT. IS THIS BASED ON A REAL PLACE? IF NOT, HOW DID YOU DEVELOP THE IDEA OF CASTLE CREIGHTON?

I tend to pull things in from my real life and blend them on the page. Castle Creighton is actually inspired by a few places. The idea for the Isle of Acacia and Castle Creighton sprung from a high school trip to France where I visited Mont St. Michel. I fell in love with the isolation of the place. It stuck with me and ended up being a major part of the setting.

Growing up in Connecticut, I'd been to Gillette Castle in East Haddam, Conn., which fed into the idea for a castle in New England. I went back there recently to help get the feel of the castle while doing revisions. The Isle of Acacia was partly inspired by the Thimble Islands in Branford, Conn. There's also a small, uninhabited island off the coast of Westbrook, Conn., that I walked out to once during low tide. It felt like such a cool thing—a place that was only reachable at certain times of day. It fit the Gothic mood of my story perfectly.

THE MAIN CHARACTER CALLS GHOSTS "UNBELIEVABLES." WHERE DID YOU GET THE TERM FROM AND WHY DID YOU DECIDE ON USING "UNBELIEVABLES" RATHER THAN "GHOSTS"?

The unbelievables are all the supernatural beings people don't believe in. I wanted to explain why some people see ghosts and some people don't. I was fascinated with the idea of belief fueling reality. Like when you tell yourself you've lost your keys and you believe it so much that you can't see them sitting on your desk in front of you. Because you believe your keys are gone, they are, even if they actually aren't. I think the mind is capable of shutting so much out and that was something I wanted to explore. There is more to the unbelievables than ghosts. Something very sinister lives in the shadows.

K.C. Tansley

ARE THERE ANY AUTHORS OR BOOKS THAT INSPIRED YOU IN WRITING THE GIRL WHO IGNORED GHOSTS?

I was a big fan of ghost stories and Gothic stories as a kid. I remember reading about banshees and thinking there was nothing cooler. One of my all time favorite reads is *Wuthering Heights* with its Gothic love story. Agatha Christie mysteries were a must-read for the 11-year-old me too. I loved the intricate plotting and how it all came together so perfectly in the end.

As an adult, I read *The Woman in Black*, and it probably contributed to some of the creepier moments in the story. The *Harry Potter* series played a big role in my writing this book because I was distraught over Hermione and Harry leaving my life. I didn't read the final Potter book until a few years after the series ended.

DO YOU HAVE ANY GHOST STORIES OF YOUR OWN TO SHARE?

When I lived on Wall Street, there were several nights in that haze between dreaming and fully awake where I saw ghosts at the end of my bed. People dressed in clothes from another era and exuding an eerie bluish light. It turns out there were some horrible fires that destroyed buildings down there. I think when people die tragically something of them remains.

In my apartment in Washington, D.C., I used to hear people walking in the living room at night. At the time, I lived alone. It scared me so much I would throw the covers over my head. Because as we all know that protects us from the supernatural. I never went to investigate, but to this day, I think ghosts were moving around in there at night.

WHY DID YOU DECIDE TO WRITE THE GIRL WHO IGNORED GHOSTS AS A YOUNG ADULT NOVEL VERSUS "NEW ADULT" OR ADULT FICTION?

This was the first manuscript I ever wrote, so it's where I cut my writing teeth. The book went through many incarnations before I settled on YA. In its earliest version, it was set in grad school, and I tried to sell it as an adult paranormal mystery. At each conference I attended in every pitch session and manuscript critique, I was told that it was an impossible sell. College and grad school didn't fit into the adult or the YA market. And New Adult didn't exist at that time. After a few years of being told to make it YA, I started to explore the possibility.

I read a ton of YA books to make sure this was where my story truly belonged. The things my characters are dealing with (struggling to find/define themselves) and the tone felt right for a YA audience. I also wanted to write a book that a teen, a parent, and a grandparent could all enjoy. Something PG-12, appropriate for 12+.

DO YOU INTEND TO HAVE A SERIES FEATURING THE MAIN CHARACTER, KAT PRESTON?

I always saw this as a series. I have ideas for several more books. I've written a short outline for the sequel and plan to work on the first draft this summer/fall. Kat will definitely be front and center, and Evan will also play a major role. The four families have a lot that they need to deal with together, and it's going to take a few books to get through. If I'm channeling Toria and making predictions, I foresee more time traveling as they fight for their future.

Photo by: Brett D. Helgren

K.C TANSLEY lives with her warrior lapdog, Emerson, and three quirky golden retrievers on a hill somewhere in Connecticut. She tends to believe in the unbelievables—spells, ghosts, time travel—and writes about them.

Never one to say no to a road trip, she's climbed the Great Wall twice, hopped on the Sound of Music tour in Salzburg, and danced the night away in the dunes of Cape Hatteras. She loves the ocean and hates the sun, which makes for interesting beach days. The Girl Who Ignored Ghosts is her debut YA time-travel murder mystery novel.

As Kourtney Heintz, she also writes award winning cross-genre fiction for adults.

You can find out more about her at: **http://kctansley.com**

CPSIA information can be obtained at www.ICGtesting.com
Printed in the USA
LVOW11s1627180416

484132LV00003B/289/P